INFAMY

ALSO BY ROBERT K. TANENBAUM

FICTION

Trap

Fatal Conceit

Tragic

Bad Faith

Outrage

Betrayed

Capture

Escape

Malice

Counterplay

Fury

Hoax

Resolved

Absolute Rage

Enemy Within

True Justice

Act of Revenge

Reckless Endangerment

Irresistible Impulse

Falsely Accused

Corruption of Blood

Justice Denied

Material Witness

Reversible Error

Immoral Certainty

Depraved Indifference

No Lesser Plea

NONFICTION

Echoes of My Soul

The Piano Teacher: The True Story of a Psychotic Killer

Badge of the Assassin

INFAMY

A Novel

ROBERT K. TANENBAUM

Gallery Books

New York   London   Toronto   Sydney   New Delhi

G

Gallery Books
An Imprint of Simon & Schuster, Inc.
1230 Avenue of the Americas
New York, NY 10020

First Gallery Books hardcover edition September 2016

GALLERY BOOKS and colophon are registered trademarks of Simon & Schuster, Inc.

For information about special discounts for bulk purchases, please contact Simon & Schuster Special Sales at 1-866-506-1949 or business@simonandschuster.com.

The Simon & Schuster Speakers Bureau can bring authors to your live event. For more information or to book an event, contact the Simon & Schuster Speakers Bureau at 1-866-248-3049 or visit our website at www.simonspeakers.com.

Manufactured in the United States of America

10   9   8   7   6   5   4   3   2   1

Library of Congress Cataloging-in-Publication Data
Names: Tanenbaum, Robert, author.
Title: Infamy / Robert K. Tanenbaum.
Description: First Gallery Books hardcover edition. | New York : Gallery Books, 2016.
Identifiers: LCCN 2016019694
Subjects: LCSH: Karp, Butch (Fictitious character)—Fiction. | Ciampi, Marlene (Fictitious character)—Fiction. | BISAC: FICTION / Mystery & Detective / Police Procedural. | FICTION / Legal. | FICTION / Suspense. | GSAFD: Legal stories.
Classification: LCC PS3570.A52 I54 2016 | DDC 813/.54—dc23 LC record available at https://lccn.loc.gov/2016019694.

ISBN 978-1-4767-9319-1
ISBN 978-1-4767-9320-7 (ebook)

To those blessings in my life:

Patti, Rachael, Roger, Billy;

and

To the loving Memory of

Reina Tanenbaum

My sister, truly an angel

INFAMY

ACKNOWLEDGMENTS

To my legendary mentors, District Attorney Frank S. Hogan and Henry Robbins, both of whom were larger in life than in their well-deserved and hard-earned legends, everlasting gratitude and respect; to my special friends and brilliant tutors at the Manhattan DAO, Bob Lehner, Mel Glass, and John Keenan, three of the best who ever served and whose passion for justice was unequaled and uncompromising, my heartfelt appreciation, respect, and gratitude; to Professor Robert Cole and Professor Jesse Choper, who at Boalt Hall challenged, stimulated, and focused the passions of my mind to problem-solve and to do justice; to Steve Jackson, an extraordinarily talented and gifted scrivener whose genius flows throughout the manuscript and whose contribution to it cannot be overstated, a dear friend for whom I have the utmost respect; to Louise Burke, my publisher, whose enthusiastic support, savvy, and encyclopedic smarts qualify her as my first pick in a game of three in the Avenue P park in Brooklyn; to Wendy Walker, my talented, highly skilled, and insightful editor, many thanks for all that you do; to Sarah Wright and Cynthia Merman, the inimitable twosome whose adult supervision, oversight, brilliant copyediting, and rapid responses are invaluable and profoundly appreciated; to my agents, Mike Hamilburg and Bob Diforio, who in exemplary fashion have always represented my best interests; to Coach Paul Ryan, who personified "American Exceptionalism" and mentored me in its finest virtues; to my esteemed special friend and confidant Richard A. Sprague, who has always challenged, debated, and inspired me in the pursuit of fulfilling the reality of "American Exceptionalism"; and to Rene Herrerias, my coach at Cal, who believed in me early on and in so doing changed my life, truly a divine intervention.

PROLOGUE

"Oyez, oyez, oyez, all rise. All those having business in Supreme Court Part 42, State of New York, New York County, draw near and ye shall be heard."

Pausing his litany, Chief Administrative Court Clerk Duffy McIntyre glared balefully out at the packed courtroom as if daring those in attendance to show the slightest inclination toward unruliness. Having ensured their silence, he continued, "The Honorable Supreme Court Justice Vince Dermondy presiding."

Short and somewhat pugnacious-looking, Judge Dermondy immediately entered through the door leading from the judge's robing room and took his seat up on his dais before he, too, turned his attention to those in attendance. He glanced with his intense gray-blue eyes first at the defense table, then the prosecution, and finally beyond them to the gallery.

"Good afternoon," he said. "It's my understanding that we have a verdict, and I want to take a moment before the jury is brought in to warn each and every one of you that I will not tolerate any outbursts, demonstrations, or statements directed at anyone present. I understand full well the implications of this verdict whatever the jury has decided, but I expect—no, demand—that the decorum of this courtroom and these proceedings be respected. Am . . . I . . . clear?"

Under his glower, the audience nodded as one. Most had already seen this judge in action after a group of protesters managed to find seats in the courtroom on the first day of the trial and began hurling politically charged invectives when the People's case was introduced. Then partway through the trial, Dermondy had a reporter for one of the Washington newspapers taken into custody after the journalist approached a juror for a quote, which the judge followed with the dismissal of another juror when it came to light that she had contacted a book publisher and offered to sell her story.

No one had taken any chances with the judge since. Dermondy nodded. "Good, you may be seated." He turned to

McIntyre. "Please inform the jurors that we're ready for them."

Of all the people in the courtroom, the only one not intimidated by the judge was Roger "Butch" Karp, who stood at his customary place behind the prosecution table. As the district attorney of New York County, he was a firm believer in the sanctity of court proceedings and appreciated a judge who felt the same way. He'd inherited that view from his first boss, the legendary DA Francis Garrahy.

As such, he didn't see the proceedings as a game or contest between attorneys jockeying for unfair advantages and pulling out all stops to "win" a conviction. He believed that as a prosecutor, his job entailed a solemn, sacred search for the truth.

Truth. Karp thought about how little that word meant to the three men standing across the aisle from him behind the defense table. Two attorneys and the defendant, a man who was on trial not just for murder, but metaphorically for murdering the truth. In Karp's book that was the same as committing treason.

Karp looked down at the omnipresent yellow legal pad on the table. On its lined sheets was his outline of the People's case— witness by witness, evidence connected to more evidence—with notes in the margins as issues or thoughts arose so that he forgot nothing, missed no detail from his opening statement to his final summation.

As he moved through the trial, each page served its purpose and was then folded over and paper-clipped to the cardboard backing. All that was left now was the final page of his summation. Or rather, the last two notes he'd made to remind himself of what he'd wanted to end the case on.

At the top of the page was the word "infamy" and a series of other terms that to him defined the word as it applied to this case. It had come to him the evening before closing summations as he'd pondered how to get the jurors to understand the full implications of this crime, this criminal. "End result . . . unbridled ambition . . . weak character . . . duplicitous . . . their own enrichment politically and otherwise."

The last line of the page, as well as of his summation, was a partial quote from Mark Twain. "A truth is not hard to kill . . . a lie well told is immortal."

Karp looked over at the defense team and their client. They lived in a world of well-told lies. It was the whole reason they were all in the courtroom on a summer day in New York City waiting for a jury to render its verdict. The entire defense had been composed of more well-told lies. And the infamy of it was that these lies cut to the very heart of the nation's security, all so that a few corrupt men and women could consolidate power, gain enormous wealth, and promote their worldview.

The defense attorney kept his eyes focused on the door leading from the jury deliberation room. He'd try to read the jurors as they entered for the telltale signs of which way the vote had gone. The defendant also was watching the door but felt Karp's eyes and turned toward him.

Up to this moment, the defendant had acted as if the trial hardly mattered to him. It was at worst an inconvenience, an irritation; at best, a joke. Although he was polite to the judge and charming to the jurors, he laughed and joked with his attorney during the breaks, and smiled or even smirked during the People's case. Then he'd been the picture of aggrieved and unjustly accused when he took the stand—at least until Karp had cross-examined him. But even though he'd been knocked up against the ropes, he'd remained arrogant and smug in his invincibility.

However, now as the jurors shuffled to their assigned seats, most with their heads down, the smirk had disappeared, leaving only a thin sheen of the arrogance. His face was pale, and he licked his thin lips as if suddenly parched. Something else was in his eyes, something different.

Doubt, Karp thought. But then the defendant's dark eyes narrowed and filled with hate as he sneered and gave his attention back to the jurors.

Unperturbed, Karp half turned and glanced over his shoulder at the bench full of people immediately behind the prosecution table. It was quite the eclectic assembly of characters: his wife, Marlene; his daughter, Lucy; her fiancé, Ned Blanchett; as well as the Taos Indian tracker John Jojola; Vietnamese gangster Tran Van Do; federal antiterrorism agent Espey Jaxon; journalist Ariadne Stupenagel; Richie Bryers, his close high school friend and, as it turned out, a star prosecution witness; and Detective Clay Fulton of the NYPD. They'd all come to witness the final act of an epic tragedy they'd unknowingly played a part in during the opening scenes nearly a year earlier.

Smiling slightly at his family and friends, Karp then looked out over the rest of the audience in the gallery. Most of the hard wooden benches were crammed with media types attracted to the high-profile case like hyenas to a lion kill and just as excited at the smell of blood in the air. A grim-faced collection of defense supporters, many of them well known in political and show business circles, stared up at the ceiling or glared at Karp from the benches behind the defense table.

He was just about to turn around to face the judge when his eyes fastened on a woman sitting in the second row from the back of the courtroom next to the aisle. She was wearing a short dark wig and sunglasses, but he recognized the oval-shaped face and, more than that, the way she carried herself. *Like a supremely confident predator*, he thought, as he had for many years whenever their paths had crossed. Something told him she'd been watching him, but she was now just looking straight ahead at the judge, the slightest smile on her face.

Karp frowned at the sudden dilemma her presence created. Sitting in the back of a New York County trial court was a woman who'd committed more felonies in and around Manhattan than there were taxicabs in Times Square at rush hour. She was a paid assassin and terrorist for hire. He was the top law enforcement official in New York City, sworn to uphold the law; she was "officially" on escaped status, but there she was in the flesh.

Still, he hesitated. He knew that he should alert Fulton and court security to apprehend her. And yet, he owed her. So did many people who would never know it. Nor would anyone be aware if he chose not to do anything.

"Please be seated," Judge Dermondy commanded. He then faced the jury foreman, who sat closest to his dais. "Ladies and gentlemen of the jury, have you reached a verdict?"

The jurors all nodded. "We have, Your Honor," the foreman said, holding up the verdict forms.

"Mr. McIntyre, if you please," Dermondy said, indicating that the chief clerk should retrieve the documents and hand them to him. The judge looked down at the documents and after a moment nodded. He turned and addressed the defense table. "Will the defendant rise."

1

Eleven months earlier

THE TWO MEN STANDING IN THE SHADOWS OF THE GATE watched as a woman dressed head to toe in flowing black robes walked toward them. They'd been following her progress since she'd left the village road a mile away and started down a long dirt path to the compound. But night was falling, and concealed by the loose clothing and veil, there was little they could see of her or what she might be carrying.

"Halt," said one of the men, stepping into the middle of the road and pointing his AK-47 at her. "What do you want, woman?" he demanded nervously in Arabic.

Startled by the man's sudden appearance and threatening gesture, the woman stepped back with a small cry. "I am sent from Abu Bakr al-Baghdadi," she replied, also in Arabic but in a dialect more in keeping with northern Iraq. "I bring a message for Ghareeb al Taizi."

The second man now stepped out onto the road. "What did she say?"

The first man frowned and turned to his companion. "What? Speak Arabic. I don't understand Persian. Besides, it is an infidel language and grates on my ears."

"And I have a hard time understanding your old-fashioned babbling," the second man retorted in a halting Arabic. "You Saudis are full of goat shit, so high and mighty when if it wasn't for oil, you'd all still be wandering the desert on camels. But watch your tongue, sand flea, or did you forget you're speaking to a VAJA officer?"

"Ah, yes, VAJA, the vaunted Iranian intelligence agency. How could I forget? You are constantly reminding me," the Arabian scoffed. "But I'm not afraid of you. I've fought in Libya, Yemen, Chechnya, and now here with the Islamic State of Iraq and Syria, where nobody gives a shit who you are. I'm a jihadi, not some spy sneaking around like a snake."

The two men glared at each other for a moment before turning back to the woman. "Never mind your ignorant insults, what does she want? I don't understand her dialect," the Iranian said, pointing his own gun at her.

"She said she is from the Commander of the Believers, al-Baghdadi, and that she has a message for al Taizi."

"How do we know she is not a spy?" the Iranian asked. "I don't trust women. Like that Chechen whore the Russian brought as his bodyguard; there's something funny about her."

The Arabian laughed. "Watch what you say around her, and even how you look at her. I agree, she has no shame and won't cover her hair and face, and those tight-fitting clothes are an affront to Allah. But I've heard stories from Chechnya about Ajmaani that would curl your hair. That 'whore' could cut out your heart and show it to you with a smile while it was still beating. She's no village cow like this one here." He gestured to the woman, who waited quietly for them to finish their argument.

"As I said, how do we know she is telling the truth?"

The Saudi wrinkled his nose. "Well, she's definitely from this region; I can tell by her peasant Iraqi Arabic and the way she smells like a goat." He addressed the woman. "You would have been told our password. Say it now, and I'll take you to al Taizi."

The woman's brow knitted and she hesitated. The two men gripped their weapons and began to walk toward her. "'Who dies today is safe from tomorrow's sin,'" she blurted out, and fell to the ground groveling as if in fear. "Please, do not hurt me."

The Saudi kicked at the woman. "Get up. That was correct."

"What kind of a password is that?" the Iranian scoffed.

"It's an old proverb that al-Baghdadi likes. No one else would think to use it." The Saudi bent over to look at the prostrated woman. "What is this message you have for al Taizi?"

The woman looked up. He expected to see fear, but there was none. Just a sort of sad reluctance for what was about to happen. "Only that may Allah have mercy on your souls."

The Saudi stepped back and began to bring his weapon to bear on her. "Her eyes," he said to the confused Iranian.

"What about them?"

The woman answered for him. "They're gray."

There was no time for any more questions. Death arrived for the Saudi with an angry whiz followed by a heavy thud, and a grunt escaped his lips like he'd been punched. The bullet struck him in the center of his chest, deconstructed his heart, tumbled, and then exited out his lower back, creating a much larger hole coming out than going in. He was already dead as he looked down in bewilderment. He sighed and crumpled to the ground.

The Iranian was still trying to understand what had just happened when the sound of a muffled gunshot arrived a moment later. By then it was too late for him as well; a second 7.62 caliber bullet from an M40A5 sniper's rifle struck him in the temple, and half of his head disintegrated into a fine red mist.

Lucy Karp lay still. The shots had come only seconds apart, but she knew they were from the same rifle fired by a single sniper. In fact, the shooter was Ned Blanchett. And she also knew that the footsteps of two men running in her direction from the desert belonged to John Jojola and Tran Van Do.

While she'd walked openly from the village and down the path toward the mud-walled compound to draw the attention of the now dead guards, the two old guerrilla fighters had worked their way carefully up a small ravine and then waited for her to fall to the ground. That was her signal that the target was present in the compound and the mission should go forward, beginning with Ned taking out the guards she'd drawn into the open. She'd also ascertained that the target, al Taizi, was present before she gave the signal to attack into the microphone hidden behind her veil.

"You okay, Lucy?" Jojola asked as he ran past.

"Yeah, I'm good," Lucy replied, quickly pushing herself up off the ground. She slipped into the shadows beneath the gate as her two friends dragged the bodies of the dead men next to the outside wall. Then they joined her.

"You see anyone else?" Jojola asked, turning his craggy bronze face toward her, his dark eyes seeming to gleam with adrenaline, even in the shadows. A former Army Ranger who had served in

Vietnam, Jojola was a member of the Taos Indian Pueblo in New Mexico. He had, in fact, been the pueblo's police chief trying to catch a child killer until a chance encounter with Lucy and her mother, Marlene Ciampi, resolved the case and somehow many years later led to this small isolated village in Syria.

"I couldn't see much beyond the gate," Lucy replied. "But I think our spy in Ramadi was right. These guys might be afraid of drones, but they're so far off the beaten path here, they're not too worried about boots on the ground. The guard was minimal and careless."

"There'll be others in the compound," Jojola said, "including the targets."

"We have to go set up," Tran, a former member of the Vietcong and once the mortal enemy of Jojola, interjected. "Espey and the others will be here in less than a minute."

The two men split up and moved quickly to take up positions covering the largest of the buildings inside the compound. They'd hardly melted into the shadows before the MH-60 Black Hawk helicopter appeared overhead and four men rappelled down a rope. The last of these was S. P. "Espey" Jaxon, the federal anti-terrorism agent who led the team. He made his way to where Lucy waited, while the others, on a signal from Jojola, moved toward the building, advancing one at a time across the open space.

About the same time, someone from one of the other buildings shouted in Arabic and opened fire. He missed, but the member of Jaxon's team who turned to deal with the threat did not. Even so, the element of surprise was gone.

There was a flash and a bang as the team blew open the main door of the large building and entered. The sound of gunfire and hand grenades erupted from inside, then it stopped abruptly. Someone whistled. "Let's go," Jaxon said to Lucy, and they ran for the building.

The lighting inside was dim but enough for Lucy to see bodies lying in doorways and sitting against blood-spattered walls. They were all "bad guys" and none from the team, who were searching the rooms and removing equipment and papers like high-speed burglars.

Up a flight of stairs, past four more bodies, and at the end of the hallway, Jaxon and Lucy entered what appeared to be a mission-planning room with several laptop computers on a large table and maps on the walls, including a big one of Yemen on the southern coast of the Arabian Peninsula and others of countries in the Middle East and Africa. A chill ran down Lucy's spine as she noted maps of Europe and the United States with colored pins stuck in some cities. Members of the team were taking photographs of the maps before rolling them up and sticking them in aluminum tubes.

However, it wasn't the maps that drew Lucy's attention but the bodies near, and in some cases slumped over, the large table. She hadn't expected so many of them. A neatly coifed, dark-haired middle-aged man with a small mustache sat in a leather chair staring up at the ceiling through dead eyes, a neat bullet hole centered in his forehead. He was dressed like a wealthy business-man, in a tailored dark suit with a starched white shirt and black tie. Next to him, an immensely fat man with a swarthy face, also in a business suit, though his was ill fitting, slumped in his chair with both hands pressed against his chest. A large stain spread out through his fingers. His breath came in ragged gasps and then stopped altogether. Two younger men in leisure suits lay on the floor behind them, clutching semiautomatic handguns they'd had no chance to shoot before bullets caught them in the face.

Across from them, a large, florid older man with an enormous belly, short silver hair, and wearing a camouflage shirt and coat lay on the table with a knife protruding from his back. His head was turned to the side and his sightless blue eyes registered sur-prise. He seemed to be looking at the head of the table, where the last dead man sat upright; he'd been shot in the mouth, and a trickle of blood ran from his lips. He was dressed in a black sweatshirt, baggy black pants, and a black turban.

Sheik Ghareeb al Taizi, Lucy thought. *One of the targets, except we'd hoped to capture him. But who are all these other guys? Who killed them?* Her eyes shifted to the other target, a strikingly beautiful woman sitting calmly in a chair at the other end of the table. She was looking at Lucy and smiled when their eyes met. "Lucy Karp," she purred in heavily accented English. "Good to see you again."

"Nadya," Lucy replied without emotion. "Or are you Ajmaani this evening?"

Nadya Malovo shrugged. "I'm whoever I need to be when I need to be someone. But I prefer Nadya among old friends. Isn't that right, Ivgeny?" she asked in Russian as she turned to a tall man with a scarred face and a patch over one eye who stood next to her with a gun pointed at her head.

Listening to Malovo talk, Lucy understood how she could pass herself off as Ajmaani, a supposedly Muslim terrorist from Chechnya. *Even speaking English or Russian she has a touch of a Chechen accent; almost perfect*, Lucy thought. However, she could still discern that underneath it all Nadya Malovo was a native Russian speaker from the area around Moscow. Lucy was a "super-polyglot," a savant fluent in more than six dozen languages, as well as several dialects.

As such, Lucy had immediately identified the first guard at the gate as being a native of Medina in Saudi Arabia. She'd been surprised that the second guard spoke Persian. "Educated, upper middle class, said he was with VAJA," she'd told Jaxon while they waited for the firefight to be over.

"Iranian intelligence," he'd replied, his eyebrows scrunched together. "What was he doing here? We were looking for Malovo and al Taizi. We'll make sure we get his fingerprints when we leave."

Now Jaxon looked at the man with the eye patch and nodded to the dead men in the room whose faces were being photographed and their fingerprints taken by other members of the team. "They all resist, Ivgeny?"

Ivgeny Karchovski shook his head and replied in his own heavy Russian accent. "They were all dead when we got here. Every one of them, except the one who just died." He looked at Malovo. "Only one other person was alive."

Jaxon walked over to Malovo. "The guy at the end of the table is al Taizi," he said to her. "Who are all the rest of these guys?"

Malovo shrugged. "Dead men."

"Why did you kill them?"

Malovo smiled as though she'd just been complimented on her clothing choice, which was a tight-fitting T-shirt and camouflage shorts. "I heard the shooting and thought it was probably American special ops," she said. "These fools might have tried to go out in a blaze of glory, and I didn't want to get caught in the crossfire. So I took care of the problem and waited to surrender quietly. Imagine my surprise when the first man through the door was my old flame from Afghanistan, Ivgeny Karchovski."

"Are you sure that's the only reason you killed all of them?" Jaxon asked, his eyes narrowing. "Or is it that dead men tell no tales?"

Malovo laughed, then winked. "We may need to talk, but shouldn't we be going? There's a large ISIS presence here, as I'm sure you know, and they're bound to have heard the shooting." She glanced at Karchovski. "You don't seem happy to see me, darling."

Karchovski shook his head. "On the contrary, I'm glad you're here; we came to arrest you and bring you back to the U.S." He looked down at the dead man on the floor. "And this piece of trash."

"Sorry about that," Malovo answered. "But I think that between the computers and documents you'll find here, and what I might be able to help you with in the future, your trip won't have been wasted."

At that moment, one of the young men who'd rappelled from the helicopter entered the room. Unlike the rather eclectic members of the team like Lucy, Jojola, Tran, and Blanchett, the other agents were elite former Special Forces and all business in a war zone. "The locals will be swarming this place like ants at a picnic in a few minutes. I think we'd all rather hitch a ride out of here on a Black Hawk than hoof it across the desert with a bunch of angry ISIS members after us."

"Agreed," Jaxon replied. "You got what we need?"

"We've grabbed all the hard drives from the desktop computers, laptops, cell phones, and any documents we could find," the young man replied. "There's a safe we'll blow and clean out as we're leaving."

"Then let's call in the bird and get the hell out of here," Jaxon said. He looked at Malovo. "Cuff her."

Karchovski pulled plastic ties out of a pocket and put them on the assassin's outstretched wrists. "How romantic," Malovo said with a sardonic smile. "Reminds me of that night in Kabul when we were oh so much younger."

"I wouldn't remember," Karchovski said.

"Nonsense. You could never forget, darling," Malovo said with a laugh, and stood up.

Outside the compound walls, Lucy saw that Ned Blanchett had arrived. She walked up and hugged him. "Good shooting, cowboy," she said.

"Thanks, sweetheart," Blanchett replied. "Just like we planned." He looked at Malovo and frowned. "Where's al Taizi?"

"Dead," Lucy replied. "Nadya killed him, along with a half dozen other guys, before we got there."

"We got company," Jojola shouted. He pointed in the direction of the village, where the headlights of a convoy of vehicles had suddenly appeared and were racing toward them.

"Where's the Black Hawk?" Jaxon asked.

As if summoned at his command, the helicopter materialized out of the night, hovering just a few feet off the ground. There was a small explosion from inside the main building, then the rest of the team came running, one of them carrying a black bag with what Lucy assumed were the contents of the safe.

Less than a minute later, the team was back on board the helicopter as it climbed up and away from the onrushing vehicles. Looking down, Lucy saw red flashes from guns, but they were soon left behind. She turned to find Nadya Malovo watching her. The beautiful assassin sat between two of the younger members of the team, who looked like teenagers who'd suddenly found themselves sitting on either side of a *Playboy* bunny. *How can one woman—especially such a dangerous woman—exude so much animal sensuality?* she wondered.

As if reading her mind, Malovo winked. "Just like old times," she said. "Be sure to give my love to your father when you see him. Tell him I'll be in touch."

2

ARIADNE STUPENAGEL CURSED AS THE SPIKE OF ONE OF her high-heeled black boots sank into the soft grass of Central Park and nearly pitched her to the ground. Without losing her shoe or her pride, she quickly managed to right the ship and continued walking toward the Sunday-afternoon gathering near the Boat House.

Should have worn more practical shoes to a picnic, she thought, but then quickly reversed herself. *To hell with that . . . If I can't wear heels, what's the point of living?*

The day was stupefyingly hot and humid, even for New York in July, and Stupenagel was annoyed by the rivulets of sweat trickling through various crevasses of her curvaceous body. She reached up to pat her bottle-blond hair into place and then down to release another button of the sheer red blouse she wore over a well-filled black bra. She'd finished off the outfit with a very tight, very short black skirt.

Pressing her lips together, she assured herself that they were sufficiently covered by her trademark cherry red lip gloss. She then turned up the wattage of her smile and covered the last thirty yards to the men and women milling around a group of tables, one of which displayed a banner proclaiming Welcome 148th Battlefield Surveillance Brigade Reunion Sign-in. As she approached, she was aware of the appreciative glances of the men in the crowd, and the corresponding disapproval of many of the women.

Bold, brassy, and tall even without the heels, Stupenagel stood out in any crowd, and that was the way the hard-driving journalist liked it. At times her in-your-face attitude got her into trouble, and she'd seen her share of jail cells, third world police stations, and various other dangerous situations. In pursuit of her stories, she'd narrowly escaped run-ins with a bevy of psychopaths, hit men, gangsters, dirty cops, tin-pot dictators, and terrorists. But that bravado, and on occasion her over-the-top sexuality, also got her into the offices, bedrooms, and confidences of the rich, the powerful, and the famous. She knew when to resort to guile over confrontation, but if the situation called for a full frontal assault to overwhelm the enemy's defenses, she was the right gal for the job.

She'd toned the libido down in the past few years, especially after her engagement to Gilbert Murrow, a mild-mannered assistant district attorney who was the aide-de-camp for Butch Karp. But she could still work the feminine charm and turn men's heads when needed. The picnic she was about to invade seemed to be just the right situation.

The majority of the fifty or so people gathered were young men with a sprinkling of middle-aged males among them. Of the women, most seemed to be attached to the men—girlfriends and wives—though some appeared to be members of Troop D. A few of both the men and women were in Army uniforms displaying the Ranger patch, though most were dressed in civies of loud aloha shirts and tattered T-shirts. She glanced at the chests of those in uniform and noted the ribbons indicating tours in Afghanistan and Iraq.

Stupenagel also knew that LRS stood for Long Range Surveillance. As the Army's surveillance units in the field, the LRS teams operated behind enemy lines for as long as thirty days at a time. They primarily conducted reconnaissance, target acquisition, battle information, and damage assessment missions. A few of the units, however, specialized in capturing and interrogating prisoners, sabotage, and field assassinations.

Company D was one of those and apparently had carte blanche to do whatever dirty work needed doing, according to one of her sources in the Pentagon. "They have a reputation for being a bunch of cowboys even for a black ops LRS unit," he'd told her.

I like cowboys, Stupenagel thought as she sauntered past one group of young admirers. But today she only had eyes for one of the older men. He was tall, and though dressed casually, everything about his bearing said career military. Even the word "older" was relative because except for the lines in his deeply tanned, movie-star-handsome face and a little silver in the crew cut hair above his ears, there was nothing old about him.

The man was talking to an attractive young woman in uniform, standing apart and out of earshot of the others at the gathering. They both turned and frowned as Stupenagel walked up. She wondered if they were lovers.

IT HAD STARTED a few days earlier with a call from Lucy Karp, who asked if she wanted to go out to lunch. There was nothing unusual about the invitation; she and Lucy's mother, Marlene Ciampi, had met as freshmen at Smith College when fate had made them roommates. They soon became best friends, and even when their careers and lives had taken them down separate roads, they'd remained as close as sisters. So close that when Marlene and Butch had Lucy she'd been honored to be their first child's godmother.

Stupenagel suggested that they meet at the White Horse Tavern, a historic watering hole in Greenwich Village, long known as a hangout for artists, musicians, bohemians, and journalists, everyone from Dylan Thomas to Jack Kerouac. The tavern was a favorite of hers, but as soon as she saw Lucy sitting outside at one of the sidewalk tables she knew this wasn't a social meeting.

Lucy stood as Stupenagel walked up and kissed her on the cheek. As they sat down, she looked her goddaughter over and thought about how she'd changed both physically and mentally. Lucy had her father's unusual gold-flecked gray eyes and her mother's dark hair and olive coloring. She'd been something of an ugly duckling growing up—a skinny, precocious child, then a gangly, awkward teenager with a large nose and a stunning talent for learning languages. However, the duckling had blossomed into a swan several years after she moved to New Mexico, where she'd fallen in love with a genuine cowboy—a ranch hand named Ned Blanchett. Since then she'd filled out nicely, though there was no extra fat on her lithe frame; she looked tan and fit due to her outdoor lifestyle and what Stupenagel thought of as "the bloom of love."

Yet there was more to Lucy than met the eye. Several years earlier, fate and circumstances led Lucy, because of her language skills, and Ned, a dead-eye rifleman, to being asked to join a small federal antiterrorism agency headed by former FBI agent Espey Jaxon. "The kids," as well as their boss, were not generally forthcoming with details—everything was "highly classified and hush-hush." But there'd been occasions when they deemed it appropriate, or necessary, to share information with Ariadne—often a quid pro quo for something she dug up. At such times, they trusted her to do the right thing with the information.

In some ways, holding back or embargoing information bothered Stupenagel. As a muckraking, take-no-prisoners journalist, she was much more comfortable throwing everything against the proverbial wall and seeing what stuck. Having to use her discretion and "act responsibly"—instead of writing it all down and letting the chips fall where they may—made her want to break out in journalistic hives.

Sitting across the table from Lucy, Stupenagel recalled with sadness one of the last times she'd been at the White Horse Tavern. She'd gone there to meet Lieutenant General Sam Allen, a decorated war hero, the interim director of the CIA, and a former lover. He'd called her out of the blue—it had been many years since they'd shared hot, passionate nights or even a cocktail—but although they reminisced a bit, it wasn't old times in the sack he wanted to talk about.

Disguised in an old Yankees ball cap and ratty sweatshirt, he told her that he had reason to believe that people close to the president were "aware in real time" of an attack on a U.S. consulate in Chechnya. And that rather than provide requested assistance, they had allowed the consulate to be overrun to cover up a foreign policy gaffe. Exactly why, he didn't know.

Allen said he planned to testify before Congress and spill the beans, but added that he was being blackmailed by powerful people who threatened to expose an affair he'd been having. He explained that he was telling her this in case something happened to him and asked her to try to protect the young woman if it did. Unfortunately, Sam Allen was prescient. He'd been murdered the night before he was due to appear before the congressional subcommittee.

The murder of Sam Allen and the cover-up of the debacle in Chechnya was one of those instances in which not wanting to interfere with the pursuit of justice for Sam and those who died in the consulate caused her to hold off writing her story until the men who'd plotted his death were caught, and subsequently convicted by Butch Karp. After that, however, the story had taken on a life of its own, first with her exposé of the murder of Allen and the involvement of the president's political cronies. Inevitably more sources came out of the woodwork, and she'd written a series of stories tied to the administration's feckless foreign policy, especially when it came to dealing with Islamic extremism. Eventually, she ran out of new material, but she believed that she'd hardly scratched the surface of the exact motivation for the major players. Even some of their identities had remained in the shadows.

Lucy confirmed that there was more to the story this day at the White Horse. She wasn't at liberty to reveal everything about the mission but asked the journalist if she recalled the story about the death of Ghareeb al Taizi, an ISIS leader in Syria.

"Sure. The White House took credit for ordering the mission," Stupenagel said. "But I've never been able to get much of anything out of my sources about it."

"That's because very few people know anything, including the military brass," Lucy told her. "But it wasn't a Special Forces operation, nor did the administration know anything about it until it was over. It was one of ours, and the target wasn't just al Taizi."

"I don't understand," Stupenagel said.

"A few weeks before the mission, we got word that Nadya

Malovo was back working for her Russian bosses and up to some mischief," Lucy went on. "We'd been trying to find her since that little incident in Chechnya and Dagestan, but she disappeared. Then she popped up back in Moscow, not hiding at all but in the company of a Russian gangster named Ivan Nikitin. The next thing we knew, she was on the move. She got a little careless in Istanbul, and we picked up her trail; we lost it again in Damascus, but then a reliable source in Ramadi spotted her, apparently working as a bodyguard and interpreter for Nikitin. We got round-the-clock drone surveillance on her and watched her drive her boss to a compound outside a village north of Ramadi on the Syrian border. It's the heart of ISIS country, and that alone was curious considering Russia is supposed to be helping us destroy ISIS."

Stupenagel shrugged. "Gangsters aren't usually patriots. They're trying to make a buck and don't care who they're dealing with so long as they can pay. Let me guess, this Russian gangster is an arms dealer?"

Lucy nodded. "Yes, that and black-market oil. However, this particular gangster is also a former Russian general known for his brutality during the Russia-Chechnya wars—mass murders of entire villages suspected of sympathizing with Chechen separatists, men, women, and children. He was appropriately nicknamed 'Ivan the Terrible.' He's not just any gangster but one with direct ties to the Kremlin."

Stupenagel raised her eyebrows. "Now, that's interesting. So I take it they were meeting this al Taizi, perhaps with the approval of the Russian muckety-mucks?"

"Yes. So Espey got the go-ahead for a raid. We wanted Malovo and al Taizi, and a chance to question Nikitin, too."

"But al Taizi got killed?"

"Yep, and he wasn't the only one. By the time our guys got to al Taizi, he and Nikitin were already dead, and so were four other men. The only one alive was Malovo. Just sitting there, cool as a cucumber."

Stupenagel whistled. "So much for her bodyguard duties. Who were the other guys?"

Lucy looked at Stupenagel for a long moment, then leaned close. "You have to promise me that this doesn't show up in a newspaper article until Espey says it's okay."

Stupenagel narrowed her eyes but nodded. "Same rules. I get the exclusive and I get to put it out there first."

"Deal," Lucy said, and looked around to see if anyone seemed to be watching or listening. "This is where it gets really interesting. It was easy to identify al Taizi, and one of our team members recognized Nikitin from Afghanistan."

"That would be Ivgeny Karchovski. . . ."

"You said it, I didn't. Anyway, the others took longer while we ran their photographs and fingerprints. Two of the dead guys were just foot soldiers there for security, not that they stood a chance with Malovo. The other two, however, were real some-bodies: one, Farid Al Halbi, was a very wealthy businessman from Syria and tied at the hip to the Assad regime; the other, Feroze Kirmani, was one of the top agents with VAJA, the Ira-nian equivalent of the CIA."

"So let me get this straight. They're all making nice with ISIS and al Taizi? And Malovo kills them all without breaking a sweat?"

"That's about the size of it."

"Malovo say why she killed them?"

Lucy shook her head. "Claimed she didn't want to die in a crossfire if her companions resisted. But to be honest, we think she intended to kill them all along."

"Why?"

Another shrug. "She didn't say much on the way back to the base in Saudi Arabia, except that she was keeping some informa-tion to herself. Maybe as a bartering chip. She did tell Espey that the men she killed were waiting for one more important player, someone representing somebody very wealthy, very powerful.

Said she didn't have a name but knows it was an American. But the guy never showed; she thinks he got tipped off about us."

"Anything to back that up?"

"Well, we were supposed to be a top secret, need-to-know-basis mission, which means not many people knew what we were doing. But there was a 'welcoming' party when we got back to the Riyadh Air Force Base in Saudi. 'They' were waiting for us, and 'they' took everything, including Nadya Malovo."

Stupenagel frowned. "First, who is 'they'? And second, I can't believe that Espey Jaxon would sit still while some goons nabbed his goodies, especially if it involved national security."

"He didn't," Lucy replied. "In fact, there was a pretty tense standoff. Espey wasn't giving them what they wanted, and they weren't letting us go anywhere. So there we were sitting in a helicopter with the sun coming up on what would be a rather unpleasant 120-degree day in Saudi Arabia with neither side budging."

"Who blinked first?"

"Wasn't a matter of blinking," Lucy said. "We got word from higher up—in fact, about as high up as you can get—that we were to stand down and turn everything over. Espey stalled as long as he could to buy time so that we could get a look at what we had, but it wasn't enough time."

"So what did you see?"

Lucy shrugged. "The documents were in Arabic, which was easy enough for me to read. Some of it might have been useful, with names and locations associated with ISIS operations. But there was a flash drive that had a number of files in it that also were in Arabic but complete gibberish, obviously encrypted. I couldn't make heads or tails of it, but I did pick up one word that was used several times: *sarab*. It's Arabic for 'mirage.'"

"Doesn't seem unusual for a desert," Stupenagel remarked.

"Yeah, but it was repeated several times throughout a few of the files. How many times does 'mirage' by the normal definition come into a conversation?"

"A code name?"

"Maybe. But we didn't have enough time to be certain."

Stupenagel frowned. "So back to my first question: Who are 'they' who took the stuff and Malovo?"

"Officially, Company D, a Long Range Surveillance unit with the 148th Battalion. But apparently no one knows much about them, except that they report only to their immediate command and from there directly to the president's national security adviser. I'm told they even bypass the Agency."

Stupenagel sipped her wine silently for a moment before speaking again. "This is all fascinating, and I'd love to know what's so important about those files and documents that these 'higher-ups' are willing to intercede between military intelligence and an antiterrorism agency, particularly one with the sort of clout Jaxon's apparently has. However, I still don't see what this has to do with me."

"Well, that depends," Lucy said. "After we got back, Espey went on the warpath and found out that Malovo was being held incommunicado at Guantánamo. He raised a stink and on the sly got her a big-shot lawyer who got her transferred to the Varick Federal Detention Center here in Manhattan. He hasn't been allowed to see her yet, but she got him a message through her lawyer. Only one word."

"Let me guess. *Sarab.*"

"Yep. But there's something else, something she didn't write down. The lawyer told us instead. He said we needed to talk to one of the senior officers with the 148th Battalion who just so happens to be an old friend of Sam Allen," Lucy said quietly. "Apparently they were classmates at West Point, though Sam was a couple of years older; both were Rangers, had several tours in the same places, including Vietnam. This guy also served under Sam in Iraq during the first Gulf War and then in Afghanistan after nine-eleven before getting into Long Range Surveillance."

Stupenagel wiped at a stray tear and cleared her throat. "What's his name?"

"Colonel Michael Swindells. We were hoping—"

"Mick Swindells! Heck yeah, I know him," Stupenagel exclaimed. "Sam, me, and Mick probably hit most of the bars from Saigon to Panama City and everything in between. Good man, better soldier, straight arrow . . . surprised he'd be involved with black ops. More of a John Wayne in *She Wore a Yellow Ribbon* type than *The Bourne Identity* . . . Why doesn't Espey give him a call?"

"For one thing, he isn't sure how Swindells would react," Lucy said, "though he'll feel better about it when I tell him what you said. But more important, all these other intelligence agencies don't know what to make of us—they can't get much information but know Espey has juice from somebody high up. They may be watching, and direct contact between Espey and Swindells might raise more than eyebrows."

Stupenagel smiled. "So you thought the personal touch from a certain charming and, I might add, outrageously gorgeous journalist might be better?"

"A visit from an 'old friend,'" Lucy said with a laugh. "We were hoping that you might at least know him because of the connection to General Allen. Drinking buddies is even better."

"Okay, I'll give him a call. Got a number?" Stupenagel asked.

"We prefer you don't use phone lines. He's been lying low, so he may be a little paranoid, too. But there's a reunion picnic in Central Park for Troop D. We have reason to believe that Colonel Swindells will make an appearance there."

"And I'm just supposed to show up out of the blue and chat up someone I haven't seen or spoken to in more than twenty years about some top secret information?"

"We know it's a stretch, but it's what we've got at the moment. Besides, you're the famous Ariadne Stupenagel, investigative journalist extraordinaire; you have more secret ways of getting information than the Kremlin, *da*, comrade? So what do you think?"

Stupenagel thought about it for a moment, then chuckled. "Looks like I'm going to a picnic."

WHICH IS HOW she found herself trying to navigate Central Park turf in high heels as she walked toward Colonel Mick Swindells and the young woman. Suddenly, the man's frown changed to a grin. "Well, I'll be damned if it isn't Ariadne Stupenagel!"

The journalist smiled right back as she crossed the last ten feet and kissed him on the cheek. "Mick Swindells, you're still a dreamboat."

"Other than your eyesight, you don't seem to have aged yourself," Swindells said, grinning.

"Liar, but I choose to remember that every lie contains a grain of truth," Stupenagel said. "So thank you."

Swindells laughed and turned toward the young woman, who was watching them with a perplexed look on her face. "Ariadne, I'd like to introduce you to Lieutenant Sasha Swindells, my daughter."

"Your daughter? I didn't know you were married."

"Twenty-two years ago," Swindells replied. "Not long after the last time I saw you."

The young woman extended her hand. "Pleased to meet you."

"The pleasure's mine. I see you have your father's eyes and that you've chosen to join the family business."

Sasha Swindells smiled. "Yes, the Army was always Dad's first love, so I thought I'd find out why. How do you know my dad?"

Stupenagel thought she detected a trace of bitterness in the young woman's voice but chose to ignore it. "Well, I'm sure he's very proud," she said as she looked back fondly at the man she'd come to see. "We were friends a long time ago; he was best friends with someone I was very close to."

The smile left Mick Swindells's face. "I still can't believe Sam's gone," he said. "Best man I ever met, and I know the two of you had something special, too."

Stupenagel felt the grief grab her by the throat for a moment before she was able to speak. "Yes, he was quite a man. A great friend and a true hero who didn't think twice about putting himself in danger for his country. But he didn't expect the danger to come from within."

Swindells's face flushed with anger. "No, and that's the most dangerous kind," he said, then tilted his head and looked quizzically at her. "So what brings you to a reunion picnic for an LRS unit? I take it you weren't just wandering around in Central Park in four-inch heels looking for soldiers? Or does this have something to do with Sam?"

Stupenagel nodded toward Sasha. "In a way it does. I don't mean to be rude, but could I speak to you alone for a few minutes?"

The younger woman patted her dad's arm. "I can take a hint," she said. "Are we still on for dinner—that is, unless you and your friend want that time to catch up?"

"That would be nice and maybe some other day," Stupenagel replied. "But I have a prior engagement with my fiancé tonight."

"Fiancé?" Swindells said, raising an eyebrow. "I'd like to meet the man who was able to talk Ariadne Stupenagel into matrimony. If I remember correctly, I think even Sam Allen failed to do that."

"He never asked," Stupenagel said. "At least, not when sober and wearing clothes. The other times don't count."

Swindells laughed and turned back to his daughter. "Pick you up at your hotel at nineteen hundred hours, Lieutenant? In the meantime, put that item I gave you in a safe place."

His daughter snapped to attention and saluted. "Yes, sir!"

Swindells returned the salute. "Dismissed, then."

As they watched the young woman walk away, Stupenagel smiled. "Beautiful girl. Seems to be a chip off her old man's block."

A funny look passed over Swindells's face, and he nodded. "Yes, maybe a bit too much. Guarded emotionally. Her mother died when she was ten. I handled it by taking on as many hot spot tours as I could get. She was mostly raised by my mom, who lives in New Rochelle."

"Thus the comment about your first love," Stupenagel said.

Swindells nodded. "Yes, that dig was meant for me. I regret not being around for her, but there's nothing I can do to change the past except try to see her more now. She just graduated, like Sam and me, from the Point and is visiting her grandmother before leaving for Ranger school."

"Like father, like daughter."

"Yes. She thinks she has something to prove. Being worthy of my love and all that." Swindells's voice caught, and he had to clear this throat before going on. "She's always had it even if I wasn't very good at showing it. . . . Anyway, I'm going to be teaching a special course at West Point in advanced asymmetrical warfare. The 148th Battalion was my last posting, and I just stopped by to say hi to some of the grunts who worked for me."

Stupenagel looked at him sideways. "I was wondering what a combat soldier like Mick Swindells was doing with a military intelligence outfit. Black ops didn't seem to be your style."

Swindells shrugged. "With the force reduction in the hot zones, it was a way to stay in the action. I think field intelligence, instead of relying on high-tech surveillance, is one place where the Army has done a piss-poor job, and I wanted to be part of bringing it up to snuff. Plus, I've learned a few things about staying alive in the field and thought I might pass that knowledge on to some of these young men and women."

As he spoke, he gestured toward the gathering. Stupenagel followed his gesture and noted that a number of the attendees were looking at them curiously.

"So I won't ask how you happened to know I would be in Central Park," Swindells said, "and why you know so much about the 148th, but do you want to let me know what this is really about?"

Stupenagel nodded. "Ghareeb al Taizi. Or, more to the point, what happened afterward at Riyadh."

Swindells kept the smile on his face, but his eyes narrowed and all traces of humor disappeared. "Never heard of it."

"I think you have," Stupenagel said. "And I want to know what was such a big secret that your guys and an antiterrorism agency were headed for a showdown at the O.K. Corral until someone high up ruled in your guys' favor."

"One, not 'my' guys; that was a Company D operation and they only report to the guys at the very top, not some lowly colonel. Two, there are some things going on that I don't necessarily agree with, but as you know, the government often keeps some information from the public."

"Even from other agencies?"

Swindells shrugged. "Interagency feuds are an everyday occurrence." He glanced at the tables and then laughed and reached out to touch her arm as if they were sharing a fond memory.

"Granted," Stupenagel said, "but I have reason to believe that this is more than an interagency power struggle. Someone high up didn't want anyone to have access to whatever was on those computers and documents."

"I don't know what you're talking about."

"Maybe not, but what about Nadya Malovo? Does she know what she's talking about? What about *sarab*, the mirage?"

Swindells's face tensed at the word, then he smiled stiffly and offered her his arm. "Let's walk." When they'd moved away from the others, he spoke again. "I want you to forget this. It's above your pay grade and probably mine; all I can say is I'm working on something, but I'm not there yet and may never get there. You don't know what you're up against, so please drop it, for old times' sake. You're swimming in shark-infested waters."

Stupenagel took the offered arm and allowed herself to be escorted away from the party. "It's for old times' sake that I can't, Mick. Besides, you do remember who you're talking to, right? The first journalist—not just female journalist—in Phnom Penh when Pol Pot was overthrown. And I was sipping mojitos in Panama City before you, Sam, and the rest of the cavalry showed up to arrest that pimply-faced, drug-dealing dictator Noriega."

This time Swindells's laugh was real. "Yes, I remember that—and more." Then his eyes hardened again. "But I won't have your blood on my hands, which is why—and the only reason why—I have to ask you not to contact me again."

Stupenagel held his gaze and then shook her head. "What do you think Sam would say, Mick?"

"I don't know," Swindells shot back. "Sam's dead, and you're the last person I need to remind about why he died."

Stupenagel dropped her hand from his arm. "He died because some power-hungry bastards saw him as an impediment to their plans. *And* he died because he was trying to do the right thing. Goodbye, Mick." With that she turned and walked away.

She supposed it might have appeared to anyone watching that she and Mick had a falling out of the jilted woman variety.

A couple of minutes later, as she was fishing in her purse for her cell phone, she nearly bumped into a young man going in the opposite direction. He had a military-style crew cut and his eyes were hidden by dark sunglasses; he didn't say a word as he sidestepped her.

Still thinking about her talk with Colonel Mick Swindells, she punched in the number for Lucy Karp.

Lucy answered just as Ariadne reached the sidewalk leading out of the park toward Central Park West. "Ariadne?"

"Hi, honey. I just saw my friend," Stupenagel reported. "I think you're barking up the right tree, but he's not talking. Maybe I can try again in a few—" She never finished the sentence.

Gunshots rang out in the direction from which she'd come. One, two, then several more.

Without knowing exactly why, she suddenly felt sick to her stomach. "Sorry, Lucy, I have to go," she said as she reached down, removed her high heels, and began to run. Back toward the reunion. Back toward a nightmare she knew in her heart had to do with the reason she was there.

3

"I DON'T GET IT."

At the sound of his elder son's voice, Butch Karp lowered the Sunday *New York Times* and peered over the top of the newspaper. Isaac, known to his family and friends as Zak, was seated at the island in the kitchen of their SoHo loft surrounded by the books and papers he'd gathered for a school project. He was leaning on his elbows with his face in his hands and staring down at his laptop.

"What don't you get?" Karp asked.

Zak picked up his head and gestured toward the items on the counter. "This."

Karp knew in general terms what "this" was. As part of their senior projects in history class, his twin sons and their classmates had been assigned to choose a revolution that had occurred somewhere in the world and write a paper on it. It was no small task; they were expected to address the causes, identify the principal characters, explain why the winners succeeded, and state whether in hindsight the revolutionaries had accomplished their stated goals.

As expected, Giancarlo, the younger by a couple of minutes and the better student, had sailed right through his selection: the American Revolution. An obvious choice, but Karp had been impressed that Giancarlo had reached back to June 15, 1215, and King John of England agreeing at Runnymede to fix his seal to the Magna Carta. Confronted by angry barons who demanded that he agree in the document to their demands to protect their rights and property from the arbitrary rule of the Crown, the king had consented to avoid civil war. A little more than two months later, however, Pope Innocent III nullified the agreement and England plunged into chaos. But Magna Carta would be revived after John's death as the basis of English law and eventually be used by American revolutionaries to justify rebellion in defense of liberty.

"Although it didn't really talk much about commoners," Giancarlo wrote in the opening of his paper that he showed his dad, "there were two provisions in particular that would have a great impact on the Declaration of Independence, as well as the U.S. Constitution, particularly the Bill of Rights. These two provisions were: 'No free man shall be taken, imprisoned, disseised, outlawed, banished, or in any way destroyed, nor will We proceed against or prosecute him, except by the lawful judgment of his peers or by the law of the land.' And, 'To no one will We sell, to no one will We deny or delay, right or justice.'

"The Fifth Amendment's provisions that 'no person shall be deprived of life, liberty or property without due process of law' comes from Magna Carta's protections according to the 'law of the land.'"

Giancarlo was still working on the conclusion to his report and whether the American Revolution had accomplished its stated goals, but he was cruising into his last laps. Zak, on the other hand, was struggling.

Surprisingly, at least to his parents and teacher, Zak had chosen the Russian Revolution, which to Karp was a much more complicated event. An exceptional athlete who was being recruited by colleges to play baseball, Zak had never been into academics like his brother. He was by no means unintelligent, quite the contrary, but as his high school counselor had been known to complain, he was at times "unmotivated" if a subject didn't interest him.

History was not one of the motivational subjects. So when he chose to explain how a variety of circumstances led to the Bolsheviks, and their descendant the Communist Party, taking over, Karp asked him why he'd picked such a difficult subject. "I don't know," Zak said with a shrug. "I guess I didn't know much about it but was curious, since Russia always seems to be in the news these days. They don't teach us much about American history and the War of Independence, but it's more than I know about the Russian Revolution. I thought it might be interesting and . . . I don't know . . . important."

The thoughtful response made Karp sit back and consider Zak. He had always been bigger than Giancarlo and favored his mother's Italian side of the family—olive skinned, thick features, and a perpetual five o'clock shadow since his first year in high school. Giancarlo was paler, thinner, a good enough athlete but no star. Both had their mother's thick, curly black hair and dark eyes, but personality-wise, Zak burned hotter; Giancarlo was more likely to try to think himself (and his brother) out of a situation.

"I think that's a great choice and I look forward to reading what you have to say," Karp said, wondering if he was watching his son mature right in front of his eyes.

"Besides, Russian chicks are hot," Zak added with a grin.

Maybe not, Karp thought, shaking his head and walking away.

Still, that night reading in bed with Marlene, he'd noted the apparent shift in Zak's maturity.

"Well, he and Giancarlo finally did just get bar mitzvahed," Marlene said. "Maybe he took the 'rite of passage to manhood' seriously."

"I'd hope so, since it was four years later than the customary thirteen years old," Karp said. "But I think there's more to it than that."

Marlene closed her book and turned on her side to look at him. "Could it be tied to the fact that he just survived being abducted by a neo-Nazi murderer, having a gun pointed at his head, and then watching a young man die?" She smiled wanly as she said it. "Take it from someone who knows, those sorts of things tend to sober you up about life."

Karp nodded. "Guess our kids, and you, too, have been put through hell because of my job. Shot. Bombed. Abducted. Assaulted." He held up his fingers as he listed the crimes that had been perpetrated against his family, some of them more than once.

Marlene reached out and put a finger to his lips. "Shhhhhh. It's not just your job—or even my wacky career decisions—

that has put this family, including you, in harm's way. I used to think Lucy was imagining that there's a battle between good and evil going on, and that for some unknown reason this family had been chosen to be in the middle of it. Now I'm not so sure, and I'm willing to think that maybe she's right. But at least we get to be the good guys, thanks to my stalwart crime-fighting husband. But we're talking about Zak, and I don't think this new 'maturity,' or whatever you want to call it, is all about a near-death encounter. Maybe he did take the words of the rabbi seriously, but I think he's just more introspective and thoughtful in general." She laughed. "I've actually caught him doing his homework without being told. And he even asked me if he could order books online for this Russian Revolution project."

Karp chuckled. "Did you take his temperature? Maybe we should take him to see a doctor." He closed his book. "But I think you're right, our boy's just growing up."

Wanting to encourage Zak, after work and on weekends Karp had helped him research his subject and find reading material. He'd heard from one of his assistant district attorneys at the office that *A People's Tragedy: The Russian Revolution 1891–1924* by Orlando Figes was the seminal work on the events leading to, during, and immediately after the revolution—actually revolutions—that culminated in the rise of the Soviet Union. So he'd ordered the book from the Housing Works Bookstore down the block on Crosby and gone there with Zak to pick it up.

Zak's eyes had widened when he saw the voluminous book. However, he'd apparently found it interesting and he'd been carrying it around with him for a month. They'd even once found him in bed reading it.

Now the fact that he was indoors on a pleasant Sunday afternoon instead of plotting ways to get out of his schoolwork was further proof that he was determined to do well. However, the momentum seemed to have stalled.

"So what about 'this' are you having a hard time with?" Karp asked.

Zak pointed to his research materials. "There's just so much," he confessed. "And some things I just don't get. So I guess I'm feeling a little overwhelmed."

Karp walked over to his dejected son. He looked over Zak's shoulder at the yellow legal pad on which he'd been taking notes.

"I don't get how the Bolsheviks came to power or why they stayed in power," Zak said. "After Tsar Nicholas abdicated and all these different groups—monarchists, social democrats, moderates—got together to try to decide what form of democratic government they wanted, the Bolsheviks were just a small minority. They were just a bunch of loud-mouthed bullies. So why did they win?"

Karp raised his eyebrows. "Good question, and one that I think has a lot of relevance to the political scene in this country now, and maybe you can go into that a little bit at the conclusion of this paper."

"What do you mean?" Zak asked.

"Well, you're right that the Bolsheviks were a minority party," Karp said. "No one really took them all that seriously as a major power broker, not until it was too late. But they were focused on their goal of achieving power and imposing their worldview on others, and they were ruthless in how they went about it. Democracy can be a messy affair with a lot of compromising and debate as its proponents try to work out their issues in a civilized manner. All of this can lead to inertia, with no one being willing to assume real leadership, particularly in a crisis. So when a small group of dedicated 'true believers' is willing to dispense with the niceties, or even the rule of law, they can easily fill in that leaderless void.

"That's a simple explanation, but I think it's pretty valid about what happened in Russia, and I think we are even seeing some of that in this country now. The 'loud-mouthed bullies'—the extremists—are taking over. They believe that they have the right to impose their worldview, whether it's subtly convincing gullible people that they 'know what's best for them,' or not so subtly at the point of a gun."

"Eventually, at least in Russia," Zak added, "it seemed to always come down to the point of a gun. The Bolsheviks even turned on each other, and anybody else who stood in their way."

"And that, my boy, is the answer to the question of how a minority party seized control of a country as large and diverse as Russia," Karp said.

Before the conversation could go any further, Karp's cell phone went off. He walked over to the coffee table in the living room where he'd left it. The caller ID identified Clay Fulton, the detective in charge of the special unit of NYPD detectives assigned to the District Attorney's Office. Karp sighed. Although they had been friends since Fulton was a rookie cop and Karp a recent law school grad working as an assistant DA in Manhattan, it was unlikely to be a social call or even a run-of-the-mill murder in a city that averaged four hundred homicides a year.

"Hello, Clay, what's up?"

"You watching television, by any chance?" Fulton replied. "Never mind, dumb question. You would have called me if you were. There's been a shooting—two fatalities, several more injured—in Central Park."

"Gangs?"

"No, lone shooter. At a picnic for an Army unit. One of the wounded was an off-duty detective. They exchanged fire. The detective, a guy named Ted Moore, got hit, but the shooter took off or it could have been worse."

"Where's the shooter now?"

"Not sure. Could be in the park. Could be in a taxi headed for LaGuardia, for all we know. There's a BOLO for him, he shouldn't get far."

"We know who he is?"

"Yeah, a former Army Ranger named Dean Mueller," Fulton replied. "He shot up a reunion party for his old unit. Some of the witnesses knew him."

Karp sighed. *There goes the weekend.* "You better send the . . ."

". . . car's on the way," Fulton finished the sentence. "Figured you'd want to go to the scene. I'm on my way now."

"Which ADA is on call from the office?" Karp asked.

"Kenny Katz. He's already there. Spoke to him for a couple of minutes, but he was getting started and needed to go."

Karp thought for a second about his protégé, Katz, and nodded. *Right man for the job. Former decorated Army Ranger himself. He ought to be able to read between the lines on this one.*

"Thanks, Clay. I'll be ready in five."

Karp hung up and leaned over the coffee table to pick up the remote control and turned on the television. Already set to the news channel, the screen winked to life with a young woman reporter barely able to contain her excitement at being "the first on scene at this horrific mass shooting." Behind her a half dozen police cruisers and several unmarked sedans, as well as two fire department paramedic vans, were arrayed on the grass, their red and blue lights flashing. Inside a perimeter of yellow crime scene tape, a line of police officers stared intently at the ground as they walked shoulder to shoulder across the grass.

"We don't have all the details yet," the journalist said breathlessly. "Police detectives have sequestered the witnesses and are interviewing them as we speak."

The camera panned to a group of people gathered near or sitting at picnic tables. The rest of the scene looked like a tornado had blown through, with beer cans, plates, food, even articles of clothing scattered throughout. Small knots of people, some in uniform, stood together, many of them hugging and obviously crying. NYPD detectives methodically moved among them, taking initial statements.

Karp spotted Assistant District Attorney Kenny Katz standing next to a detective sergeant who was questioning a woman. He did a double take: Ariadne Stupenagel. He knew at that moment that whatever had happened, she was somehow at the heart of it.

"What do we know about what happened?" the disembodied voice of a newscaster asked the young journalist.

"Well, Dirk, according to what we've been able to learn from the police—after being the first news team on the scene—about thirty minutes ago this reunion for a group of Army veterans in Central Park took a tragic turn," she replied. "I was told by a sergeant that the suspect is one Dean Mueller, who apparently once served with this particular regiment. He appeared out of nowhere and began shooting."

"Do we know how many have been killed and/or wounded?"

The young woman nodded her head vigorously. "Yes. This is not confirmed, but we believe that there were two fatalities, and at least two others wounded, including a police officer who happened to be passing by and traded shots with the suspect. He's being called a hero by other witnesses and is being treated at the hospital. We have not been able to identify the status of the injured."

"Have you been able to talk to any witnesses?" the newscaster asked.

Shaking her head, the young woman replied sadly, "No, Dirk, the police were on the scene quickly and have pretty much—"

"Just a minute, Mina," the newscaster interrupted. "Another WFN reporter on the scene, Greg Champion, has apparently located an eyewitness. We'll be cutting to Greg."

Mina's piqued countenance disappeared from the screen and was replaced with a smug-looking middle-aged male reporter. "That's right, Dirk," Champion said in an overly self-involved baritone. "I'm here with Freddy Ortega, who was enjoying a quiet Sunday in Central Park's Sheep Meadow with his friends when the shooting started about forty yards away."

The camera panned back to include a keyed-up young Hispanic man tilting his head back so that he could peer out from under a red bandanna that all but covered his eyes. "Tell our listeners what you saw, Freddy," the reporter said, sticking his microphone in the witness's face.

"Yeah, well, homes, me and some of my homies was chillin' with a couple of our bitches, downing forties and shit, when we heard it. *Pop pop pop.* A whole bunch of times. Sounded like a nine."

The reporter grimaced at the word "bitches," but continued. "By a nine, you mean a nine-millimeter handgun?"

"Yeah, homes, a nine."

"And you told me just a few moments ago that you actually saw the shooter up close?"

"Yeah, we was trying to figure out what was going down when

59

this white dude comes running toward us. He had the nine in his hand. I got in his way and said, 'Whoa, dude, wassup?'"

"Did he say anything?"

"Yeah, real spooky-like, the dude says, 'Just chill if you don't want to die.' I tell you what, homes, I was looking in the eyes of a stone-cold killer. Not my day to die, so I stepped aside and he ran past."

As the reporter continued to milk the interview, Karp put down the remote and placed a call. "Hi, Kenny? It's Butch. Yeah . . . I heard and I'm on my way. I know you're up to your eyeballs in alligators, but just letting you know, a reporter with WFN Channel 7 is interviewing someone named Freddy Ortega about forty yards from where you're standing. Ortega claims the gunman approached him and made a statement. You might want to get to him before the story grows. I'll see you in twenty."

Karp changed out of his sweats—he'd planned on challenging the twins to a game of hoops—and into his "work clothes" of gray slacks, a blue-and-white-striped button-down shirt, a paisley tie carefully selected by his spouse, and a navy blazer. His mentor Garrahy had always insisted that his ADAs look professional in public, and not only had it stuck with Karp, but he'd carried the rule over into his own tenure as DA.

The memory of his own beginnings at the DAO caused Karp

to consider his young ADA at the scene. When Karp had hired him, Kenny Katz was a little older than the typical law school graduate. He'd interrupted his education at Columbia Law School after 9/11 to enlist in the Army, then served in Afghanistan and Iraq, and received the Purple Heart for wounds he'd received and the Bronze Star for gallantry.

Karp had liked the young man from the start and recognized that not only did he have a sharp legal mind, but he also was as steady as they came. He'd taken Katz under his wing, just as his mentors had with him, with the idea of grooming him for the Homicide Bureau, where he'd excelled.

Although it was the luck of the draw as to which ADA had been on call for the shooting, Karp thought Katz's experience might help with the military aspects. He wasn't going to the scene because Katz couldn't handle the initial interviews. It was obviously going to be a high-profile case with a frenzied media, and the burden of this prosecution was going to fall on the top man's shoulder. Otherwise, the best man for the job was already on the ground and running with it.

Karp left the fourth-floor loft and entered the private elevator that took him to the ground level. He glanced up at the security monitor above the door and saw that a dark sedan was already pulled up at the curb. A plainclothes police officer, Eddie Ewin, was standing by the back passenger door, ready to take him wherever he needed to go.

"Hello, Eddie. I take it you've heard about the shooting in Central Park," Karp said.

"Good afternoon, Mr. Karp," Ewin responded, opening the door of the car. "Yeah, terrible. Heard it on the scanner and then Detective Fulton called and said you'd be needing me."

A short, broad-shouldered man with dark hair and eyes, Ewin shook his head. "I heard on the radio that some of the dead were vets. Served their time over there only to come home and have some nutcase do something like this. What's the world coming to, Mr. Karp?"

"Good question," Karp said as he settled into the seat. "But I don't have an answer."

Ewin got in the driver's seat and started the car. "The park?" he said, looking in the rearview mirror.

"Yes, please. Anything new about the shooter's whereabouts?"

"I was just listening to the scanner when you came out. I heard someone matching the suspect was seen running on the west side of the park, over past the—"

Suddenly the police scanner crackled. "All units in the proximity of the Central Park Zoo, ten thirty-nine hostage situation in progress. Suspect armed and considered dangerous . . ."

As the voice continued, Karp leaned forward and tapped Ewin on the shoulder. "Let's go to the zoo," he said. "Katz has the Sheep Meadow scene covered."

"On the way, sir, though if you ask me, it sounds like he's where he belongs."

4

WELLINGTON CONSTANTINE PUT DOWN THE SUNDAY *New York Times* and gazed out at the swimming pool where his wife, Clare, had just finished her laps and was climbing up the ladder on the opposite side. He admired her tanned, toned body, the womanly hips and, when she grabbed her towel and turned toward him, the ample bosom that had caught his eye when he was still on wife number two.

Twenty-five years his junior, he had to admit that Clare was still a stunning woman at age forty. And yet, though she'd lasted longer than any of the others (they were coming up on their eighteenth wedding anniversary), he was tired of her. Actually, he had been for a long time, but a combination of laziness and a preoccupation with his multifaceted business pursuits, as well as consolidating his political power in Washington and abroad, had delayed his doing anything about it.

As one of the wealthiest men in the world—the Long Island beach mansion they were currently living in was just one of many fabulous estates—he had his pick of young, beautiful women to attend to his physical needs. A wife was just an accessory for a man like him, akin to choosing the right tie, to be used for public functions and as a tool to present his "softer side" to a gullible public.

In that regard, the former Clare Dune had served him well. She was an Olympic-caliber swimmer when he met her at a fund-raising event for the U.S. Olympic Team. There'd been a whirlwind courtship when he'd overwhelmed her concerns about their "fall-spring" age difference and the fact that he was married with gifts, travel, and promises to divorce his second wife. He'd accomplished the latter when his wife gracefully, and probably gratefully, agreed to the divorce with a generous settlement. Her publicist had even issued a press release stating that they'd "mutually agreed to go their separate ways while remaining friends, as well as parents to their son." He'd then cemented the deal with Clare by promising to let her spend a good deal of his money on her charitable interests.

In fact, Clare was a genuine do-gooder who'd proceeded over the years to spend a small fortune on charities and noble causes all over the world. He really could not have cared less about feeding starving children in sub-Saharan Africa or saving dolphins from Japanese fishermen, but he considered it money well spent on public relations. His wife and her "team" did all of the work, and when necessary he'd fly into whatever godforsaken backwater she was championing at the moment for photo ops to appear in *People* magazine or the *Washington Post*. Then he'd fly back off to wherever he needed to be to further his true interests: the acquisition of money and power. The only thing they had in common was their son, Tommy, now fourteen years old.

Thanks to Clare, they were the ultimate Beltway progressive power couple in D.C., the darlings of the Manhattan liberal establishment, the toast of their party from Miami to San Francisco, and frequent dinner guests at the White House. Two years earlier they'd been feted by the Hollywood and music industry elite at the John F. Kennedy Center for the Performing Arts as the Philanthropic Couple of the Year, where politicians toadied up, hoping to catch a moment with him and his bankroll.

Little did those people know that in the privacy of their

homes and hotel rooms, he enjoyed slapping Clare around, careful not to leave marks on her face, though his cruel words probably hurt her far worse than blows from his hands or feet. When she tried refusing sex, he raped her, not because he really wanted her but to show her who was boss.

He knew she was always judging him—she knew what he really thought of her "bleeding-heart hobbies"—and it made him angry. Over the past few years she'd turned to alcohol to drown the disappointments of her marriage. Unfortunately for her, the booze sometimes resulted in her speaking her mind when it would have been better to stay silent. She'd once even threatened to expose him as nothing more than a disingenuous power broker, a philanderer, and a wife abuser. That had sent him over the edge, and he'd choked her until she blacked out. When she came to, he told her that the next time she threatened him she wouldn't be waking up.

There'd also been the time she left him for three days, apparently going to a women's shelter in Manhattan. He'd sent his man Shaun Fitzsimmons after her. Fitzsimmons was a six-foot-five, rock-hard black-belt bodyguard and general good man Friday. He was also a former Special Forces member who'd been drummed out of the service after being court-martialed for brutality against Iraqi civilians. Yet even he wasn't able to find her.

So he shut down her credit cards and knew she'd return if for no other reason than their son. When she came back, he beat her black and blue. "And if you ever leave me without permission, you'll never see Tommy again," he sneered into her tear-stained face.

Lately she'd seemed unusually happy. She didn't give him any "looks," or challenge him in any way. She even seemed to be drinking less. He wondered if it was because she was screwing Richie Bryers, the basketball coach at the exclusive prep school where Tommy was enrolled. He'd hired Bryers to coach Tommy in his spare time, also figuring that the "golden carrot" would assure his boy a place on the varsity squad in a couple of years.

As if on cue, Bryers appeared from the bathhouse where he'd apparently been changing into a swimsuit and white robe. He removed the robe to enter the pool. Constantine studied the man. An avid tennis player, he was no slouch himself, but he was impressed with the coach's tanned, sculpted physique. He knew the man stayed active not just on the basketball court where he'd once been a highly recruited New York Public High School player and then all-American point guard at Harvard, but also was a skier, surfer, and mountain climber.

Bryers saw him looking and smiled and waved. Constantine

smiled and waved back. He actually liked the man—at least, as much as he liked anyone—and that's why he extended the use of the pool and guesthouse to him whenever they were spending time there. It didn't hurt that he believed that between the money and the "perks," Bryers was bought and paid for in regard to his son's special tutoring and future on the team. *After all*, he chuckled to himself, *everyone has a price.*

Yet Constantine hadn't intended one of those side benefits to include sex with his wife. He didn't really care about her, and it made him all the more determined that divorce number three would be a fact before the end of the year. But on principle he didn't like the idea of anyone helping himself to anything he owned, and he owned Clare. He glanced over at his wife; she was watching Bryers as he lowered himself into the pool. She felt Constantine's eyes on her and looked his way. *Guilty*, he thought angrily, and made a mental note to put Fitzsimmons on them to confirm his suspicions.

However, at the moment he had more important things to deal with. He looked down at a leather-bound notebook open on the table next to the lounge chair he was lying on. He'd kept a journal since he was a lonely child brought up by an alcoholic mother and his shipping tycoon father. The kind of notebooks had changed over the years from the old black-and-white composition notebook to the current version that he had made special for him. But he'd kept them all—hundreds of them—now lining an entire wall-length bookshelf in his library.

Some of what he wrote when he was young were just musings of a boy or comments on other kids and people. But as he grew older, he'd used them to "think through" and plan out his business dealings, especially after becoming a business major at Princeton and he was well on his way—with the help of his father's fortune—to building an empire. The notebooks included his innermost thoughts, as well as details of some transactions and projects that at best were unethical and often criminal. He knew they were dangerous to keep, but he didn't trust computers. Besides, it gave him an almost sexual thrill to look up from his desk and see a library's worth of his writing.

Even if it was a risk, he wasn't worried. Money bought a lot of things, including law enforcement, judges, and public opinion. The press fawned all over him, and any independent media sources that dared say anything else were quickly dismissed as "politically motivated" by their colleagues,

Constantine's supporters, and the adoring public. His homes were protected by state-of-the-art security, as well as the ominous presence of Mr. Fitzsimmons and his nefarious team of goons.

Constantine frowned. The notebook was open to his latest journaling about his most ambitious project yet. But it hadn't been going well, and in fact, if the ship didn't get righted soon, his whole empire could come crashing down around his ears and he'd find himself decorating a federal prison cell. But he was no coward; the thought of his scheme—both what he planned to accomplish and the risk—gave him a rush, and he intended to make it happen. *And I always, always get what I set my mind to*, he thought.

"Excuse me, there's a call for you, Mr. Constantine."

He turned at the deep bass of Fitzsimmons's voice. "The one I'm expecting?" he asked.

"Apparently there's been a glitch."

Constantine scowled. He didn't like "glitches" and paid good money for them not to happen. "I'll take it in the library," he said curtly.

As he stood to go back into the house, Constantine nodded toward his wife, who was seated on one of the sun chairs. "I want those two watched. Let me know what they're doing."

Fitzsimmons raised an eyebrow, then smirked. "You got it, boss. Want me to do anything if they're up to some hanky-panky?"

Constantine's eyes narrowed. "No, just let me know. I'll decide what to do after that."

5

WHEN THE SEDAN ARRIVED AT THE FIFTH AVENUE EN-
trance to the Central Park Zoo, Officer Ewin pulled over to
where a uniformed police officer was waving traffic around
a half dozen parked cruisers with their red and blue lights
flashing. Karp looked out the window and noted a larger con-
tingent of officers standing by the Arsenal, as the zoo administration building was known, blocking the entrance.

Ewin rolled down his window when the officer approached.
"I got the district attorney with me," he said. "What's the
latest?"

The officer leaned over and looked at Karp. "Hello, sir," he
said when he recognized him. "The shooter's holed up with

some hostages on the northwest side of the zoo in the Bird House, near the grizzly bear enclosure."

Despite the urgency of the moment, Karp smiled. "You seem to know a lot about the zoo, Officer."

The officer, a young man who barely looked old enough to be out of high school, smiled. "Yes, sir, grew up about five blocks from here; been coming since I was a kid. You'll probably have to walk from here if you want to get up to the command post. You need someone to show you the way?"

"Not a problem, Officer," Karp replied, reaching for the handle and opening the door. "It's changed a lot, but I've been coming here since I was a toddler . . . my kids, too."

"I knew you were from Brooklyn, sir. Anyways, you'll find the command center no problem if you just head for the bears. I'll radio ahead and let everybody know you're coming."

"Thanks," Karp said as he exited. "Eddie, stay with the car, please. I'll call you if I need you."

"You got it, sir."

Karp walked over to the knot of officers at the entrance. One of them was detached by his sergeant to accompany him into the six-and-a-half-acre zoo. Walking through the strangely deserted grounds, he was reminded of another hot summer day many years earlier. It was the last time he'd visited the zoo with his mother.

He was a senior in high school and she was dying of cancer. Her bad days far outnumbered the good, so it surprised him and his father one Sunday when she announced at breakfast that she wanted to go into the city and visit the zoo. They'd worried that even the short trip from their Brooklyn neighborhood would be too taxing on her meager reserves of energy and only ramp up the pain that was her constant companion. But she'd argued that she wouldn't have many more days when she'd feel up to such a journey, "and I want to go one more time to see the animals."

A star basketball player, Karp had planned on going to his school to work with his coach on his game, but he called to say he wouldn't make it. His coach knew the situation at home and told him to spend the time with his mother. "Basketball can wait," he said. "Say hello to your mom for me, and I'll be look-ing for her in the stands when the season starts." They both knew that wasn't going to happen, but Karp had appreciated the thought.

So they'd taken the elevated train into the city. There his dad wanted to hail a taxi to Central Park, but his mom insisted they take the green line subway up to Central Park. A "people watcher," she'd always preferred to mix it up with humanity, so they rode north with the throng, getting off at the Hunter College station on 68th Street and then backtracking a few blocks to the zoo.

It was a wonderful day. Years later, Karp could still recall entire conversations, as well as the sights, the smells, and the sounds, especially of his mother's voice. She'd been happier, more full of energy than at any other time in the past year as cancer whittled at her stamina and spirit.

Unlike the walkways on this afternoon, deserted due to the gunman, those had been full of New Yorkers and visitors strolling the grounds—families with young, screaming, laughing children, teenagers in love, and old couples holding hands. His mother had been her precancer self, making funny observations about the crowds, guessing at their stories, and giggling at her son's and husband's versions. They'd wrinkled their noses in the odiferous Monkey House, laughed at the antics of the polar bears, and oohed and ahhed when the lion roared. She'd even managed to eat half the hot dog they'd bought for her from a vendor's cart. But gradually her energy waned, and she'd sat wearily on a bench across from a pen where a wolf paced back and forth.

Karp's father left them there to go get her a glass of water. She leaned against her son's shoulder, then looked up at him as a tear slid down her cheek.

"I'm sorry, Mom," he'd said softly, choking on the words but not knowing what else there was to say.

She'd wiped away the tear and patted his knee before pointing across to the wolf. "I like seeing the animals, but I think about them living their lives in cages, and it makes me sad," she said. "I think they're in pain, not because they're being mistreated but because they don't belong in captivity. A lot of them go crazy, especially the smart ones, or the ones who know what it was like to live in the wild. For them, only death can set them free from the suffering." As she'd paused, the wolf stopped his pacing and looked at her. "It's the only thing that will free me, too."

"Don't say that," he'd responded, though they both knew it was true.

She'd reached up to touch his cheek and sighed. "It's okay, Butch. I look forward to the day when I'm no longer in this pain. It's destroying more than my body; it's taking my mind, especially when I need morphine. I feel like I'm losing myself, and that's no life . . ." She stopped what she was saying and shuddered as if in sudden agony.

Karp had put his arm around her. "We shouldn't have come," he said bitterly. "This was too much."

"You're wrong," she'd replied. "I'm so glad we had this time. When I'm gone, I want you to have a million memories of me. I'm still alive if I'm remembered by those who I love and who love me."

Karp's father arrived with the glass of water. This time she didn't resist when he insisted that they take a taxi all the way back to Brooklyn. In fact, she'd slept most of the way and gone straight to bed when they arrived.

There were no more fun trips into the city, and she never made it to any more of his basketball games. Butch had to learn how to give her the pain- and mind-numbing shots of morphine by practicing on an orange, and he watched her deteriorate until at last she was freed by death.

Looking back, Karp could trace his desire to be a prosecuting attorney to his mother's battle against cancer. He'd come to see cancer as a type of evil, and he'd been powerless to stop it or protect his innocent mother. Crimes that people committed against other innocent people were another type of evil, but one he could do something about, and by putting evil people behind bars, he could protect the innocent.

The Central Park Zoo, which was officially opened in 1934 when a haphazard menagerie on the grounds was designated, had changed a lot since the days when Karp visited with his family. By the 1960s, the buildings and pens had fallen into sad disrepair; neighbors of Central Park complained of the smells and visitors of the deplorable conditions the animals were kept in. Eventually, activists forced its closing and renovation, with the gates opening again in 1988 on a modern facility with habitats designed to recreate the natural environment the animals came from.

That was the zoo his own children had known, the one whose empty pathways beneath the tall trees he was walking on now to where a killer held hostages. But when he pictured the zoo in his mind, it was always the old grounds, the wolf pen, and that last visit with his mother.

Approaching the Bird House and grizzly bear habitat, Karp made his way to the SWAT team command center behind two armored trucks that had been parked as a barrier between those assembled and the gunman. A television camera crew was on the scene, and he recognized the young woman reporter from the shooting scene now smiling triumphantly in between "live" takes. Meanwhile, heavily armed Special Ops police officers were taking position on the sides of the building. He spotted Fulton, who'd been watching for him. The big detective waved him over to where he was listening to a police negotiator speaking to someone—he presumed the suspect—on a cell phone.

"What do we have, Clay?" Karp asked.

"I might have already said this, but the suspect's name is Dean Mueller," Fulton answered. "He's a former Army Ranger assigned to the unit he just shot up. He apparently received an Other Than Honorable discharge from the Army about three months ago, but we don't know any details about it. Two uniformed officers spotted him heading for the park exit at Sixty-sixth Street and he ran into the zoo. Now he's got about a dozen people, including some kids, at gunpoint inside the Bird House."

"Mueller say anything about why he did it?"

Fulton nodded toward the police negotiator. "Not much. Something about he was set up. Don't know what that means. Otherwise, it's mostly been threats to kill the hostages if anybody tries to get at him. The guy's well trained and it's tough to come at him in that building. Good chance of casualties even if he doesn't start killing hostages."

Karp and Fulton walked over to the negotiator just as the shooter demanded, "I want to talk to the DA!"

"Okay, Dean, what do you need the DA for?" the negotiator asked, glancing at Karp. "He's a busy man."

"Quit dicking around and get me the fucking DA, or this conversation is over. Get him on the phone."

Karp stepped forward and held out his hand for the negotiator's cell phone. "This is District Attorney Roger Karp," he said.

"Yeah, right, you suddenly appeared when I asked? How do I know this isn't some other cop?"

"You know what I look like?"

"I've seen photos."

"Then I'm going to step out in front of these trucks and come to the door," Karp said. "You want to talk, we'll talk."

"Okay, but I'll shoot one of these people if anything goes wrong."

Karp started to move, but Fulton grabbed his arm. "I don't like it. This guy's already killed today. Maybe he's just looking for more publicity by shooting the district attorney."

Gently removing his arm from his friend's grip, Karp shook his head. "Something tells me he wants to get out of where he is, not kill me. I'm going to see what he wants."

Karp moved out from behind the trucks and began walking toward the front doors of the Bird House with his hands up in the air. The door opened a crack, and a young black woman's frightened face appeared. He could see that a gun was at her head and just make out a man's face in the shadows behind her. She pleaded when she saw him, "Help me, please help me."

Karp smiled at her. "We're going to get you out of this," he said, as calming as he could.

The woman whimpered. Her terrified eyes darted to the side where the gun was pressed behind one ear. She looked like she was about to faint.

"Mueller, point the gun at me," Karp said. "You're scaring Miss . . . ?"

The woman's voice quavered, "Franklin. Ann Franklin."

"You're scaring Miss Franklin, and we wouldn't want her to do anything to interrupt our conversation."

Mueller's gun turned to point at Karp. "Suit yourself," he said. "I know who you are. So are we going to talk about a deal so Miss Franklin and the others don't have to die?"

"What sort of deal?"

"I let all of these people go, give myself up, and I'll tell you what this was all about—" Mueller said.

"What is this all about?" Karp interrupted.

"Uh-uh, Karp. All I'm saying is this is big, a lot of money and a lot of movers and shakers . . . on a national level," Mueller said. "They're behind what happened this afternoon. Why I did what I did. I'll even testify against the bastards; they tried to set me up. But I get a deal before I say anything else."

"And what do you want?"

"No charges against me. A safe house until after the trial is over and I've testified. Then ten million bucks and a private jet to take me wherever I want to go."

Karp rolled his eyes. "Why not ask for a private yacht to Cuba, too. I can't do it. You killed someone, and you're going to prison for that. And where would I get ten million dollars even if I thought your information about this conspiracy was legit enough to let you get away with murder?"

"It's legit, and it's worth it, all of it—the free pass, the money, the jet . . . even the colonel's life," Mueller said. "I'm small potatoes compared to these people."

"Small potatoes, maybe," Karp said. "But you still killed someone."

"I was told to do it. We had a plan, but they fucked me over."

"Who is we?"

"That's what you get if I get what I want," Mueller demanded. "I can help you get them. You ever hear of MIRAGE?"

"You mean like a mirage in the desert?" Karp asked.

"No," Mueller said. "It's something to do with a black ops raid in Syria last winter. There's a file called MIRAGE. That's what this is all about." He stopped talking for a moment, and when he resumed, he sounded scared. "They already tried to kill me."

"Who tried to kill you?"

"Them . . . or more specifically, they had a guy at the picnic. He tried to shoot me. Ask yourself, what's he doing carrying a gun at a picnic in Central Park?"

"He was an off-duty police detective."

"He wasn't a cop," Mueller said. "Or if he is, he's dirty. He's part of this. I met him before. But that's it, no more talking. What can you do for me?"

"It's not what I can do for you, Dean. It's what you can do for yourself," Karp said. "This can go two ways. Put down the gun and let everybody go. If you want a lawyer, one will be provided for you. You also have the right to remain silent. Do you understand that?"

"Yeah, I understand what you're saying, but I won't last a day in jail," Mueller retorted.

"I'll personally see to it that you're safe," Karp replied. "And if you want to talk to me, and provide me with verifiable information about anyone else who may have been involved in this, I give you my word, you'll be safe and protected. The other way, well, eventually the SWAT guys are going to come in after you. You might survive, you might not. But if you hurt anybody else, I'll make damn sure you never step a foot out of prison. Now, are you going to surrender?"

In answer, Mueller shoved Franklin ahead and walked out behind her with his gun still pointed at Karp. Then Mueller leaned over and put the gun on the ground. "Don't shoot," he called out as he put his hands up in the air and kicked the gun toward Karp.

"Miss Franklin, come to me, please," Karp said, and held out his hand as he walked forward and stood over the gun as the SWAT team came rushing around the corner.

As Mueller was hustled off, Fulton walked up to Karp. "You okay, boss?"

"Yeah, I'm fine," Karp said, then frowned. "What was the name of the detective who got shot?"

"Ted Moore. Why?"

"I don't know," Karp replied. "Mueller says he was part of a setup."

"So Mueller's paranoid."

Karp smiled. "You're sounding like a defense attorney now. But do me a favor and check Moore out. And Clay . . ."

"Yeah?"

"Make sure Mueller is put in administrative segregation at The Tombs. I don't want him around any of the other inmates."

Fulton raised an eyebrow. "What's bugging you?"

Karp thought about it for a moment. "I don't know. Maybe it's nothing . . . or maybe it's a hunch. Let's just play it safe, okay?"

6

RICHIE BRYERS SWAM UP TO THE EDGE OF THE POOL CLOS-
est to where Clare lounged in the sun. He allowed himself a
moment to admire the swimmer's body that had not diminished
upon reaching her forties. "What are you reading?"

Clare put her book down on her stomach and looked out from
under her big-brimmed black sunhat. "A mindless romance,"
she said with a laugh. "Full of heaving bosoms and beautiful
bare-chested Scots Highlanders in kilts waving their swords and
other things around."

Glancing behind him, Bryers noted Wellington and his man,
Fitzsimmons, talking before Clare's husband went into the

house. Fitzsimmons looked over at them; he nodded at something his boss said before following him inside.

Bryers turned back to Clare. "Do you think he knows?"

The smile disappeared from her face. "I hope not."

"I don't see why he should care," he muttered. "He can always find another woman to hit and yell at."

"He cares," she replied. "He cares about anything he thinks he owns, which includes me."

"Is that a new bruise on your arm?" His voice hardened with anger.

Clare's right hand went up to the purple-blue mark on her upper left arm. "It wasn't much. He grabbed me a little roughly."

"Grabbed you a little roughly . . ." His voice trailed off. "Like the time he kicked you 'a little roughly' so that you had a bruise the size of a football on your leg. Or when he left his fingerprints on your chest from squeezing 'a little roughly' until you screamed."

Clare was quiet. A tear rolled down her cheek. "Please, I don't want to cry right now," she pleaded.

"Leave him, Clare," Bryers insisted. "I love you. I'll take care of you. We don't need the money."

"It's not the money I care about," Clare replied, wiping at her eyes. "It's Tommy. He'll never just let me go with my son . . . his son."

"He hardly gives Tommy the time of day," Bryers shot back. "Even hiring me has more to do with his ego than his son's progress on the basketball court. And that's too bad because Tommy's a good kid."

"Tommy is another one of his possessions," Clare said, "and nobody gets away with taking something that's his, especially not his wife and son running off to another man. His pride couldn't handle that."

"Pride goes before a fall, and someday that man is going to fall hard. What's he going to do? He's got to worry about his public image—the philanthropist who uses his money only for the good of others. He can't afford to be exposed for what he really is."

Clare looked over his head to see if she could spot her husband or Fitzsimmons watching them. Just in case, she laughed lightly as if Bryers had said something funny. "You have no idea what he's capable of; maybe I don't really, either, but I've heard him say things when he thought I wasn't around or not paying attention . . ."

Bryers scowled. "What sort of things?"

Clare shrugged. "Nothing specific. Just bits of conversations that sounded like threats. I've heard him yelling in his library and seen that big brute, Fitzsimmons, come out of there looking like a whipped dog, and I'd bet there aren't a lot of people who can do that to that Neanderthal. Speaking of which, Wellington doesn't keep a bunch of thugs like Fitzsimmons and his crew around to mow the lawn and run errands." She hesitated and faux-laughed again while saying under her breath, "Do you remember that New York City Council member, Jim Hughes?"

"Yeah, wasn't he the guy running for Congress who jumped off of his apartment building in Midtown?"

"Maybe he jumped, maybe he didn't," Clare said. "But two days earlier he was over here and pissed off because Wellington was backing somebody else in the primary. I heard them arguing in the library, and Hughes said he was going to go to the press—something about some oil deal in Syria—if Wellington didn't change his mind. Next thing you know, he's taking a twenty-story swan dive onto the sidewalk."

"You really think your husband would have a congressional candidate killed?"

"I don't have any proof," Clare said. "But I've lived with the man for eighteen years and I know his temper. When he gets angry, really angry, he's capable of anything." She was quiet for a moment. "I don't think he'd do anything to me; there'd be too much publicity, though I suppose he could make it look like an accident. But you . . . I couldn't live with myself if something happened to you."

Bryers frowned. This wasn't the first time they'd had this discussion since their affair had started several months earlier. He didn't think it would be their last.

WHEN WELLINGTON HAD first asked him to the house to talk about hiring him to coach Tommy, he'd liked the man. Constantine could be extremely charming and treated him like an equal—not like one of the richest men in the world hiring a private school basketball coach. They'd even sat around the pool drinking beer, discussing what Bryers could do for Tommy.

Constantine had offered him an extraordinary amount of money to coach his son. Several times his normal asking price. At first Bryers requested that he'd just take his standard fee, but the rich man had insisted. "My son's worth it."

Even rationalizing that he needed the money to supplement his teacher's salary to pay off student loans for his daughters from a previous marriage, Bryers still felt guilty. But that hadn't stopped him from accepting Constantine's money or his invitation to use the guesthouse and pool. He'd grown up poor and it didn't seem like such a big deal.

Besides, he'd worked a lot with Tommy. Far more than they'd agreed to for the money. And Bryers had enjoyed it;

Tommy was a good kid, and the mother, Clare, was easy to talk to and interesting when she discussed her causes. A few times when he saw her around the pool he'd noticed the bruises, but if he commented on them, she'd explained that she was clumsy and "always bumping into something." But there was something sad about the way she said it, or the way she talked about her husband, and he'd suspected there was more going on than being clumsy.

Still, Bryers had no intention of having an affair with his client's wife. Yes, he looked forward to seeing her and considered her a friend, but he was bought as a basketball coach and didn't let his mind go beyond that.

Then one night when he was staying for the weekend in the guesthouse, and after a couple glasses of wine, he decided to go for a midnight skinny-dip in the pool. The Constantines were out, so he thought he was safe, but they'd returned home early and the lights in the front of the house had gone on. He was about to get out of the pool and make a dash for the guesthouse when suddenly the quiet of the night was shattered by the sound of Wellington shouting in a drunken rage at his wife.

Hanging on to the edge of the pool, Bryers cringed as his client cursed Clare, slurring his words but not the viciousness. "You whore! Shoving your tits in every man's face!"

"Wellington, please, you bought me this dress. You asked me to wear it and said I looked good when we left the house," Clare pleaded.

"I didn't say flirt with anybody with a dick the whole dinner!" There was the sound of a slap, and Clare cried out in pain.

"Wellington, please. I won't wear it again. I was just trying to be nice to people and make you happy."

"Bitch! Whore! Slut!" Each word was accompanied by the sound of a slap, then of a struggle.

Bryers felt his own anger boil up inside of him. Whatever Clare had done to anger her husband, and he doubted it was anything much, no woman deserved to be hit and abused. He had decided to intervene, when suddenly all went quiet. Wondering if Constantine had knocked his wife unconscious, or worse, Bryers swam to the far end of the dark pool, intending to get dressed and investigate. Then the house's glass door opened. Clare walked out into the moonlight, wearing the low-cut, apparently offending dress. Before he could let her know he was there, she reached up and slid the straps off her shoulders and let the dress fall to the ground. She stood for a moment in the moonlight in her bra and panties, and then they, too, were off. She dove into the pool.

When she came up about ten yards from him, he could hear

her crying. "Um, sorry, but I should let you know I'm in here, too," he said quietly.

Clare gasped but then relaxed when she recognized him and swam toward him. "You heard?"

"I couldn't help it. I, um, thought you'd be gone longer. Are you all right?" he asked, acutely aware that a beautiful, nude—and married—woman was standing in the water just a few feet away. Even though the water was up to her shoulders, he was aware of her curves in the lunar light.

"Yes," she said, and made a poor attempt at a laugh. "Wellington had a little too much to drink. He gets jealous for no reason." She stopped and then sobbed. "No. I'm not all right."

The next thing he knew, Clare was in his arms, her head pressed against his chest as she cried softly. "I, um . . ." he began to say, but then aware of his body's response to the feel of her skin on his, he tried to press her away. But she clung to him even more, and then she was kissing him and he was kissing her back.

"Your husband," he managed to blurt out.

"He's passed out," she replied. "When he gets drunk like this, he hits me around, and that seems to work like a sleeping pill. He'll be out until noon."

"He hits you often?"

"Yes, but I don't want to talk about it," Clare said, then she looked like she might cry again. "Don't you like me?"

"I like you very much, it's just . . ."

"It's just nothing," she responded, and kissed him again. "I need you to make love to me. Please, I need to feel that someone cares about me, even if it's just for tonight."

"I care," he said. "I have for a while, and it's more than just for tonight."

The affair had grown from two lonely people finding solace in each other to a loving couple wanting to get married. They'd been careful to wait until her husband was out of town, or else they'd met at his place in Brooklyn. But as the weeks became months, Bryers's conscience troubled him more and more. He didn't want to take the man's money while cuckolding him and told Clare he was going to quit. But she'd reacted with both fear and desperation. "He'll suspect the reason," she wept, "and I'll never get to see you."

Even after he argued that he'd just tell Constantine that he was too busy, and they'd still find time to be together, she'd pleaded with him. That was the first time he asked her to divorce her husband and marry him. "We need to do this the right way," he'd said. But she balked over her son.

"He's getting tired of me," Clare had said of her husband. "I know he is. He'll want a divorce and then we'll be free. I just need him to reach this decision on his own. He won't even want Tommy when he has the next trophy wife."

So for a time, Bryers had been willing to wait. But lately he'd noticed more bruises, and she'd told him just the night before that her husband seemed more on edge than usual. "I think something went wrong with one of his business deals," she'd said when they were lying in bed in his apartment. "I went to his library to ask him about something this morning. I just got to the door and I heard him talking to someone on the telephone about a meeting in Istanbul. I didn't think anything of it, but when he saw me standing in the doorway, he got really angry. He screamed at me to get out and close the door. He was nice to me afterward and said he'd just had some business deals fall through and didn't mean to take it out on me, but I could tell he was just saying that."

Now today there was a fresh bruise on her arm. "I don't think he'd do anything to me," Bryers said, though he really wasn't so sure, especially when he thought about Fitzsimmons. Still, he was done seeing her abused. "How many more times is he going to hit or kick you before he does real damage? It's time to leave him. If he tries to stop you or threaten you in any way, we have the photographs of your bruises and can go to the police.

I have an old school chum, Butch Karp, who's the district attorney over in Manhattan. He's not afraid of anybody; he'd know what to do."

Clare put her book down and got up. "I don't want to talk about it right now," she said. "I think Wellington's suspicious and watching us. I'm going to fix lunch. Come on in and I'll make you a tuna sandwich."

"Sounds good," he said. "I want to get a few more laps in first if that's okay?"

"Sure, it will take me fifteen anyway."

Bryers finished his laps and climbed out of the pool and walked over to the area where Wellington Constantine had been sitting. There was a stand with fresh towels, and he grabbed one.

As he was drying off, he wandered over to where Constantine's notebook was still open on the table next to the lounge. Absently, he glanced down at the page.

"You shouldn't be looking at that!"

The panicked tone in Clare's voice behind him made him jump. "Caught me being snoopy, I guess," he said with an embarrassed laugh. "Is Wellington writing a book?"

"Not that I know of," Clare said. "Why do you say that?"

"Looks like he's working on a thriller." He nodded at the notebook. "Pretty dramatic stuff." He bent over and read from the page. "Listen to this: 'We were lucky our friend in the WH got wind of the raid or the MIRAGE files might have stayed in the wrong hands. Stupid for al Taizi to keep a record.' And then it goes on, 'Col. S and the Russian bitch are threats and need to be eliminated starting today.' What do you make of that? Sounds like a spy novel."

"All I know is that he considers his notebooks to be very personal," she said. "He told me never to touch them or look in them. He's got hundreds of them on the shelf in his library. I think he'd be really upset if he knew you were looking at that."

Bryers shrugged. "It's none of my business anyway. What have you got there?"

Clare held up two plates, each with a sandwich. "Let's eat."

"Sure, I've got to go use the bathroom real quick. Didn't want to pee in the pool."

"Too much information." Clare laughed. "Okay, be quick about it. And wash your hands!"

"Yes, ma'am," Bryers said, walking into the house.

The hallway to the guest bathroom went past Constantine's library, where he'd once sat and talked about coaching the man's son. As he approached the room, he saw that the door was half open and heard Constantine's angry voice.

"I don't care what it takes!" He was apparently speaking to

someone on the telephone. "You get your ass down there and make sure that shit Mueller keeps his damn mouth shut. Tell him you'll represent him in court; say we'll get him off and double what he was being paid. . . . What's that? . . . Just say Moore was acting on his own and that we'll deal with him. Tell him whatever you need to, but make sure he keeps his damn mouth shut!"

Bryers froze. He didn't know what to think. Then Fitzsimmons spoke. "There's a call on the secure line. It's the White House. Want to take it?"

"Of course I'll take it, you moron," Wellington answered, then apparently took the call. "Yeah, it's me." He was quiet for a moment, then shouted, "Don't threaten me, you bitch. I put you and your boss where you are. We wouldn't be in this mess if he'd made sure those files got handed over to me right away. Who were those guys in Iraq? You don't know? You work for the most powerful man in the world and you don't know who was on that operation? Well, they almost fucked up MIRAGE, and it still might be, so I'd suggest you find out."

Bryers was suddenly aware of footsteps approaching the door from inside the library. He knew he was about to get caught eavesdropping by Fitzsimmons, and the thought made him afraid. But instead, the door was closed.

Returning to the pool, Bryers accepted his sandwich from Clare. "You'll never guess what I just heard," he said.

"What?"

"You know that novel I thought Wellington was working on? I don't think it's fiction."

7

KARP SHOOK HIS HEAD AS HE LEANED BACK IN THE CHAIR
and looked across his desk at the woman on the other side.
"How is it that you always seem to end up in the middle of
things?" he asked.

Ariadne Stupenagel shrugged. "Just lucky, I guess," she answered, though there was no humor in her eyes. She hung her
head. "Mick Swindells was a friend of mine. I've known . . . I
knew . . . him for a long time. We were the Three Musketeers,
me, Mick, and Sam Allen. Now two of them are gone, and I
think there's a connection."

As Stupenagel buried her face in her hands and stifled a sob,
Karp pushed a box of tissues toward her. "I'm sorry, Ariadne. I

know they both meant a lot to you," he said, glancing at Clay Fulton, who sat in a leather chair over near the wall that housed Karp's extensive book collection. "You're sure you're up to this? We can do it some other time."

Waiting for Stupenagel to pull herself together, Karp thought about their long association, which for many years had bordered on the typical love-hate relationship between a district attorney and a hard-charging member of the media. They'd tangled plenty. She'd want information and he wouldn't give it to her; or she'd write a story that he thought might mess up a case, and they'd have words. But she was one of the best at what she did, and in spite of her zeal to get out in front of her colleagues to be first with the "scoop," she also had ethics and would hold a story if convinced that it might damage a case or a suspect's right to a fair trial.

Karp stood up and looked out the window of his office eight floors above Centre Street in the Criminal Courts Building. Down below, the sidewalks were teeming with tourists, businesspeople, couriers, vendors, the homeless, criminals, and saints—a microcosm of Gotham's population all sweating together on a hot, humid afternoon while traffic on the streets honked, screeched, and crept along. It was the day after the shooting in Central Park and he wondered how many had even paid attention to the news.

Shootings were such an everyday occurrence that the media reported them as frequently as they talked about the weather. But this one was certainly different. A colonel in the Army gunned down by a former soldier; a brave witness killed by a bullet from an off-duty detective's gun as the witness tried to stop the gunman; the detective, whom the press was hailing as a hero, wounded in an exchange of gunfire.

Karp glanced over at Fulton, who was deep in thought. Fulton had interviewed the wounded detective, Ted Moore, that morning and then called Karp.

"He took a bullet in the leg, but not too bad. They sent him home already; that's where I talked to him. We only got a couple of minutes because he was pretty out of it from the painkillers," Fulton had reported. "He said he just happened to be walking past the picnic when he saw Mueller walking toward the colonel. Said the guy seemed agitated, so he kept his eye on him, saw them argue, and the gun came out and the colonel got shot. Moore went for his own gun and fired. Poor guy's pretty shook up about the witness who took his first shot, but it was a bang-bang sort of thing. Probably why he hesitated and Mueller got the drop on him."

"Before Moore shot, did he tell Mueller to drop his weapon?" Karp asked.

"Apparently wasn't time," Fulton said. "He said he thought Mueller was going to start shooting indiscriminately."

"What do we know about Moore?"

"Clean record," Fulton replied. "His dad was a lifer and retired from the Three-Four Precinct in Washington Heights. Still lives with his parents up there. Apparently does pretty well for himself working off duty; drives a nice car, has a boat in the driveway."

"You've done some digging," Karp noted.

"You asked me to look into him," Fulton said with a smile. "Mine is not to question why . . . You buying Mueller's story about Moore being dirty?"

"I'm not buying anything at the moment," Karp had responded. "There's just something nagging at me about this one, including who's representing him. I wish we could have talked to him before counsel attached."

After Karp got Mueller to surrender the day before, he'd walked back out of the park and instructed Ewin to drive him downtown to the Criminal Courts Building at 100 Centre Street. A towering gray monolith, the courts building housed the District Attorney's Office and the grand jury rooms, as well as the trial courts, judges' robing rooms and chambers, Legal Aid offices, and Departments of Correction and Probation headquarters.

Karp was waiting for Mueller to get booked and be made available to interview when he got a call from Kenny Katz, whom he'd asked to monitor the process.

Katz was angry. "He barely got in the door at The Tombs when an attorney was waiting for him, demanding that he be allowed to speak to Mueller," Karp's young protégé said. "He was yelling about Mueller's Fifth and Sixth Amendment rights being violated and causing quite the scene."

"That was fast," Karp replied. "Who was the lawyer?"

"Get this, Robert LeJeune III," Katz practically spat.

"One of the most expensive—and least ethical, I might add—criminal defense lawyers in the state of New York tore his thousand-dollar-an-hour ego away from the Hillcrest Country Club to represent a Central Park shooter?" Karp said.

"Yeah, and the intake guys got so flummoxed that they gave him five minutes with Mueller, and by the time he got done, our suspect was invoking his right to remain silent," Katz replied.

"What in the hell?" Karp said, along with a few other choice words. "I guess LeJeune was watching the news, but . . ."

"He says he's working pro bono for some group called American Vets with PTSD and that he was notified by them."

"Never heard of American Vets with PTSD."

"Neither have I, and I know about a lot of these veterans'

groups. Some are better than others. PTSD is a real thing for guys who've been in-country; I've had some counseling myself," Katz said. "But this is a new one on me. I'll ask around, see if they're legit. But it looks like we're not going to get a statement out of Mueller."

So all they had out of Mueller were the statements he'd made to Karp at the zoo. He knew LeJeune would probably try to suppress them, saying that his client had been in "constructive custody" knowing he was surrounded and in effect under arrest. But that was why Karp had told him he had a right to an attorney and the right to remain silent. He'd made sure that he later took a statement at the DAO from Ann Franklin, the hostage, to back him up on that.

Something's just not adding up about this, Karp thought as he turned back to Stupenagel, who was dabbing at the mascara that had run down her cheeks while looking in a hand mirror. She finished and looked up at him. "I'm good," she said.

Karp sat on the corner of his desk. "Okay, tell me what's going on here. What were you doing in Central Park talking to the victim five minutes before he gets shot and a gun battle erupts?"

Stupenagel looked at the yellow legal pad on the desk. "Are you taking notes?"

"Not right now. I just want to hear what you have to say."

Karp didn't elaborate that any notes he took from a witness would have to be turned over to the defense attorney at trial. If she'd been a hostile witness, or the defendant, he would have conducted an in-depth Q&A with a court-certified stenographer present. But Stupenagel was a friendly witness, so all he'd written on the pad was that he was meeting with her and that Fulton was present.

Stupenagel nodded, but added, "Butch, I understand I'm a witness, and I want to cooperate. Mick Swindells was a friend of mine, and I'll do whatever I can to put his killer away. But I'm still a journalist and I promised certain people confidentiality and I can't break that without their permission."

"I'm not asking you to," Karp replied. "At least not now. I just want to try to get a handle on what went on and why."

"Okay. Where do you want to start?"

"From the beginning."

"I went there to talk to Mick about some information I'd received. Do you remember this past winter about a raid in which an ISIS leader named Ghareeb al Taizi was killed?"

"Yeah, the administration made a big deal about it," Karp said. "How the president had given the go-ahead and then waited all night in the White House war room for word that it had been a success. There weren't a lot of details, as I recall."

"Well, it might not have gone down quite the way the White House press office described it," Stupenagel said. "In fact, there were more players killed during that raid—representing a sort of compendium of bad guys in the region, such as Syria, Russia, and Iran—that maybe the administration didn't want anybody to know about."

"You mean," Karp said, "they're meeting with ISIS? So much for the coalition against terrorism."

"Yeah, that's exactly what I mean," Stupenagel replied. "Anyway, after these guys got killed by a certain counterterrorism team of good guys, if you know what I mean, some documents and computer files were seized before they hightailed it out of there. They didn't get much of a chance to look the stuff over because when they got back to base, they were met by an Army unit and were forced on orders from 'high up,' and I mean *really* high up, to turn over the documents and files, as well as a prisoner."

Stupenagel looked expectantly at Karp. "Aren't you going to ask me the identity of the prisoner?"

"Okay, I'll play along. What was the identity of the prisoner?" Karp said.

"Nadya Malovo."

Karp's face tightened. "Why does that not surprise me," he said with a sigh. "Where is she now?"

"Well, the feds had her at the maximum-security prison in Colorado," Stupenagel said. "But a mutual friend of ours got her transferred to the Varick Center across the street."

"Okay, what does this have to do with the murder of Colonel Swindells?"

"Well, for one thing, Colonel Swindells was in command of the battalion this unit belonged to, though apparently they operate on orders from higher up, and he wasn't present when the documents and Malovo were seized," Stupenagel said.

"And?"

"And apparently, the little bird who told me about some of this said the counterterrorism team was aware that Swindells was looking into one file in particular that lies at the bottom of all of this."

"What file would that be?"

"It's called 'Sarab,' " Stupenagel replied.

"Sarab? What's that?"

"I don't know exactly. I wasn't told all of the details, but it's an Arabic word that means 'mirage.' "

Karp felt the hair on the back of his neck stand up at the same time Fulton sat up straight. She had their full attention. "You said 'mirage,' right?" Karp said, looking at the detective and back to the journalist.

Stupenagel narrowed her eyes. "I smell another part of this story. What's up, Karp?"

At first Karp hesitated, but then he thought he owed her this much. "This is off the record for now. You can't use it."

"Yeah, yeah. I got dibs on it when it's time, but what's going on? Why are you and Clay suddenly acting like cats in a lightning storm?"

"The shooter, Mueller."

"Yeah, what about him?"

"He said this had to do with a black ops raid in Syria this past winter," Karp said, "and a file called MIRAGE."

Stupenagel whistled. "When I asked Mick about the raid and Ghareeb al Taizi, he played dumb, said he didn't know anything about it. But when I mentioned MIRAGE, he told me to forget about it, that I was swimming in shark-infested waters. In fact, he said not to contact him again."

A look of anger took over her face. "Now my friend's dead, and I'm smelling a rat. Have you tried talking to Mick's daughter, Sasha? Maybe he told her something."

Karp looked at Fulton. "Clay tried this morning."

"She's obviously distraught and she pretty much slammed the door in my face," Fulton said. "There was a moment, however, when I thought she might say something."

"Mind if I reach out to her?" Stupenagel asked. "I was going to anyway, just as a friend of her dad. But I could see if she'll talk to me."

"Be my guest," Karp said. "Anything else?"

"Nothing," Stupenagel said, then seemingly changed the subject. "Isn't Lucy home visiting?"

"Yeah, why? And what's this got to do with . . . ?" A look of understanding crossed Karp's face.

"I think it's time for one of those good old-fashioned father-daughter talks," Stupenagel said.

8

THE OLD WOMAN WHO ANSWERED THE DOOR OF THE brownstone in Manhattan's Washington Heights neighborhood smiled. "You must be Teddy's friend who called," she said. "How nice of you to come visit him. Come in, come in!"

Opening the door wider, Mrs. Moore led the way inside the modest home. "You must be a special friend because he hasn't wanted to see anybody else. Just that one television crew and the reporter from the *Post*. They were so kind. Oh, and that nice black police detective who stopped by."

"Do you know his name?"

"No, but I think he left a card with Teddy. They only talked for a couple of minutes. Isn't it nice that the television people and newspapers are calling Teddy a hero for stopping that bad man in the park the other day!"

"Yeah, that's great," Shaun Fitzsimmons said. "He's quite the hero, and I'm sure you're very proud."

"Oh, we are," she said, then her face looked troubled. "Of course, he's very upset about that poor man he shot. But that wasn't Teddy's fault. He was trying to protect people and stop the bad man."

"Of course he was," Fitzsimmons said, then thought to himself, *Too bad he fucked up and now has to pay for it.*

Constantine had been livid about the "glitches." Nothing had been going right with the master plan since the incident in Syria. Why in the hell that still-unidentified black ops team had chosen that particular night to go after al Taizi they didn't know, but it had screwed everything all up. They were lucky the boss had friends in high places who got wind of the raid or, as Constantine had said, "We'd have been sitting there holding our dicks, trying to explain what the fuck we were doing there."

Constantine had pulled some serious strings to get the raiders intercepted in Saudi Arabia. Fitzsimmons didn't know everything about the MIRAGE plan, he wasn't going to be in the inner circle at the meeting, but he knew it was big and had to do with black-market oil, the Russians, the Iranians, and those bloody bastards in ISIS. That alone said it was above his pay grade to know.

The plan had been FUBAR—fucked up beyond all recognition—ever since. It got worse when the files didn't get handed over to the spooks right away. Colonel Swindells somehow got wind of it all and started poking his nose in. Fitzsimmons had to act fast and find someone on the inside willing to grab the MIRAGE files, and that's when he'd located Mueller. Promised a couple million dollars, the soldier had been more than willing but got caught going through Swindells's office and court-martialed out of the Army.

Swindells hadn't been able to break the code yet, or they'd have known about it. But it was only a matter of time, so after the unit transferred back to the States, Fitzsimmons leaned on Mueller to make it right. They'd come up with a plan for Mueller to shoot the colonel, and then they'd get him off on a mental illness defense. "Couple years in a nice hospital," Fitzsimmons had assured him, "and you'll have four million waiting for you on the outside."

Of course, they weren't going to take a chance on that and had arranged a little surprise for Mueller, but Moore messed up, too.

I told the boss it was too complicated, too many moving parts,

Fitzsimmons thought as he'd driven over to Moore's house. *He just should have let some of my boys, who can be trusted to do the job right, take out Swindells. We could have made it look like a robbery.*

They'd looked for an opportunity, but Swindells was cautious. He was a Ranger, and he also knew that something was up and didn't leave himself open until he decided to attend the picnic. That's when Constantine had come up with the idea of making Mueller fix the problem.

Only he didn't fix it, Fitzsimmons thought as he followed the old woman into the house, *he only made it worse. I swear, between his ego and his writing everything down in those damn journals, the boss is going to get us all fried. Now it's my job to tie up the loose ends.*

Walking into a dark and musty-smelling living room, Fitzsimmons looked around. The walls were covered with photographs of police officers. Some he recognized as Moore, others were the old man who was now sitting in an overstuffed chair drinking a Budweiser.

"Hello, young man," the old geezer said, slurring his words. "Excuse me for not getting up. Thirty-five years on the force mixing it up with every Tom, Dick, and Harry who wanted to take a swing at me left me a little crippled up. The rheumatism's acting up this morning." He held up the beer can. "I'm working on a little painkiller."

Fitzsimmons crossed the room and shook the man's hand. "Nothing wrong with that after a distinguished career fighting bad guys."

"See there, Martha, a man who understands. I'm Theodore Senior. My lady is Martha; she sometimes gives me a hard time about my beer."

Still looking around the room, Fitzsimmons didn't see photographs of any other siblings. "Ted your only child?"

The couple looked at each other sadly. "Yes, Teddy was a difficult birth," Martha replied. "He's been a real joy to us. We were so proud when he became a police officer like his father. Teddy's a good boy and saves his money and works a lot of overtime. He has a nice car and bought a boat this year. Now, if he'd only settle down with a nice girl and give us some grandchildren."

"Some more boys to contribute to the thin blue line at the NYPD," Theodore Sr. said.

"You two just talk for a minute," Martha said. "I'll go up and make sure Teddy is awake. I told him you were coming over, but those painkillers make him sleepy." She headed for the stairs, then turned back. "I'm sorry, I've forgotten your name?"

"It's, uh, William . . . William Besler."

"That's right, William," she said, and began her slow ascent. "Teddy, you have a visitor! William's here to see you."

Fitzsimmons smiled. "Nice woman," he said.

"One of a kind," the old man agreed. "Been together almost forty-five years. Puts up with me . . . for the most part. So you on the force?"

"No," Fitzsimmons said. "Former military."

"Oh? I was in Nam," the old man said. "An MP, then came back and got on with the NYPD, like my dad and his dad before him. Where were you stationed?"

"I did tours in Afghanistan and Iraq."

"Ah, saw some fightin', did ya?"

"A little bit."

"Yeah, I was in Huế during the Tet Offensive. Terrible time. Lost a lot of buddies." The old man shook his head at the memories. "I was lucky to get back to the wife and kid. Of course, working the Three-Four Precinct was like being in a war zone sometimes, too. Crazy thing that happened in the park. I hear the shooter was ex-military and had a beef with the guy he shot."

"Yeah, that's the story I got, too," Fitzsimmons said. He hooked a thumb over his shoulder. "Think I'll go see Teddy. Wake him up and see if he's malingering."

The old man chuckled. "Yeah, you do that. I've been shot a couple times myself. Can't keep a good man down."

As Fitzsimmons walked up the stairs, he noted the photographs of Teddy Moore displayed along the length of the wall. As a child. As a teenaged baseball player. In his high school graduation cap and gown. And his police officer's uniform.

Fitzsimmons was met at the top of the stairs by Martha Moore. She had a funny look on her face. "What's the matter?" he asked.

"He says he doesn't know a William Besler. Is that the name you gave me when you called on the phone earlier?"

Fitzsimmons clapped his hand to his forehead. "Sorry, no, he knows me by my nickname, Fitz," he said with a laugh.

"Oh, that's right," the old woman replied. She started to turn back. "I'll let him know it's Fitz who's come to see him."

"That's okay, Mrs. Moore," he said, placing a big hand on her shoulder and moving past her. "I'll take it from here."

Martha looked unsure for a moment, but then smiled. "Well, okay. I know he'll recognize the name Fitz. I'm just an overly protective mom."

"Like a good mom should be," Fitzsimmons replied. "I think your husband wanted another beer, so you go along and I'll visit with Teddy."

Martha rolled her eyes. "Not another one. He's drinking too much, but who can blame him with the rheumatism and all."

Watching to make sure the old woman continued on down the stairs, Fitzsimmons then turned and walked to the end of the hallway, where he opened a door. The room looked like it was still inhabited by a teenager—filled with even more photographs and memorabilia, trophies, model airplanes hanging from the ceiling and Yankees pennants on the walls. However, the patient lying in the bed was in his early forties.

"Hello, Teddy," Fitzsimmons said. "How you feeling?"

Moore nodded. "I'm doing okay. I should be up and around in a week or so."

"Yeah, so we heard." Fitzsimmons walked quickly over to the bed, then suddenly pulled back the sheets and felt underneath the protesting Moore, picked up the pillow, looked, and then threw it back down.

"Jesus, what the fuck are you doing?" Moore demanded.

Fitzsimmons put a finger to his mouth. He went around the room, looking in the closet, under the desk, and along the bookshelf. Seeing a business card lying on a nightstand, he picked it up.

"Looking for a wire, Teddy," Fitzsimmons said. "You wired?"

"Fuck no," Moore replied.

Fitzsimmons held up the card. "Detective Clay Fulton with

the New York District Attorney's Office visited? What did you tell him?"

"Nothing much. Said I was just out for a Sunday stroll when I saw this guy go after the colonel. I shot but hit that asshole hero-type, which got me shot by Mueller. That's it."

"What did Fulton want?"

"Just said they were putting the case together against Mueller and wanted to ask some questions," Moore said. "Nothing unusual about that, especially in a police-involved shooting."

Fitzsimmons stood looking at him for a moment with his eyes narrowed. "Yeah, I suppose not."

"So tell your boss, whoever he is, that I'm sorry, but I couldn't do anything about the guy who got in the way, poor schmuck," Moore said.

"Sorry ain't going to cut it, Teddy."

Moore frowned. "What do you mean? It wasn't my fault the plan got screwed up. I've done plenty of odd jobs for you in the past, and I just took a bullet for your guy. What more does he want? You don't have to pay me the money."

"That's not enough," Fitzsimmons said. "You fucked up and now you're a loose end." He walked over to where Moore's handgun hung in its holster on the closet door. Grabbing a tissue from a box on the desk, he removed the gun and brought it back to the bed, tossing it on Moore's lap. "You're going to take one for the team."

Moore's eyes grew wide, and then his face got angry and red. "Fuck you, Fitz. And fuck your boss! I ain't eating no bullet for either of you! You crazy asshole."

Fitzsimmons shrugged. "Okay, let me tell you how it's going to go. You know my boss has a lot of money, right? Very powerful man, lots of connections. Well, first thing that happens is the press is going to get a large file about a certain Detective Ted Moore and some of his extracurricular activities, including his connection to several murders and other rough stuff. I think the DAO and the brass at the NYPD will get the same file."

"I'll let 'em know who put me up to it!"

"Yeah, really? Who, Teddy? I'm a ghost. I'll be sipping margaritas in Mexico when you're indicted. And you don't know who the boss is, or what strings he's going to pull."

"I don't care," Moore said, though his face was now ashen. "I'm not going to do it."

"You didn't let me finish," Fitzsimmons said. "Imagine your poor parents, the media camped out on their front lawn. Only it's not to talk to the 'hero' Ted Moore, but the dirty cop. The embarrassment alone will probably kill them. Because you're a fuckup Teddy, a real fuckup. But it gets worse. One night some black monkeys from Harlem, friends of that activist you shot in the alley, they're going to show up here. They're going to beat the fuck out of your old man and then make him watch while they gang-rape your mom."

"You're filth, Fitzsimmons!"

"I been called worse." Fitzsimmons pointed to the gun. "It's up to you. Die a hero who couldn't get over shooting an innocent civilian while trying to stop a killer. Or throw your parents to the wolves, and then, believe me, you won't last a day in prison anyway."

Fitzsimmons stood looking down at Moore, who started to cry. "There, there, Teddy," he said. "It will all be over before you know it."

Walking out of the room and down the stairs, Fitzsimmons found Martha waiting for him. "Is everything all right?" she asked anxiously. "I heard some raised voices."

"Everything's fine," Fitzsimmons assured her. "He's just really upset about that accidental victim he shot, and I had to talk some sense into him. I hope the department will get him some counseling, he's pretty despondent."

"I know," the old woman said. "I worry about him so. He's such a good boy."

"Yeah," Fitzsimmons said as he walked to the front door. "A

real champ. You have a nice day, Mrs. Moore, and say goodbye to Mr. Moore for me."

Fitzsimmons had walked a block to his car when he heard the shot. He paused for a moment, then heard the woman's scream, and he smiled. *One less loose end*, he thought, and got in the car.

9

THE YOUNG ASSISTANT U.S. ATTORNEY IN MANHATTAN'S Southern District glanced down at his lap, where his cell phone was open to his Facebook page. He frowned at a message from his fiancée: "Can't wait to see u 2nite, pookums. Remember we have dinner date w/parents @ 6." It was already 4:00 p.m. and the arraignment hadn't even started yet. And now the judge was taking his time reading through some documents on another case.

Looking up briefly to make sure the judge didn't see him, he texted back: "Hung up in court. But should still be there on time, snookie." He winced when the response was a frowny-face emoji and the words "u better."

The thought that "snookie" would be angry if he was so much as a minute late for this meeting with her mom and dad, and withhold her sexual favors for God knew how long, threw him into a near panic. He turned toward the defense table, where the defendant— a strikingly beautiful middle-aged woman in a gray prisoner jump-suit—sat with her attorney, Irving Mendlebaum, a well-known and highly respected criminal defense lawyer in Gotham. She didn't look dangerous; in fact, she had a body and a face that even snookie would have envied. He wondered what she had done to be facing federal terrorism charges. He hadn't been told much, just to get the arraignment done as quietly as possible on the down-low and that someone higher up would take over the case later. *Probably another lonely housewife who helped some towel-head buy a gun,* he thought. *What's taking this idiot judge so long?*

The defendant, one Nadya Malovo, felt his gaze and turned her head toward him. The thought came to him that now he knew what a bird must feel when transfixed by a snake's eyes—a lovely snake with alluring green eyes—shortly before it struck. She smiled as if she knew what he'd been thinking when he checked out her body, and damn if he was unable to resist smil-ing back. He covered his discomfiture by looking toward the back of the courtroom.

Two men in dark suits and dark glasses had been sitting in the last row when Malovo had entered the courtroom through a side door leading from the holding area. He figured they must be federal agents; their square-jawed, unsmiling faces sent a chill through him. But as he looked at them, they stood up and left the courtroom.

"All right, counsel, I'm ready to proceed," Judge John Keegan announced. "I understand the matter before the court is the arraignment of the defendant Nadya Malovo on terrorism charges."

The assistant U.S. attorney stood and nodded. "That's right, Your Honor, we . . ."

The federal prosecutor stopped talking, and all heads turned when the doors at the back of the courtroom suddenly opened and two other men walked in. Both were middle-aged, one white, with a lean, athletic frame; the other a large, powerful-looking black man with a menacing scowl on his face.

Defense Attorney Mendlebaum seemed to have been expecting them, as he now rose and addressed the judge. "Your Honor, may we approach the bench with these two gentlemen?"

The judge's eyes scanned the two men entering the courtroom and then glanced at both the prosecutor and defense counsel, as well as the defendant, who sat with an amused smile on her face. "Please come forward, gentlemen," Judge Keegan said warmly.

Malovo sat calmly as the four men gathered at the judge's

sidebar, the assistant U.S. attorney looking perplexed and wondering how this was going to affect his evening plans. The judge smiled and greeted the newcomers. "Gentlemen, I'm certain that you are about to let me know why your presence is necessary for this routine arraignment."

A legendary prosecutor and brilliant trial lawyer before he received his lifetime appointment to the federal bench, Keegan had prosecuted several cases where Mendlebaum had represented the accused. The two trial lawyers epitomized the professionalism, integrity, and expertise admired by the New York Bar and beyond. Keegan, of course, was familiar with S. P. Jaxon when he was an ADA in the Manhattan DAO and also admired the work of Detective Clay Fulton.

"Good afternoon, Your Honor. As you know, I'm now with a counterterrorism federal security agency, the name of which appears on this card," Jaxon said as he handed it to Judge Keegan. "Due to the sensitive nature of this particular agency, I ask that it not be repeated for the record but kept in the court's confidential file. For the record, with me is New York Police Department Detective Clay Fulton, who leads the NYPD detective unit assigned to the New York District Attorney's Office."

"Actually, I know Mr. Fulton from my years with the DA's Office," Keegan said. "How are you, Clay?"

"I'm well, thank you, Your Honor," Fulton replied. "I'd heard you were appointed as one of the eleven FISA judges handling sensitive national terrorism issues."

"Yes, it's been quite an eye-opener," Keegan said.

"Your Honor," Jaxon said, pulling a document from the inside of his suit coat, which he handed to the confused assistant U.S. attorney, "the United States Justice Department is suspending and holding in suspense the federal indictment against the defendant, Nadya Malovo, at this time. It's relinquishing custody to Mr. Fulton and the New York District Attorney's Office."

Fulton pulled out his own documents and handed them to Keegan. "The prisoner has been indicted on six counts of murder in New York County. At this time, I will be escorting her across the street to the offices of the District Attorney."

The judge looked over the indictments and then at the assistant U.S. attorney. "I take it you didn't know about this?"

The young man, suddenly hopeful that his evening might turn out well after all, shrugged. "No, but that doesn't mean anything. I was mostly just a warm body assigned to handle the arraignment and wouldn't have been the prosecutor at her trial. If the papers are in order, I'm good with it. Sounds like she'll have enough to worry about over at the DAO."

The judge turned his attention to the defense attorney. "Mr.

Mendlebaum, you seemed to be aware that these two gentlemen might be making an appearance. Care to elaborate?"

"We have been in discussions with both Mr. Jaxon and New York District Attorney Roger Karp, and we've agreed not to contest this jurisdictional change," Mendlebaum said.

The judge looked at the four men and then over them at the defendant, who held his gaze without expression. He shook his head. "Something's in the air, but who am I to question why," he said, and banged his gavel. "This case is hereby placed on the suspense calendar and may be recalled at the pleasure of the U.S. attorney for good cause. Detective Fulton, the prisoner is now yours."

The young assistant U.S. attorney hurriedly shoved his papers into a briefcase and hustled out of the courtroom, smiling and texting on his phone as he walked.

"Ms. Malovo, shall I accompany you across the street with these gentlemen?" Mendlebaum asked.

"That won't be necessary, Irving," she said coyly. "I'll call you if I have further need of your assistance. Thank you for all you've done for me, and perhaps we might renew our acquaintance someday under more congenial circumstances."

"I'd be delighted." Mendlebaum beamed like a schoolboy. "Until then, if you're sure—"

"Yes, quite," Malovo said, cutting him off, "I'm sure that I will be in good hands with Monsieurs Fulton and Jaxon. *Au revoir.*"

Mendlebaum did a little bow. "I bid you *adieu*, then."

As the attorney walked away, Fulton rolled his eyes. "Oh, brother," he said as he looked at Malovo. "Okay, let's go."

"Are these necessary?" Malovo held up her handcuffed wrists.

Fulton scowled. "I still have a scar in one of my legs where you shot me," he said. "And the memory of a lot of good men, and a busload of children, dying because of you. The cuffs stay on until we get into the DAO, though I wouldn't mind at all if you tried to escape."

Malovo smiled and batted her eyes at him. "It's not good to hold grudges, Detective," she said in her husky, heavily accented voice. "It's unhealthy and might prevent you from making new friends. People change over time; maybe I am not the same person you remember."

"I'd believe that a snake could change before you would," Fulton replied. "No matter how many times you shed your skin, no amount of 'change' atones for murdered children. Now get your butt up. The boss wants to see you."

An expression that might have passed for pain flitted across Malovo's face before it disappeared and was replaced by a smirk as she stood. "So grumpy, Detective, but maybe you're not getting enough exercise," she scoffed. "From the looks of you, I don't think you could catch a cold, much less me."

"You're in jail, facing murder charges," Fulton noted. "Apparently you're not as fast as you think."

"Maybe I wanted to get caught. Did you ever think of that?"

"Yeah, and maybe you're getting old, a little long in the tooth."

Malovo laughed, a surprisingly girlish sound. "Touché, Detective! Well played. Attacking a woman's vanity as she approaches her . . . um . . . young middle age. But you couldn't keep up with me if I hopped on one leg."

"I wouldn't have to," Fulton replied. Now the tight smile he'd plastered to his big brown face disappeared. "Even you can't outrun a bullet. Now move!"

The two men escorted their prisoner through a side door. "That was easier than I thought it might be," Fulton said to Jaxon. "When we saw those two spooks go into the courtroom earlier, I thought we might have a problem. Glad to see them leave."

Jaxon smiled as they stepped onto an elevator taking them to the basement. "As if you wouldn't welcome throwing a punch or two at federal agents, present company excluded, I hope."

"Yeah, you get a pass." Fulton grinned. "Anybody you recognized?"

"Nope. But I don't know every spook passing through town."

"They're here to kill me," Malovo said as they stepped off the elevator.

The men exchanged looks. "What makes you think that?" Jaxon said.

"Same reason Butch went through all of this trouble to get me out of their hands," Malovo said. "If you hadn't been there today, there would have been a small story in the *New York Times* about a female prisoner hanging herself in her cell. Or who was a notorious terrorist who somehow managed to secrete a cyanide capsule in a hollow tooth. Or was shot while trying to escape."

In the basement of the building, Jaxon quickly escorted Malovo to a small room, where he picked up a long coat that he placed around her, buttoning it up over her handcuffed wrists. He pointed to a pair of winter boots. "Hop into those."

"They're not very attractive," Malovo complained.

"You want to still be here when those two goons come looking for you?" Jaxon asked. "I don't think we have much time before they realize the 'arraignment' should have been over by now."

"If you're going to put it that way." Malovo slipped her feet into the boots. "Let's go."

The two men escorted their prisoner through a door and out into the parking garage beneath the federal center. Jaxon flashed his badge at the security guards at the entrance.

Reaching the street, Fulton nodded to a uniformed police sergeant standing at the curb. The sergeant blew a whistle and other uniformed officers stepped out in traffic, blowing whistles and holding up their hands to stop the vehicles, creating an opening.

Fulton and Jaxon hurried Malovo through to the other side and then hustled her to the Leonard Street side of the Criminal Courts Building. Just as they were about to turn the corner, they heard a shout. Looking behind, they saw the two federal agents who'd been in the courtroom trying to make their way through the now flowing traffic.

"Can't I just this once?" Fulton said, looking at Jaxon.

The agent laughed. "As much as I'd like to see that, I think we better get her upstairs to your boss."

"Yes," Malovo added. "My hands are cuffed, so I'd rather avoid any unpleasantness, though on some other occasion, I'd be happy to help."

"Don't need your damn help," Fulton growled as they went to the Leonard Street side entrance that had a secured private elevator reserved for judges and the district attorney.

A minute later, the elevator door opened into the offices of the district attorney. Karp stood there waiting in the anteroom. "Was looking out the window and saw the parting of the yellow taxi sea, and apparently a couple of Egyptians who weren't so happy about your exodus," he said. "Let's go into the conference room."

When they were all seated, Karp looked across his desk at Malovo. "It's been a while."

"Too long, darling," Malovo replied.

Karp smiled as he shook his head. "Clay, please take off Nadya's coat and cuffs," he said, hoping that his face and voice weren't exhibiting the usual male reaction to the femme fatale's presence. He reminded himself that she was a cold-blooded killer, as heartless and murderous as any serial killer he'd ever put away. *And she's drop-dead gorgeous.*

"Let's get down to business," Karp said. "I believe you've been informed that you're under indictment on six counts of murder in New York County."

"Is that all?"

Karp hesitated. "If you'd like to confess to more, I'd be happy to add to the number."

"That will do for now."

"The offer stands if you reconsider," Karp said. "In the meantime, you've agreed to talk to me today, and you understand I will not be offering you any deals or dropping any charges."

"I understand," Malovo said. "I made only one request. Is that still on the table?"

Karp looked at the others, then nodded. He stood up. "Follow me, please."

Karp led Malovo out of his inner sanctum into the reception area. No one else was present. He'd told his receptionist, Darla Milquetost, to take the rest of the day off so that this could all be handled privately.

Karp opened the door to another inner office in the DA suite. A man was seated at the table. "You good with this, Ivgeny?" he asked.

"Yes, Butch, I'll see what she wants."

Standing back from the door, he let Malovo walk past him. "As agreed, Nadya, you have your requested meeting with Ivgeny, but try to keep it reasonably short, please."

"Okay, but that's hardly enough time to say hello to a former lover," Malovo said with a smile, "but a girl has to take what she can under these circumstances."

"We'll be in the conference room," Karp said, and closed the door.

About twenty minutes passed and Karp stood up about to knock on the door when it opened and Malovo appeared, followed by his cousin. For once she seemed somewhat subdued, and Karp wondered what had transpired between the two Russians. But he doubted they'd tell him and decided not to ask. "Can you let yourself out, Ivgeny?" he asked.

"Yes, Butch," Karchovski said. "I have a car waiting for me outside." The former Red Army colonel–turned–American gangster reached out and touched Malovo on the shoulder. "Do the right thing, *dorogoy*, and perhaps we will meet again."

"It is enough to hear you call me 'darling' again," Malovo replied. She turned to Karp. "I'm ready to talk to you, Butch."

10

As the two women walked across the tree-shrouded lawn of the West Point Cemetery, the taller one reached over to touch her friend's arm. "Thanks for driving, Marlene," Ariadne Stupenagel said. "I didn't want to take a taxi. And to be honest, I wanted your company."

"You bet. That's what besties are for," Marlene Ciampi replied. "I'm sorry for your loss. It seems like we were just burying Sam Allen, and now your friend Mick."

The friends continued on in silence in the heat of the late afternoon toward the knot of people gathering around a fresh grave. "I guess this is what happens when you get older," Stupenagel said. "You start losing the people you created the memories of your youth with; it makes me feel old. I have so many recollections of the three of us, and more and more keep flooding into my mind. I think those were the best years of my life." She squeezed Marlene's hand. "Except maybe the years we were roomies in college."

"Hold on to those memories," Marlene said. "As my hubby's mom said, so long as the people we loved remember us, we will live forever."

Stupenagel nodded and again fell silent, looking around at the white marble headstones. Some of them marked the final resting places of soldiers dating back to the Revolutionary War—even before there was a United States Military Academy at West Point. "I wonder why he chose to be buried here instead of Arlington," she said. "It was the same with Sam."

Marlene pointed over toward the Hudson River. "Maybe that's the reason. Arlington's beautiful, but it doesn't have that million-dollar view. Somehow it seems more peaceful here, too, maybe because there are fewer visitors. I think only graduates, their immediate families, and staff can be buried here."

"That's right," Stupenagel said. "And they both loved West Point. Even when we were tearing it up in Southeast Asia and Latin America, this was one memory only the two of them shared. Maybe they just wanted to be here with all the rest of these American heroes who had this place in common."

They walked the rest of the way without speaking until they came to the outer edge of the large gathering of mourners. Most of the men in attendance were in uniform, though some of them appeared to have dug their clothes out of mothballs. The women, even Stupenagel, were in black. An honor guard of cadets in the gray uniforms of the academy stood off to the side with their rifles, while a bugler waited.

During the ceremony, Stupenagel watched Sasha, who was seated and wearing her dress uniform. Although the young woman's face was ashen, she didn't appear to be crying. But as the bugler played "Taps" and a cadet officer brought her the American flag that had rested on the casket and was then folded into a neat triangle, she buried her face in the cloth and sobbed.

Stupenagel covered her mouth to stifle her own sob, then flinched when the honor guard discharged the first of three volleys in a twenty-one-gun salute. Marlene held onto her arm and leaned against her.

When the services were over, Marlene asked, "Do you want to say anything to Sasha now? Were you going to ask her about MIRAGE?"

Stupenagel shook her head and wiped at her tears. "No, it's too soon. I wasn't invited to this, and she might blame me. I was the last person to talk to him, and maybe even mixed up in the reason he was killed. I'll call in a few days and see what she says."

They were walking away when a female voice called out from behind them. "Hello. Ariadne Stupenagel?"

Sasha Swindells was walking across the lawn toward them. Behind her the crowd of mourners looked confused, concerned.

"Yes?" Stupenagel said.

"What are you doing here?" Sasha demanded.

"I came to pay my respects. Your father was a good friend for many years."

"Not because of what you wanted to talk to him about before he was killed?" the young woman asked accusingly.

Stupenagel's eyes filled with tears. "That's not why I came. But I admit that I would like to talk to you at some point about that," she said. "I may be able to help the people who are trying to get to the bottom of his murder."

"What people?" Sasha spat, balling her hands into fists. "The same people in charge of the government he risked his life for from Vietnam to Afghanistan? The people who betrayed him?"

"No," Stupenagel replied, feeling the tears leak down her cheeks. "As a matter of fact, the district attorney of New York, Butch Karp. This is Marlene Ciampi, she's my best friend, but she's also the DA's wife, though she's just here to support me."

"I already told that detective I wasn't interested in talking to the district attorney," Sasha said. "I told that other guy, too. The big guy, William somebody, said he worked for a counterterrorism agency. Creepy asshole wouldn't take no for an answer. But I don't trust any of you. This isn't about some crazy soldier having a beef with his former commanding officer, but now the real reason is going to get swept under a rug. Well, I'm not helping you with your little cover-up. I'll get to the bottom of this, and when I do . . ."

"I understand," Stupenagel said. "I feel the same way. Did you know your dad's friend, Sam Allen?"

Sasha's eyes narrowed. "Yes. Murdered by the same people. The district attorney made scapegoats out of those two guys, but the real power is still in place."

"The president's national campaign manager, Rod Fauhomme, and the president's national security adviser were no scapegoats. They were major players behind the scenes and Mr. Karp went after them," Stupenagel said. "They planned the murder of General Allen because Sam was about to expose them and the corruption that goes all the way up to the administration. That took some guts on the DA's part. He can't do it all without help, but I'm sorry I came. Today I just wanted to say goodbye to an old friend, not dig into a conspiracy, or cause you more pain."

With that, Stupenagel and Marlene turned to go. They'd walked about ten yards when Sasha called out again. "Wait."

The young woman approached. Her face had softened and was wet with tears. "I loved my dad very much," she said. "I never had enough time with him; he was married to this damn uniform." She looked around. "To this damn place. But I loved him anyway, and I need to follow through on the last thing he asked me to do."

Sasha fished her cell phone out of the pocket of her dress slacks and tapped on the screen. "I haven't shown this to anyone else. It's a text he sent to me right before he was shot." She handed the phone to the journalist.

Stupenagel read the text out loud. "'If something happens to me, please give my copy of the Gold Book to the woman you just met. I love you forever, Dad.'"

Handing the cell phone back, Stupenagel looked confused. "The Gold Book?"

"Basically, it describes the code of ethics and responsibilities every cadet is expected to internalize so that upon graduation each newly commissioned officer is, and I quote, 'committed to the values of Duty, Honor, Country.' It's about living honorably at all times in all environments. Now incoming cadets receive the book as a PDF computer file. But Dad, who was going to be teaching a course in professional military ethics, had his original Gold Book he got in the 1960s printed and bound in a leather case. He didn't say why he wanted you to have it, but he went to the trouble of texting me that message, so it has to be important."

Sasha Swindells looked back at the crowd of mourners, most of whom were watching her. "We're having a little get-together at the reception hall," she said, "and I have to attend. But please join us, and we can get the book after that. It's at his place on the grounds."

Two hours later, Sasha broke away from the crowd of well-wishers and found Ariadne and Marlene waiting in the back of the hall. "I think it's okay for me to leave now," she said. "You have a car? It's a little bit of a hump and it's getting dark."

"A truck," Marlene said. "We can all pile in the front."

As they wound their way in Marlene's truck toward staff housing over near the cliffs that rose above the Hudson River, Sasha apologized for her earlier outburst. "Dad didn't tell me much about what he was doing," she said. "I think he was trying to protect me. But I knew it had to do with one of his last postings overseas. Something was troubling him and he was looking into it. That's about the extent of my knowledge."

"I understand the anger and suspicion," Stupenagel replied.

"These people seem to be good at sowing both, even among friends."

"Divide and conquer, I guess," Sasha said as they pulled onto a street that was mostly dark and empty except for the streetlights. "It's summer break and a lot of the faculty are gone. Dad's place is up ahead."

Approaching the house, Sasha suddenly tensed. "Keep driving," she said. "I think I saw a light moving around inside. No one is supposed to be here."

Marlene kept rolling and pulled over half a block farther down the street. She reached under her seat and pulled out a .380 handgun. "Call the police, or MPs, whoever responds at West Point," she told the other two. "I'm going to go check it out."

"Marlene, stay here," Stupenagel said. "Let the police handle it."

"I'm just going to make sure they don't slip out the back when the cops arrive," Marlene said. "You two stay here."

"You're ordering a commissioned officer in the United States Army to stay out of the fight?" Sasha said. "Not on your life, and not at my dad's house."

Marlene looked at the young woman's determined face and nodded. "Okay, but we're just going to keep an eye on them until the cops show. No heroics. Stupe, tell them I'll be around back and not to shoot the female civilian with the gun."

Running from shadow to shadow across the lawns, Marlene and Sasha arrived at the bungalow. Creeping next to a back corner of the house that Sasha indicated was where she'd seen the light, they could hear someone moving around inside, apparently trashing the place as he looked for something.

"The son of a bitch, he's in Dad's library," Sasha whispered, and started to move.

Marlene grabbed her arm. "Remember, we're going to let the cops handle this," she cautioned in a hushed voice. "We don't know if he's armed or if there's more than one. You keep a lookout here while I work my way over to the other side so I can cover the back door."

Leaving Sasha in place, Marlene ran to a small wall beyond the back patio and knelt with her gun out, pointed at the back door. Suddenly, the night air was disturbed by the sound of an approaching police siren. Cursing that the element of surprise had been lost, she readied herself.

As expected, the back door opened and the dark silhouette of a large man appeared in the doorway. "Stop right there or I'll shoot," she shouted, rising from her position behind the wall.

The man hesitated and began to raise his hands. But at that moment, Marlene heard a sound behind her and whirled just in time to miss being stabbed by a man wearing a dark ski mask.

She didn't have time to shoot before he kicked the gun from her hand and charged into her, knocking her to the ground and landing on top of her. "Take off, sir, I'll handle the bitch," her assailant yelled to the man in the doorway.

Instinctively, both of Marlene's hands went immediately to the attacker's arm that held the knife as he tried to press the blade home. She was strong, but he was stronger, and she knew she was about to lose the fight when the man was knocked off of her by Sasha, who flew in and tackled him.

Marlene scrambled to her hands and knees and found her gun where it had fallen. About ten feet away, Sasha was struggling with the man. Before she could do anything, there was a cry, and the young woman fell back. The man stood up with the knife in his hands.

"Put it down, asshole," Marlene demanded.

The man whirled and pretended he was about to drop the knife, but instead he charged, covering the distance between them with alarming speed. Marlene fired twice. The first round caught him in the stomach, doubling him over just a few feet from her. The next entered the top of his head, killing him.

Marlene looked for the second man and just caught a glimpse of him running through the backyard two houses away. She ran over to Sasha, who was lying on her back, her hands over her stomach. Even in dim light, Marlene could see the dark blood seeping through her fingers.

"I'll be okay," Sasha moaned. "Go get the book. It's on Dad's desk."

"I need to get you an ambulance," Marlene protested.

"If you don't get it now, the cops won't let you get it later," Sasha insisted, then groaned. "It could disappear."

The appearance of flashing red and blue lights accompanying the siren convinced Marlene there wasn't any more time. She stood up just as Stupenagel appeared. "Tell the cops that they need to call an ambulance," she yelled. "Sasha's been stabbed."

Marlene ran for the house, picking up the flashlight that the first man had dropped when she told him to stop. She quickly made her way to the library. Everywhere she looked, books had been pulled from their shelves, papers were scattered on the floor, and a wall safe that had been hidden behind a painting was open and empty. She went over to the desk and spotted a small booklet bound in blue leather. On the outside, embossed in gold, were the logo of the United States Military Academy and the words "Gold Book." She picked it up and stuffed it down her pants.

A minute later, Marlene walked out of the house and stopped as she was blinded by a flashlight in her face. "Put the weapon on the ground," a voice demanded.

Only then did Marlene realize she was still holding her gun. She slowly leaned over and put the gun down.

"It's okay, Officer," Stupenagel said. "She's the wife of the New York district attorney. She's the one who stopped the guy with the knife."

"Yeah, and I'm the adjutant general," the military police officer said. "On the ground, lady, until we get this sorted out, and lock your fingers behind your neck."

"Yes, Officer," Marlene said, complying with the order. "Just please get an ambulance for the young woman. She's the daughter of the officer who used to live here. We were just coming back from his memorial service to retrieve some of his personal effects when we ran into these men who'd broken into the house."

"An ambulance is on the way," the MP said. "In the meantime, you always go to memorial services with a gun?"

Marlene sighed. "What can I say? Some girls like purses and lipstick. I'm partial to semiautomatics."

11

CLARE DUNE FROZE. SHE THOUGHT SHE'D HEARD SOME-thing, or someone, though no one else was supposed to be home. She stood for a moment outside her husband's library, her heart pounding, her hands sweaty, and listened.

There were no more sounds and she decided that she was being paranoid. Wellington was at Camp David with the president on a "boys only" holiday. She'd just checked on Tommy, who was asleep upstairs, the servants had all gone home, and she hadn't seen the brutish Shaun Fitzsimmons for days.

Clare thought about Richie Bryers and wished he was spending the night in the guesthouse. She didn't want to return to the bedroom she shared with Wellington. She wanted to lie in his arms all night. But it simply wasn't safe. What if the maid or Fitzsimmons showed up in the morning? But recently, he'd been convinced that Constantine was spying on them. "Or maybe you've got me paranoid," Richie had teased her the last time they got together as he kissed her goodbye. "Let's just take a break and stay separated for a little while."

"You're not getting tired of me, are you?" she'd pouted.

"I'll never be tired of you," he'd replied. "I want to spend forever with you. Divorce him and marry me now. We'll never have to spend another night apart."

However, Clare repeated that it was better to wait for Constantine to make the decision. "It won't be long. He doesn't even try to have sex with me anymore," she said. "He's probably already got someone on the side. Good for him, hope she talks him into it soon."

Still, his absence was making her rethink her position on asking for a divorce. That and Richie was convinced her husband was somehow tied up in the shooting of that colonel in Central Park after he read the newspaper articles. "Remember what I read in his journal about some colonel and a 'Russian bitch' being in the way," he'd reminded her. "Then I heard him talking about a guy named Mueller—and that's the name of the guy who shot that colonel in Central Park that same day. That doesn't add up to a coincidence. And what about 'MIRAGE'? It's in his journal and he brought it up, and Iraq, too, with whoever he was talking to at the White House."

At first Clare had refused to buy into it. "I think you're jumping to conclusions," she'd said. "I know he's unscrupulous and not at all the man he presents to the public. But murder and espionage? He's always fighting with someone over his business deals, and I think his oil company has refineries in Iraq. Who knows what he meant by a colonel and a Russian being in the way? They could be competitors."

But Bryers had reminded her that she was the one who thought he might have had something to do with the congressional candidate who fell from his apartment building. "And you're worried he might do something to me if he finds out about us," he'd pointed out. "What's so far-fetched about this?"

Gradually, Clare had come around. "Maybe you should talk to your friend, that district attorney in New York," she suggested.

"Butch? Yeah, I've thought about it," Richie said. "But I don't have any proof. Who's going to believe a public school basketball coach over a well-loved philanthropic billionaire who gives millions of dollars to charities and golfs with the president? I need proof." He'd thought about it for a minute. "I wish I could get another look at his journal."

Clare had suggested that she could try to look at it. "I'll take photographs of the pages on my phone and send them to you," she said.

Richie, however, forbade her. "If this is real, it's not a game," he said. "It's not worth you putting your life in danger."

So they'd avoided the topic for a couple of days, and then she'd had another idea. "Imagine if he was convicted of murder," she said. "We'd be rich, but more important, think of all the good things we could do with the money. We could still live a good life and make a real difference in the world."

Richie still didn't like the idea, but tonight, after a couple of glasses of wine, she decided to act. She reached on top of the doorjamb where she'd once seen him hide the key to the library, unlocked the door, and went in. Even though she and Tommy were the only ones home, she didn't turn on the lights and instead used the small flashlight she'd brought with her.

Clare walked quickly over to the part of the massive bookshelf where Wellington had carefully lined up his journals in chronological order. Those on the far end she knew were fifty-year-old composition notebooks containing the memories of a child. She moved to the end where the latest journals were stacked and pulled the last from the shelf. Taking out her cell phone and pressing the button to open the camera app, she opened the journal and began to scan until she saw a page with MIRAGE printed in big bold letters. She took a photograph and sent it to Richie.

Almost immediately he texted back. "What are you doing? Get out of there!"

She was about to turn to another page when she heard a noise again. Her heart jumped into her throat. "Someone's here," she texted. She hurriedly replaced the journal and left the library, locking the door and putting the key back.

Pausing, she listened but couldn't hear any other sounds. She decided she was paranoid, but she wanted another glass of wine before she continued, so she walked to the kitchen.

Suddenly, the lights went on and she nearly dropped her glass. She whirled around to see who had flicked the switch. "Shaun," she said. "What are you doing here?"

Fitzsimmons, who was standing on the other side of the kitchen island, smirked. "Thought I might catch you and your boyfriend," he said.

Clare laughed nervously. "You know Wellington's at Camp David."

The brute began to move around the island, but she moved, too, to keep it between them. "Quit playing stupid, you fucking whore," he said. "I'm talking about your boyfriend, Bryers."

Clare's eyes widened. "You can't talk to me like that. Get out or I'll call Wellington." She glanced at her cell phone. A text message popped up from Richie. "Are you okay?"

Fitzsimmons laughed. An unpleasant sound. "Messages to your fuck buddy? Doesn't matter, the boss knows all about you two. I even showed him photographs of you locking lips outside of Bryers's apartment. You weren't very careful."

Clare decided to play tough. "Well, I'm glad it's out," she said. "I want a divorce."

The big man sneered. "Think a guy like Wellington Constantine is going to let his whore wife fuck around on him and then get a big settlement?"

"I don't want anything from him," Clare said. "I just want out."

"Oh, you're going out, all right. Boss gave me the go-ahead." Fitzsimmons took a pill bottle out of his pocket and slid it across the island toward her. "Start swallowing."

Clare stared down at the bottle in disbelief. "You're crazy. I won't do it!"

Fitzsimmons took a cell phone out of his pocket. "You know FaceTime?" he asked. "Of course you do; how stupid of me. You and your little boy toy were probably doing the nasty in front of each other when you couldn't get together." He tapped on the screen and spoke to someone who answered. "You there? Good. Point your phone toward the building."

Sliding his phone across the island to Clare, he said, "A friend of mine is on the other end of this call. You recognize where he's at?"

Clare looked down and her hand went to her mouth. "It's Richie's apartment building," she gasped.

"Yeah, a nice little love nest while it lasted," he said. "Too bad that when little Richie goes on his nightly jog, he's going to be involved in an armed robbery. Only this one's going to go south, and Richie's going to get shot."

Tears welled in Clare's eyes. "You're a monster."

Fitzsimmons shrugged. "Yeah, probably. But I'm also pissed off. I lost a good man the other night and almost got shot in the process. So don't mess with me. If you want to save your boyfriend's life, you'll start swallowing pills."

Dazed, Clare reached for the pill bottle. "What are they?"

"OxyContin. Wash them down with your wine and you won't feel a thing," Fitzsimmons said. "No pain. No muss. No fuss. You'll just float off to sleep and never wake up."

Clare started to cry. "Please, I just want a divorce. Call Wellington. Tell him I'll sign anything he wants. He can have his money. I don't want anything."

"You're missing the point," Fitzsimmons said, impatient now. "You've been giving away something the boss owns. He can't just let that go. Besides, he's having dinner with the president about now and won't want to be disturbed." He looked at his watch. "I believe we're about five minutes from Richie's run. So what's it going to be?"

Clare nodded and wiped at her tears. "Okay."

"Now, that's true love," Fitzsimmons said. "Let's go out by the pool and have a nice relaxing moment on the chaise lounges."

Clare did as she was told. Sitting down, she took the cap off the bottle, and after a moment's hesitation, she tipped its contents back into her mouth. She picked up the glass of wine and downed it.

"That's a good girl," Fitzsimmons encouraged her. "It will be over soon."

Within minutes, Clare began to feel the effects and collapsed back against the lounge. Five more minutes passed and she was vaguely aware that Fitzsimmons was undressing her.

"My, my," she heard him say. "A shame to waste such a good piece of ass. But I suppose it wouldn't be a good idea for my DNA to be found in you. The medical examiner has been paid off to determine it was a suicide, but he might say something to the boss, and I'd be next."

"Richie be okay?" she mumbled.

"Probably. For now," Fitzsimmons said. "It would be suspicious if you both died. He may have told one of his buddies about you. But who knows, the boss has a long memory. Maybe in a couple of years, Richie will have an accident, or maybe that robbery will go down like I said. But for now, he's okay."

Clare felt Fitzsimmons pick her up and was hazily aware when he walked her down the steps into the shallow end of the pool. She was on her back, looking up at the stars and thinking how beautiful they looked until the grinning face of her murderer got in the way. She felt him press down on her chest and the water close over her face.

Water filled her nostrils and throat and, when she tried to breathe, her lungs. Then her body convulsed and the world began to fade. *I love you, Richie*, she thought. *Goodbye.*

12

BUTCH KARP ALLOWED THE ANGER TO WASH OVER HIM AS he looked out the window of his office at the park across the street. He was now fully aware of the treachery and deceit that had taken place. As his thoughts swirled, he watched children chase after one another in the late-afternoon heat while vendors hawked hot dogs, soda, and knishes to passersby, and panhandlers worked the crowd. His attention was drawn to a young couple lying on the grass locked in an embrace and then turned back to the man who sat defeated in the chair across from his desk with his head down.

"I get you anything, Richie?" Karp asked.

"No, I'm good, thanks, Butch," Bryers replied, his voice subdued.

Karp nodded and wondered for what must have been the hundredth time that day that of all the people in the world who would crack open the MIRAGE case, it would be an old friend from high school. He and Richie Bryers had played basketball against each other for rival schools in Brooklyn; although fierce competitors on the court, they'd both admired each other's game and were designated co-captains of the elite All-City Basketball Team. Then, when they attended summer basketball camps together, the admiration had developed into a friendship. That friendship had lasted after Karp went off to play for the University of California–Berkeley and Richie went to Harvard. Busy lives since had limited most of their interaction to holiday cards and the occasional phone call, but they hadn't lost touch.

The last thing he'd expected that morning, however, was Bryers calling to say he needed to talk to him about a murder. Surprise had turned to incredulity when his old friend started telling a fantastic story about having an affair with the wife of one of the wealthiest men in the world and that he believed her death was being swept under the rug.

Karp glanced at the *New York Times* lying on his desk. The news of the woman's death was on the top of the front page beneath a double-decker headline: Billionaire Philanthropist's Wife Drowns; Clare Dune Dies in Long Island Home Pool.

A sub-headline suggested that a combination of alcohol and prescription drugs might have been partly responsible for what the story, quoting an anonymous source in the Suffolk County medical examiner's office, termed an "accidental" drowning while hinting at the possibility of suicide. The story noted that Dune's "shocked and grieving" husband, Wellington Constantine, had immediately flown home from Camp David, where he'd been vacationing with the president.

"Mr. Wellington asks that his and his son's privacy be respected as they grieve," according to a statement released by the billionaire's publicity team.

Initially during his telephone conversation with Richie, Karp had listened politely for old times' sake as Bryers accused Constantine of killing Dune. A moment later, he'd bolted upright in his chair when his friend mentioned that he believed Constantine was involved in "some crazy plot called MIRAGE" and was connected to the murder "of that Army officer in Central Park." He'd interrupted the conversation and asked Bryers to come in as soon as he could.

Now, with Bryers sitting across the desk from him as Fulton sat nearby listening, Karp had his old friend tell his story. "It has to be his goon, Shaun Fitzsimmons," Bryers said. "Constantine was at Camp David."

"Dinner with the president is a pretty good alibi," Fulton acknowledged.

"He'd never get his own hands dirty," Bryers said. "But Clare thought he'd had Fitzsimmons push that New York City Council member, Jim Hughes, off his balcony."

Karp looked at Fulton, who narrowed his eyes. "I know the detectives who worked that case," Fulton said. "They weren't convinced he was a jumper. Maybe there were some fingerprints left at the scene they haven't been able to connect. I'll pass this along."

When he got to the part of his story where Clare was in Constantine's library, Bryers showed him the photograph taken from the journal and her next text saying she thought someone else was in the house.

"If you don't mind, Richie, we're going to need to turn over your phone to my forensics guys," Karp said. "I don't know how they work all of their magic, but I think they might be able to prove that these came from her phone, and what time, and even where she was when they were sent. I'd like to have her phone, but that would tip off our suspects."

"Whatever it takes," Bryers responded.

Finally, it all makes sense, Karp thought, as he looked over at his grieving friend. Like the tumblers in a bank vault, the pieces of the MIRAGE case clicked into place, with Bryers providing the final digits.

Now Malovo's information also made sense, connecting the dots from a photograph she'd downloaded on Constantine's computer taken in Istanbul to a bloody raid in Syria to a showdown on the tarmac at the air base in Saudi Arabia to the murder of a decorated Army colonel in Central Park. She didn't know the name of the master puppeteer, but Bryers had just drawn a line between those dots to him. No wonder Mueller had been so afraid of "they"—or, more accurately, "he"—when Karp talked him into surrendering at the zoo. Wellington Constantine was not just one of the wealthiest men in the world; he was one of the best connected.

Karp had never liked the man. He created so-called not-for-profits allegedly to fund inner-city welfare organizations that were ignobly antipolice groups led by radical homegrown militants. But that wasn't affecting whether or not he would make a case against him for the murder of Colonel Swindells. That would be determined by the legally admissible evidence. Moreover, Karp would seek an indictment only if he could prove the case not just beyond a reasonable doubt but "beyond any and all doubt," so that even Constantine's supporters, his media assets and amoral public officials, would have to concede his guilt.

Even if Swindells didn't know who was behind MIRAGE, Karp thought, *he knew the conspiracy had to go about as far up the ladder as it could. No wonder he warned Ariadne to stay away from the "shark-infested waters."*

THOSE WATERS HAD nearly engulfed Stupenagel and Marlene when they went to the memorial service and talked to Sasha Swindells. It had never ceased to amaze him how his wife always seemed to end up in the middle of the action, or how good she was at handling it.

Fulton had run a background check on the burglar she shot, which had resulted in interesting but not particularly revealing findings. The deceased was one Toby Milhowski, ex–Special Forces who'd served in Iraq until he and other members of his company were court-martialed and dishonorably discharged for the torturing of civilians.

"There wasn't much else on him, except a New York driver's license that listed a Yonkers address that turned out to be false. He hasn't even filed tax returns since getting out of the Army," Fulton reported, "which tells me he's a guy flying under the radar. The only thing we could find was a car loan application he filled out a few years back listing his employer as Frontline

Security Services, which had a Newark address but apparently went out of business not long after that. We're trying to run that down, see who else might have been involved."

No telling who the other burglar had been, but there was no doubt in anyone's mind that they'd been after whatever Swindells had regarding MIRAGE. Karp found it ironic that the colonel had hidden clues about how to locate that information in a West Point publication about ethics and living an honorable life. *So antithetical to these people's warped ideology*, he thought, *so probably a good place to hide it.*

When Marlene and Ariadne had brought the Gold Book to Karp's office yesterday, they'd all pored over it looking for clues as to what it meant. Obviously, Swindells wanted to get it in the hands of an investigative journalist he trusted. But there was nothing in the thin book that yielded any answers. Not until they turned it over to the DAO's crime lab technicians.

"Turns out that the colonel marked certain letters and words using a highlighter detectable only with a black light," Fulton said when he brought the book back, along with a copy that showed the highlighted areas. "The crime lab boys were pretty excited about discovering that, though it is still in a code of some type."

The first part of the coded information was easy enough to decipher. On different pages, Swindells had marked M-I-R-A-

G-E. But he'd also highlighted other letters and numbers that at first didn't make sense until Marlene sat up and said, "Those are GPS coordinates." She'd quickly punched the coordinates into an app on her cell phone, and then smiled. "It's the library at West Point," she said.

Further study revealed the title of a book, *Boots and Saddles*, as well as a surname, Farrington, and the words, "The Battle of the Little Bighorn." The hints necessitated a return trip for Marlene and Stupenagel, who insisted on going to the academy with Fulton and Jaxon. "After all," Adriadne had said, "Mick intended that this go to me, and I'm sharing."

At the academy, they met Sasha Swindells, who escorted them to the library. As they entered the building, Marlene pointed to a directory on the wall. "That solves one riddle," she said. The directory listed A. E. Farrington as the curator of rare books.

"I say we go straight to the horse's mouth," Jaxon suggested.

As they told Karp, a few minutes later they found the rather mousey-looking curator sitting in a back office. He'd raised an eyebrow when the unusual group approached him but otherwise said nothing and just frowned.

"I'm looking for *Boots and Saddles*," Sasha said.

"It's a memoir written by Elizabeth Bacon Custer about her time on the plains with her husband, General George Armstrong

Custer." Farrington sniffed. "I'm sure you can find it on the shelves. We have several copies that are available to West Point students and alumni."

"I think this might be a very special copy," Sasha continued, but Farrington didn't respond.

"My father, Colonel Michael Swindells, might have left it here."

Still no response. The group looked at one another.

"I'd like to know more about the Battle of the Little Bighorn."

Farrington smiled sadly. "I've been waiting for you," he said. "But the colonel, a dear friend—believe it or not we were in the same year here at the Point—made me promise to wait until I heard those words. He gave it to me several days before he was shot." He got up and walked over to an ancient-looking safe and removed a manila envelope, which he handed to Sasha.

"I was so sorry to hear about your father," Farrington said. "I hope justice will be done in his name."

Sasha smiled and had to wipe at a tear that rolled down her cheek. "I hope so, too, and this may help," she said, and hugged the suddenly embarrassed librarian.

THE TEAM HAD returned from their excursion to West Point with their prize and reported to Karp, but it wasn't something he could share with his friend. "I can't tell you everything that is going on," Karp told Richie. "You're a witness, and it's going to be a long, hard journey getting justice. But I will tell you that this is all part of a bigger picture than you know, even with what you've told me."

At that moment, there was a knock on the door, and Jaxon and Marlene entered the room. Karp quickly filled them in on Bryers's story.

When he finished, Jaxon could barely contain his anger. "These sons of bitches," he spat. "This goes beyond murder. This is treason."

"So what's next?" Marlene asked.

Karp thought about it for a minute. "A lot of dominoes have to fall," he said. "I need Mueller to turn, which means convicting him at trial. I also want Fitzsimmons. How's our story holding up about what happened the other night?"

"I talked to the superintendent at West Point," Jaxon said. "A good man, outstanding service record, and served with Colonel Swindells in Vietnam. I told him it was a matter of national security and also important to bringing the colonel's murderers to justice. He raised an eyebrow when I said 'murderers,' not 'murderer,' but didn't ask any questions. So far the only thing that's been in the press is that two burglars were caught breaking into the colonel's house, and that one of them was shot and killed. The name of the shooter is being withheld pending investigation."

Karp looked at Bryers. "Richie, what I'm going to ask you to do might be dangerous, but it also might help us get the guys who killed Clare."

"Like I said, whatever it takes," Bryers said grimly.

"Good. I want to talk it over with Clay. I'll get back to you tonight."

"Okay." Bryers nodded and got up to leave. "You know, this is my fault. I don't know if it's because of what we were doing, or because she got caught in the library, but either way it's on my head."

"You didn't murder her," Karp told him. "Whatever else you need to deal with, that's your call, but nothing you did was worth killing her for."

After Bryers left the room, Karp looked at Jaxon. "We got the right files?"

Jaxon nodded. Karp was referring to the contents of the manila envelope they'd brought back from the West Point library. Inside was a book, or most of a book, because a small rectangle had been cut into the pages just deep enough to contain a computer flash drive.

"Yeah, we had it tested," Jaxon said. "We just got word. It's the MIRAGE file that was taken from us in Saudi Arabia. But it's encrypted, and I'm worried about turning it over to the usual folks who deal with that sort of thing. This goes about as far up as it can go, and no telling where Constantine has his tentacles."

"I have an idea about that," Karp said, and looked over at his wife. "You remember Iaian Weber?"

"How could I forget," Marlene said.

She turned to Jaxon, who had no idea who Iaian Weber was. "He's the same age as our twins, but with an IQ so far off the charts he makes even Giancarlo, who's a bona fide Mensa, look like a slacker. The kid was doing calculus by third grade, and I believe he won the National Science Fair in the sixth grade, up against high school geniuses with his project with which he duplicated from scratch how the U.S. Navy broke the Japanese code during World War II that won the Battle of Midway."

"Exactly," Karp said with a grin. "I think he was the youngest ever admitted for Ph.D. work in computer sciences at the Massachusetts Institute of Technology. Isn't that what his parents said the last time we had dinner with them?"

"I thought they said he was specializing in drone aerial surveillance technology," Marlene said. "Has several top secret government contracts and all that."

"That's right," Karp agreed. "But his dad and I got to talking about how Iaian's hobby is still code breaking and he was working on duplicating the Enigma computer used to break the Nazi code in World War II. What do you think about me contacting Iaian and seeing if we could enlist his help?" he asked Jaxon. "I know he has the highest security clearances."

"I'm all for it," Jaxon replied. "Especially if it keeps what we're doing off the grid. If Constantine or you-know-who in that photograph Malovo gave us gets wind of this, it's going to get hot . . . really hot."

Karp smiled. "I wouldn't want it any other way."

13

SHAUN FITZSIMMONS STOOD IN THE SHADOWS UNDER THE
large oak watching the figure seated on the bench near the Alice
in Wonderland statue in Central Park. The area around the
bench was bathed in a golden light from a nearby streetlamp and
it didn't appear that there was anyone else around.

"Okay, Johnny and Dana, go check him out," he said. "Be
thorough, wand him and scan everything within twenty feet."

"Right, boss," one of the designated pair responded as they
took off at a brisk walk toward the man on the bench.

As he watched them go, Fitzsimmons was worried, an unusual
feeling for him. But Toby's death had unnerved him more than
he cared to admit. "We must have set off a silent alarm," he later

explained to Constantine, "because whoever that bitch was, she was waiting for us with Swindells's daughter when I came out. Toby took her on and stabbed the young one, but took one in the head after that."

Constantine had been none too happy, not because Toby died but because the MIRAGE file couldn't be located. He blamed Fitzsimmons.

"We tossed the place, even broke into the safe," Fitzsimmons said. "Hopefully it stays lost. But if it doesn't, no one's going to crack that code. The Russians said even their best guys hadn't been able to do it, and they were given months to try."

Fortunately for Fitzsimmons, Constantine took out his anger on his wife. He'd looked at the photographs Fitzsimmons had taken of the pair kissing and tossed them back at him.

"No one fucks around on me," Constantine had snarled. "I'm tired of the bitch anyway. I want her gone by the time I get back from Camp David, but make it look like an accident or suicide. When it's done, put a call in to Ray Chelton at the Suffolk County medical examiner's office. Make sure he does the autopsy himself and certifies cause and manner of death, and that nothing comes back to haunt us. He owes me for getting him out of hot water with that bimbo who was after him for sexual harassment."

Killing Clare Dune had been fun. Fitzsimmons had come on to her a few times after he started working for Constantine, and she'd shut him down without so much as a smile. As he took her clothes off that night, he'd considered raping her, but Chelton might have said something.

They weren't surprised when Richie Bryers called. But they thought it would be to offer condolences or maybe tearfully confess, not an attempt at blackmail. "I know all about MIRAGE," he had said. "And about Mueller and the colonel and the Russian bitch."

"What do you want, Bryers?" Constantine said, switching over to speakerphone so Fitzsimmons could hear.

"Your goon listening in now, too? Good," Bryers said. "I know who you had do the dirty work. But let's be adults about this. Clare was just a nice piece of ass. And this is just a business proposition."

"What makes you think I'm going to do business with some little prick who was fucking my wife?" Constantine said.

"Well, I'm going to send you something right now that ought to persuade you."

That "something" turned out to be a photograph of a page from Constantine's journal. Constantine turned to Fitzsimmons with daggers in his eyes but said, "Okay, I see it. Now what?"

"I'm not saying anything over the phone," Bryers replied. "But I've got plenty more where that came from. Let's work out the details where neither of us has to worry about being recorded. Send your ape there to the Alice in Wonderland statue in Central Park tonight at nine. He's there on time or I'm gone and the district attorney gets some really interesting information to go with his case against Mueller. Otherwise, we come to an accommodation and go our merry ways."

Goon? Ape? I'm going to beat the prick to death with my bare hands. Fitzsimmons seethed as he watched his men frisk Bryers and pass a wand capable of picking up any transmitting devices over him. They then used the wand to check the area, including the nearby statue.

When Johnny and Dana finished, they waved to Fitzsimmons, who strolled over. "Hello, Richie," Fitzsimmons said. "Boys, go keep an eye out. Let me know if we get company."

"Sure, boss," one of them said. "Here's his phone."

"Hey, asshole," Bryers said. "Yeah, boys, keep a good eye out, because if something happens to me, your boss and his boss are going down."

"So what do you want, Bryers?"

"Four million in this bank account in the Caymans."

"And what do I get?"

"You mean what does Wellington get. He gets my silence and all of my photographs of his journal. Pretty interesting all that about MIRAGE and Iraq. Calling the White House for private discussions."

"All your photographs, huh?" Fitzsimmons said. "Let me see." He looked at Bryers's phone. "Funny, I only see one photograph from Clare. And a text about someone being in the house."

"That would have been you. I downloaded the others already and have them in a safe place." Bryers sounded nervous, and Fitzsimmons knew what he needed to know.

"You're lying, Richie. You don't have jack, otherwise you would have shown them to me. You see, I looked at Clare's phone. She deleted this photograph and the text, but she didn't have a chance to empty the trash. There's nothing in it except a few photographs of the two of you. Cute little selfies but nothing more from the boss's journal."

"She didn't have a chance because you killed her, you bastard."

"Yeah, but I want you to know that I fucked her real good before I stuck her head underwater," Fitzsimmons replied. "And you know what, she liked it. I think she even liked it when she was dying. Kind of hard to tell, she was pretty fucked up on Oxy-Contin and cabernet."

Suddenly, Bryers launched himself at Fitzsimmons, who easily sidestepped his charge and sent him to the ground with a hard punch to the kidney. The big man then kicked him in the ribs. "You're such a fucking loser, Richie, you can't even blackmail right."

Gasping, Bryers raised himself up on his elbows. "No. But I set you up pretty good."

Fitzsimmons's eyes narrowed. "And what do you mean by that, you little prick?"

"He means you're under arrest."

Fitzsimmons whirled around just as a large black man flanked on either side by two other large men emerged from the shadows. The black man had a gun in his hand and flashed a badge. "I'm detective Clay Fulton of the NYPD and work for the New York District Attorney's Office. Put your hands on top of your head, and don't make me nervous; this gun has a very squirrelly trigger around assholes."

"You ain't got shit," Fitzsimmons sneered as he put his hands on top of his head while the other two detectives stepped forward and relieved him of his gun and then cuffed his hands behind his back.

"Only a record of you admitting the murder of Clare Dune," Fulton said.

"Bullshit. I know for a fact the area was clear," Fitzsimmons swore.

"Maybe when your boys—who by the way aren't very good lookouts and are now on their way downtown, too—first checked." Fulton pulled a small radio transmitter from his pocket. "Iaian, would you mind bringing that little bird a bit closer so our friend here can see it."

A small black hovercraft drone not much larger than a shoe box dropped out of the darkness above their heads and hovered at twelve feet. "Don't know much about them myself," Fulton said. "But apparently the damn thing can see like an owl at night and records conversations at up to thirty feet. Long story short, your ass is ours. Let's get him downtown, men, the DA's waiting."

AN HOUR LATER, Fitzsimmons was sitting in an interview room at The Tombs when Karp, Fulton, and a stenographer walked in. "Good evening, Mr. Fitzsimmons," Karp said. He looked at the stenographer, who nodded. "I'm District Attorney Roger Karp. With me this evening are Detective Clay Fulton of the NYPD DAO detective squad, and Jack Simmons, a court-certified stenographer. Also present is Shaun Fitzsimmons."

"Fuck off."

Karp ignored the remark. "I'd like to ask you a few questions," he said.

"Free country, asshole."

"First, you have the right to remain silent. Anything you say can be used against you," Karp recited. "You also have the right to have an attorney present. If you can't afford one now, one will be provided for you. Do you understand what I just told you?"

"I understand English. Do you understand 'fuck off'?"

"I'd like to ask you about the death of Clare Dune."

"Terrible, that," Fitzsimmons said. "Shouldn't go swimming when you've been swallowing mother's little helpers and drinking wine."

"What about your statements you made to Mr. Bryers in the park?"

"He's trying to blackmail my employer, Mr. Wellington Constantine," Fitzsimmons said. "I was bullshitting him to see what he wanted."

"Did you drown Clare Dune?"

"She drowned on her own."

"What about New York City Council member Jim Hughes?" Karp asked. "Did he throw himself off his balcony, or did you push him?"

Surprised, Fitzsimmons blinked and his face tightened, but

the look didn't last long. He looked at the fingernails on one of his hands and shrugged. "Never met the man. Don't know who you're talking about."

"Never been to his apartment on Forty-eighth Street in Midtown Manhattan?"

"Doesn't ring a bell. Should it?"

"You tell me, Shaun," Karp said.

"Never been there," Fitzsimmons said. Then he smirked. "Oh, wait a second, is that a strip club? Yeah, I think that's the Pink Pussycat. Some nice girls in there, you ought to check it out, Karp, relax a little."

"Any idea what you were doing on August fifteenth last year?" Karp asked.

Fitzsimmons looked up at the ceiling, as if thinking. "I believe I might have been in Aruba. Can't be sure."

"What if I told you we have your fingerprints on the railing on Mr. Hughes's balcony? The railing you pushed him over," Karp said.

"Couldn't be mine," Fitzsimmons said, though he was starting to show signs of nervousness.

"Funny thing is," Karp went on, "we didn't get a hit on the national crime computer the first time the NYPD ran those prints. For some reason, nobody had your fingerprints on record, even though the military does that routinely when you sign up. Guess it helps to have friends in high places. But you might remember you got fingerprinted when Mr. Fulton brought you in an hour ago, and the NYPD ran them through for me really fast. And guess what? They're a match for the prints from the balcony in Hughes's apartment. Now, are you sure you've never been in that apartment?"

Fitzsimmons glared but didn't say anything.

"For the record, Mr. Fitzsimmons has not answered the question," Karp said. "Maybe you'll remember this. At some point in the struggle before Mr. Hughes was pushed over the railing, he scratched his assailant. We know this because a DNA sample was obtained from skin beneath his fingernails.

"Know anything about that? No. Okay, the suspect has again declined to answer my question. I will tell you that the first time the NYPD tried to get a hit on the DNA, just like the fingerprints, they came up empty. But I bet I can get a judge to sign a warrant giving us permission to obtain a DNA sample from you, and I'd also be willing to bet we'll get a hit with the sample taken from underneath Mr. Hughes's fingernails. And when we do, I'm going to indict you for not just the murder of Clare Dune but also the murder of Councilman Jim Hughes. Now, would you like to answer my questions?"

Instead of answering, Fitzsimmons's face turned red and he started to stand up as if to attack Karp. But then he looked over at Fulton, who had taken a step forward. Fitzsimmons sat back down with his arms crossed.

"That's right, big boy," Fulton said. "Keep your butt in that seat."

"Fuck you," Fitzsimmons snarled. "And fuck you, too, Karp. I want a lawyer."

Karp smiled. "You need us to call Legal Aid, or maybe your boss will spring for someone a bit more expensive?"

"I've said all I'm saying," Fitzsimmons replied. "I want my phone call now."

A few minutes later, Karp and Fulton were talking in the hall. "Let's get that lineup together with Fitzsimmons. But have him make that call so that a lawyer is present."

"Will do."

Karp walked to the viewing room, which contained a one-way mirror that allowed law enforcement and witnesses to study those in a lineup. Jaxon and Malovo were waiting for him. "Good evening, Nadya," he said.

"*Dobryy vecher*, Butch," Malovo replied. "We have to stop meeting like this. People will talk."

Karp laughed and shook his head. "I'm sure they would if they knew. In the meantime, how are your accommodations in the country?"

Malovo rolled her eyes. "To be honest, I'm bored out of my mind. I'm not so sure I want that little house with a white fence anymore. But I am determined to try. What do you need?"

"I'm going to ask you to view a lineup in just a few minutes and tell me if you see anyone you can identify," Karp said. "I expect there will be a defense attorney present in the viewing room. He won't be able to see you because you'll be standing behind a curtain, and I'll ask you not to speak so that he can't identify your voice. Instead, Detective Fulton will be with you and have you write a number on a pad if you recognize someone."

"I can do that," Malovo said. "I hope this whole process isn't going to take forever. I am bored on the farm, Butch. A girl like me needs excitement, and hopefully a man in her bed."

"I can't help you there," Karp said. "But you're not planning on going anywhere, are you?"

Malovo looked hurt by the suggestion. "Butch, I gave you my word," she said, and smiled coyly. "If you can't trust your friends, who can you trust?"

Karp shrugged and shook his head. "No one at all, I guess," he said, and left her and Jaxon. He walked down the hall and entered another small room. An older couple were sitting next to each other, the man's arms around the woman, who cried quietly against his chest.

"Mr. and Mrs. Moore?"

"Yes. I'm Ted Senior and this is Martha."

"Good evening. I'm District Attorney Roger Karp. I appreciate you coming down here at this late hour. We're going to ask you to view a lineup of individuals in a few minutes. But first I'd like to talk to you about your son."

14

Six months later

OVER THE PAST THREE WEEKS, KARP HAD METHODICALLY laid out the People's case against Dean Mueller, beginning with the usual steps, such as re-creating the murder scene through the use of a forensics civil engineer, who made a to-scale diagram of the fatal shooting area, as well as the crime scene photographer and his work. Some of his questioning dealt with such minutiae, and he knew the jurors might wonder where he was going with it. But there'd been a reason behind each detail he elicited from his witnesses.

New York County assistant medical examiner Gail Manning had appeared to explain the cause of death of both Swindells and Matt Robbins, the brave young soldier who had tried to reach Mueller but instead got in the way of the bullet from Detective Ted Moore's gun.

"Was Colonel Swindells shot more than once?" Karp asked.

"No. Just the fatal wound to the head."

"He wasn't shot in the foot, or arm, or after the fatal wound?"

"No. Just the one head shot."

Karp had also called an NYPD fingerprint expert, who testified that the only prints found on the shell casings belonged to Mueller.

"So the defendant loaded the clip?" Karp asked.

"Yes."

"No one else?"

"No one else."

Next Karp had called a department ballistics expert, who testified that the deceased had been shot with bullets from the 9mm handgun taken from Mueller at the zoo.

"Was this gun loaded with live ammunition?" Karp asked, noting the quizzical looks on the faces of some of the jurors.

"Yes, copper-jacketed live ammunition."

"And was this the ammunition used to actually shoot Colonel Swindells?"

"Yes. Our tests show that the ammunition used to shoot the

deceased came from the same box of bullets as those found in the gun."

"They weren't blanks?"

"No. Live ammunition."

"The gun wasn't loaded with raisins?" Karp smiled as he asked the question, but his intentions were serious.

The ballistics expert gave him a funny look but answered. "No raisins, just bullets."

Several eyewitnesses were called to describe the shooting, to identify not just Mueller but also his demeanor and the exact nature of his actions.

"So even though you were between the defendant and Colonel Swindells as he approached, he walked right past you?" Karp asked several witnesses.

"Yes," each had replied.

"He made no attempt to confront or shoot you?"

"No. He walked straight for the colonel."

The witnesses all described how after a brief confrontation with Swindells, Mueller pulled his gun and shot Swindells before the colonel had time to react.

"Did he shoot wildly or wave the gun around?" Karp asked one Ranger who'd witnessed the shooting from ten feet away.

"No. He took careful aim and pulled the trigger," the man had replied.

Karp had asked for and received Judge Peter Rainsford's permission for the witness to leave the stand and demonstrate how Mueller aimed the gun. The Ranger assumed a shooter's stance, holding the imaginary gun with two hands as he sighted down the imaginary barrel. "Like this," he said.

"Did he then begin shooting wildly at others?" Karp asked the witnesses, who all replied that Mueller had not.

"Only when the other guy shot at him and hit poor Matt," one of the female Army vets testified, "did Mueller return fire as he'd been trained. He then took off running."

The only surprise Karp had run into from his witnesses was when he called Freddy Ortega to the stand to testify about comments Mueller had made to him as he ran from the scene. Ortega denied that the defendant had told him to "chill if you don't want to die."

When Karp reminded him that he'd made that statement to the television crew as well as to Assistant District Attorney Kenny Katz, Ortega's eyes flicked over to the defense table. *He's been bought, or he's scared*, Karp thought, and stopped his questioning.

His suspicions were confirmed when, on cross-examination,

Ortega talked about how Mueller had "acted all crazy, his eyes were rolling around and shit. He said some people were after him and wanted to torture him and kill him. Then he ran away like a crazy dude."

However, Ann Franklin, the hostage Mueller had with him when Karp met him at the door of the Bird House, had kept to the statement she'd given later that evening at the DAO. Although Mueller was obviously agitated and frightened, she said, he had also told the hostages that they wouldn't be harmed if they all cooperated.

"Did he at some point threaten to kill you and the other hostages?" Karp asked.

"Not me specifically," she'd replied. "And not until you were talking with him. Then he made some threats."

"When I spoke to him at the zoo," Karp continued, "did he want anything in exchange for letting you and the other hostages go?"

"Yes. He wanted ten million dollars and to be taken someplace—he didn't say where," Franklin replied. "He also didn't want to be charged with crimes."

"He was aware that he'd committed crimes?" Karp asked.

"Yes. He said he would testify against other people who he said were involved if you would not charge him."

"Did I offer him a deal to testify against these 'other' people?"

"No. You said he needed to let us go and give himself up. You said if he did that he could talk to you later."

"Did he say that someone else was trying to kill him, or would kill him?" Karp asked, knowing the defense would be raising this issue.

"Yes. He said others were trying to kill him."

"Did he mention anyone in particular?"

"He said the other guy at the picnic. He said someone else had a gun and tried to shoot him."

"Did I inform him about the identity of the other man with a gun?"

"Yes. You said he was a police detective."

As expected, LeJeune had belabored Franklin about her testimony regarding what he called Mueller's "wild statements regarding these mysterious others."

"Did he describe these others?" LeJeune asked.

"No. He just said they wanted to kill him and that it was a setup."

"And by 'setup' he was referring to the police detective who attempted to stop him?"

She shrugged. "I guess."

"So he didn't describe a mysterious conspiracy of 'others' who were trying to kill him?"

"Not to my knowledge."

As both he and LeJeune had mentioned Detective Ted Moore during the trial, Karp had avoided anything that would give away what he believed Moore's real intentions had been that day. The meeting with Moore's parents six months earlier had been heartbreaking for them, but what he'd learned was for another day and another trial he hoped to prosecute.

For the same reason, he had not called Stupenagel to the stand. She didn't witness the shooting, but more important, he had not wanted to get into why she was at the picnic or her conversation with Swindells.

After Karp rested the People's case, the defense had called only three witnesses. The first was a former member of Mueller's Ranger company prior to joining the 148th Battlefield Surveillance Brigade.

Specialist Duane Jones had described an incident in which the Humvee they'd been riding in while on patrol in Iraq was struck by an improvised explosive device.

"Was my client injured in the explosion?" LeJeune asked.

"He was dazed and, uh, talking kind of funny," Jones said. "I think he suffered a head injury."

After Jones stepped down, LeJeune had produced a document purporting to be a military physician's assessment that Mueller suffered "a possible concussion."

The defense attorney had then called Dr. Cheryl Dominguez to the stand. A brain trauma specialist at a veterans' hospital in New Jersey, Dominguez testified that the military frequently "underdiagnosed the severity of head trauma caused by exposure to massive explosions."

"So this could have been more than a concussion?" LeJeune asked.

"Yes," Dominguez replied. "I've looked at the incident report from Iraq, as well as the battlefield physician's report, and talked to Mr. Mueller."

"And your conclusion?"

"I believe the severity of his injury was much worse than originally diagnosed," Dominguez said. "On the Glasgow Coma Scale, I believe he was between a nine and a twelve, which would indicate moderate traumatic brain injury."

"And what sort of issues might we see from moderate traumatic brain injury?"

"A common effect is confusion, which can last from days to weeks," Dominguez said. "But we also see physical, cognitive, and behavioral impairments, which may last months, or even be permanent."

"When you say behavioral impairments, might that include a change in a patient's personality or mental stability?" LeJeune asked.

Dominguez nodded her head vigorously. "Quite frequently, actually. They may become quick to anger or, on the other end of the pendulum, suddenly unusually docile. Or their personality may swing radically from one to the other over a short period of time."

"Might it also cause periods of paranoid delusions?"

"Yes. Such a mental health issue is not uncommon at all."

Rising to cross-examine Dominguez, Karp remained behind the prosecution table as he asked, "Dr. Dominguez, did you or anyone you know of perform a CAT scan or MRI to determine if the defendant suffered this traumatic brain injury?"

"Well, no," Dominguez said, "but he's exhibited the classic symptoms."

"Which were?"

"Well, I would say that shooting someone was out of character for him. And he then exhibited paranoid delusions by, from what I understand, claiming that 'others' were after him."

"So other than what defense counsel contends is proof that the defendant did not know the nature and consequences of his acts or that what he was doing was wrong when he shot Colonel Swindells, you have no other evidence to a reasonable degree of scientific certainty."

"Um, no."

"No brain scans?"

"No."

"And, in fact, the original diagnosis from this 'battlefield report' that has suddenly shown up," Karp said, "was the defendant exhibited symptoms of a mild concussion."

"As I said, I believe he was misdiagnosed."

"Based on what? Conclusions you've reached six years after the alleged incident during which time there are no other reports of which I'm aware of the defendant exhibiting any of these behaviors?" Karp asked.

"I did my best with the material I was given and a complete oral examination of Mr. Mueller."

"Are you aware that after this alleged incident, the defendant transferred into an extremely well-trained Ranger unit, the 148th Battlefield Surveillance Brigade, known for their ability to perform in the field under the most difficult circumstances?"

"I did see that in his service record," Dominguez said.

"And that during the time he was with the 148th until his discharge he was considered an exemplary soldier?"

"Yes, I'm aware of that."

"So apparently none of these 'symptoms' of a moderate brain trauma were present?"

"I wouldn't say that," Dominguez countered. "They can go into remission or get worse over time."

"How much time? What is the baseline for your speculation 'get worse over time'?"

Dominguez didn't answer, so Karp continued as he walked several steps closer to the witness. "In fact, you don't know to any degree of scientific certainty that the defendant shot the deceased because of a concussion or because he had other reasons to commit murder?"

After Dominguez retreated from the stand, LeJeune had called Dr. Hank Winkler. An expert on post-traumatic stress disorder and associated personality disorders, the psychiatrist had stayed on the stand for most of the day as the defense attorney led him through a long and tedious explanation of PTSD, which he said created a delusional belief system. He attributed the PTSD "possibly to the injury he suffered in Iraq and/or it may be organic in nature and due to inherent chemical imbalances."

The psychiatrist concluded that Mueller believed that Swindells had unfairly targeted him for court-martial "regarding a relatively minor infraction." Over time, in combination with his PTSD and paranoid delusions, he believed that the colonel had intentionally set out to destroy his career and his self-image as a soldier.

"Eventually, that grew into the conviction that Swindells 'hated' him to the point that he wanted him to die and had hatched a plot with unknown 'others' to have him killed. On that tragic day, Mueller only intended to confront the colonel. But apparently at the precisely wrong moment in time, the colonel said something to him—he can't recall exactly what, which is common for someone who had been in a delusional state—that caused him to believe he needed to defend himself."

LeJeune turned his witness over for cross-examination. If Dr. Winkler's expert testimony was believed by the jurors, Mueller was not legally responsible for his actions at the time he killed Colonel Michael Swindells and should be sent to a locked psychiatric hospital facility, not a prison. While a patient at the locked facility, Mueller would be released from custody once the hospital shrinks determined he was no longer a danger to the community or to himself.

Now it was up to Karp to disabuse the jurors of Dr. Winkler's contentions and convince them of what he'd called in his opening statement "the insanity of the insanity defense." So much was riding on convicting Mueller, who'd sat for most of the trial with his head down and showing so little emotion that Karp thought he might be drugged. The few times Karp had caught his eye, he'd looked quickly away.

Karp stood looking at the slim balding man on the witness stand, who returned his gaze with a deep frown on his face. Five weeks into the trial of Dean Mueller and it had all come down to this, the prosecution's cross-examination of the defense's psychiatrist and his opinion.

Karp walked out from behind the prosecution table and stood against the witness rail.

"Doctor, in arriving at your opinion, did you take into account that the defendant planned his attack by determining where Colonel Swindells would be on that date and at that time?"

"Yes."

"And that he took a taxi to Central Park for the express purpose of attacking Colonel Swindells?"

Winkler frowned. "Well, I don't know about that. I know he wanted to confront the victim with his delusional belief that Colonel Swindells and others were trying to harm him."

"But he took a gun with him for this confrontation, not a banana or a Roman candle?"

Winkler chuckled. "No, definitely not a banana. He took a gun."

"And prior to leaving his home, he loaded his weapon with live ammunition?"

"Yes."

"Not with raisins or Cracker Jacks? But copper-jacketed nine-millimeter rounds that he removed from a box, inserted into a clip?"

Again, Winkler laughed at the question. "No, he didn't load it with raisins or Cracker Jacks. They were real bullets."

"And he placed the clip in the butt of the gun. He didn't put a Hershey bar in there?"

Winkler's eyebrows knitted. "This is getting a little silly, don't you think?"

"Answer my question, please."

"Yes, he stuck the clip in the gun."

"Did you take into account that the defendant bypassed a number of other people present at the picnic and went directly to Colonel Swindells?"

"Yes. That's who he had targeted."

"And did you take into account that only after confronting

the victim did Mueller remove the weapon from his waistband, point it at the deceased, and pull the trigger?"

"Well, yes, of course."

"Doctor, do you agree that the defendant, at the time he loaded the gun and brought it to Central Park, knew and appreciated that the weapon was an instrument capable of causing the death of the deceased?"

"Yes. He was a soldier and had handled many weapons."

"Yes, that's very true," Karp said. "And further, Doctor, do you agree that at the time the defendant confronted the colonel, he was armed with a loaded handgun, not a Roman candle?"

"This is ridiculous. Of course he knew it was a gun."

"And do you agree that when he shot the deceased, he knew he was shooting a living person, not a paper target?"

"Obviously."

Karp left the jury rail and walked out in front of the witness box. "On the issue of wrongfulness, did you take into account that, after the shooting, the defendant fled the scene?"

"Yes, he tried to escape."

"And that during his attempt to escape capture, he was confronted by uniformed police officers, at which time he took shelter in the Central Park Zoo?"

"Yes, that's true."

"And that in the zoo, he took hostages in an effort to avoid capture?"

"I believe that's true."

"And that while holding a gun, not a banana, to the head of a hostage, he acknowledged to me that he had committed a crime?"

"Yes. That's all true."

Karp folded his arms across his chest. "Then, Doctor, would you please tell us when it was that Mueller failed to know and appreciate the nature and consequences of his acts or that they were wrong?"

Winkler sat for a long moment squirming in his seat as he took off his glasses, wiped them with his tie, and then replaced them on his nose.

"Doctor, answer the question, please."

"At the, um, precise moment he pointed the gun at the deceased and pulled the trigger. It was at that moment he believed that he was killing the person, or persons, who intended to kill him."

Karp shook his head, looked at the jury, and said, "Now, isn't that silly."

15

AFTER KARP DISMANTLED WINKLER'S TESTIMONY ON THE stand, LeJeune rested the defense case. Judge Rainsford adjourned for the day. "We'll pick up tomorrow morning with summations," the judge said when the jury left the courtroom. "And I'd guess deliberations by tomorrow afternoon."

Karp met back in his office with Fulton, Katz, and Jaxon. "If all goes well, we could have a verdict as early as tomorrow afternoon, or possibly the next morning," he said. "If it's guilty, and I expect it to be, we'll see if he wants to roll over on his pals. If he does, the dominoes are going to start tumbling fast. Where's Fitzsimmons?"

"He's in solitary," Fulton responded. "Apparently, he likes to get in fights in the general population. We didn't want someone to stick a shank in him, so we put him away for safekeeping."

"Good. We may need him," Karp said with a nod.

Even indicted for the murders of Clare Dune and Jim Hughes, Fitzsimmons, who'd hired one of the best criminal defense attorneys in Manhattan, was still refusing to talk. The press had, of course, gone to town with the story, leaving Constantine to fend off questions about his "right-hand man," as described in an article by Stupenagel, being accused of murdering his wife and a New York City Council member.

"MR. CONSTANTINE HIRED Shaun Fitzsimmons based on recommendations from friends," his publicist had said at a press conference following Fitzsimmons's arrest. "Having said that, Wellington is concerned that these accusations are politically motivated to get to him. However, he's willing to let justice run its course, confident that the truth will prevail."

When he thought about Fitzsimmons in the grand scheme of putting the case together, Karp couldn't help but recall the night of his arrest and the request he'd made of the Moores. Separately, they'd both picked Fitzsimmons out of a lineup as the "friend" who'd stopped by their house to visit their son, Teddy.

"He said his name was William . . . I can't remember the last name," Martha Moore had said, her voice cracking. "But Teddy didn't know him by that name. That's when he told me his nickname was Fitz. He seemed like such a nice man, but after he went back to Teddy's room, we heard loud voices like they were arguing. Then he left and . . . and . . . and Teddy did that."

Martha had broken down into tears and loud sobbing, and had to excuse herself to go to the restroom. After she left, her husband explained that they were Irish Catholic and that suicide was a mortal sin. "She's worried that we won't get to see him in heaven."

Ted Moore Sr. had then looked at him as if contemplating an unpleasant thought. "This isn't about making a case against this guy for Teddy's death, is it?"

Karp looked in the old man's eyes, which were brimming with tears but they held his gaze. He shook his head. "No, I'm afraid not. We believe that your son was involved with the man you just identified in a murder."

"Is this about that shooting in Central Park? The one where Teddy was the hero?"

"Yes."

"I knew something was hinky about all that," Moore said. "You don't spend thirty-five years with the NYPD without developing a sixth sense about these sorts of things. Not to mention there aren't enough off-duty jobs in the city to suddenly be able to afford a fifty-thousand-dollar boat, a sports car, and a truck. I don't know why Teddy thought his old man wouldn't know that, but maybe I didn't want to see at first."

The old man choked up, and Karp reached out and put his hand on his shoulder. "I'm sorry," he said. "But I'm going to need you to identify that man in court to connect him to your son."

"I understand," Moore said. He hesitated, then asked, "Any way you can keep Martha out of it?"

Karp grimaced. "I don't know. If this goes to trial, there's going to be a lot of publicity and media coverage."

"Martha doesn't watch a lot of news or read the papers," Moore said. "She says it's too depressing. Still, she's bound to hear something when she gets together with her friends. But I was hoping maybe you won't need to call her as a witness. I think that might be too much for her."

"I think I'll be able to get by just with you," Karp had said. "I take it you've testified before?"

"Yeah, a few dozen times," Moore said. "I'd appreciate whatever you can do about Martha."

"**WHAT ABOUT CONSTANTINE?**" Karp asked his associates.

Jaxon spoke up. "He's in Geneva, where he enrolled his son in school. A little bird told me there's been a flurry of calls going back and forth between Switzerland and the White House."

"Any idea what's being said?" Karp asked.

"Unfortunately not," Jaxon replied. "It's all on secure lines, and there's no way I'm going to get a federal judge to give me a warrant for a wiretap."

An hour later, after Fulton and Katz left the office, Jaxon remained behind. "You know that when you make your move on Constantine, all hell is going to break loose," he said. "You took on some major players in the Sam Allen murder, but this will make that look like a tempest in a teapot."

"You saying I should back off?"

Jaxon laughed. "I know better than that. But it's not just Constantine's wealth and connections you're going to be dealing with. He's popular with the media and with the public. I'd hate to see some wacko go after you or your family."

"I've thought of that," Karp said. "When the time comes, if it doesn't look safe, Marlene and I have agreed they're all going to New Mexico. Lucy and Ned's ranch down there is pretty much off the grid. It would be tough on the boys; this could fall right at the end of their senior year. But it can't be helped."

"The boys are proud of their dad," Jaxon said. "They might not be thrilled, but they'll do what they need to do."

THE NEXT MORNING, Karp was still thinking about the ramifications of what that day might bring when Judge Rainsford called upon LeJeune to deliver his summation. The defense attorney spent two hours picking and choosing through the evidence, and then reiterated the testimony of his three witnesses before closing with an impassioned plea.

"There is no doubt that my client, Dean Mueller, shot and killed Colonel Michael Swindells," LeJeune said. "However, he is not a murderer. He is—through no fault of his own—a disturbed individual who did a terrible thing, but at the same time was not responsible when you carefully apply the insanity defense. After all, everyone knows he was suffering from a severe mental disease and defect, which seriously impaired his rationality, his judgment, and his ability to distinguish between right and wrong. He had a false belief mentality."

LeJeune walked behind the defense table and put his hands on Mueller's shoulders. "I would ask you to remember that we sent this young man off to a foreign country to fight for your freedom and mine. He laid his life on the line for us and was injured in the process. It's not the sort of injury you can see. He didn't lose and arm or a leg. There are no scars on his body. But there's a scar up here." The defense attorney pointed to Mueller's head.

LeJeune came out from behind the defense table and walked dramatically over to stand in front of the jurors. "Colonel Michael Swindells was an American hero. There is no doubt about that. But so is Dean Mueller, and he does not deserve to be thrown into prison like so much trash."

When LeJeune finished, Rainsford announced a fifteen-minute break. "After which we'll hear from Mr. Karp."

After the break, standing in front of the jury, Karp began his own summation by agreeing that "the act of taking another life is crazy by normal standards. Whether it's with bullets, or a knife, or drowning someone, the purposeful taking of a human life is an insane, irrational act. But that is not the question before you today. The questions you need to answer are whether Dean

Mueller knew that what he was doing was wrong and whether he understood the nature and consequences of his actions."

Karp let it sink in. "That, ladies and gentlemen, is what differentiates 'crazy' as we understand it going about our lives, and 'insanity' in the legal sense of whether the defendant can be held responsible for his actions. And if you answer the questions yes, then you must find him guilty of murder."

Karp then went through the question-and-answer cross-examination of Dr. Winkler. "The gun was loaded with bullets, not raisins. He understood that a gun was a weapon capable of causing death. He knew that death could result from pointing it at the victim's head and pulling the trigger. He didn't shoot wildly, or shoot the deceased in the hand or foot, or point the gun at him and say, 'Bang bang, you're dead.'

"From the evidence, we know that the defendant leveled the murder weapon at the deceased's head and pulled the trigger, intending to murder Colonel Swindells with a single shot.

"Now let's take a moment on the issue of wrongfulness. Immediately after the defendant murdered the deceased, he fled the scene, took hostages, and tried to make a deal because he understood that he would be arrested and charged with murder. Clearly, he knew what he did was wrong."

Karp marched over to the defense table and pointed at Mueller. "The defendant, this man right here, confronted with overwhelming factual guilt, is attempting to avoid responsibility and mock the justice system by invoking the not guilty by reason of insanity defense. The fact is that one of the most corrosive aspects of the criminal justice system is the insanity defense, which can provide an escape mechanism for wrongful violent misconduct.

"If allowed, it would permit this murderer to beat the system by establishing that he was suffering from a delusional belief system that induced irrational motivations, which compelled him to act out his violent impulses. Through his defense counsel, he is claiming that, based upon a mental disease or defect, he did not know or appreciate the nature or consequences of his acts or that they were wrong. Accordingly, his attorney would have you believe that he was not responsible when he executed his victim."

Karp returned to his place in front of the jurors. "Even if we believe, and I suggest there's ample evidence that it is simply not true, but even if we believe that the defendant suffers from a mental disease or defect that spawned a delusional mind-set, or false belief, that impelled him to kill the deceased, should our criminal justice system allow individuals with a delusional belief system that induces irrational motivations that result in violent wrongful criminal conduct to be exonerated?"

Patrolling in front of the jury box, Karp continued: "Isn't one of the major purposes of the criminal justice system to incarcerate those violent criminals who cannot control, but act out, their violent impulses? It offends notions of common sense that the criminal justice system creates by use of the insanity defense the very tool for these violent offenders to avoid responsibility and escape punishment."

Karp then blasted the "pervasive" use of psychiatric experts by both the defense and prosecution at trials. "In virtually every 'insanity' case that goes to trial, each side—the prosecution and the defense—hires its own so-called expert psychiatrist. Both psychiatrists proceed to give ironclad divergent opinions regarding the defendant's state of mind. Such testimony is at best conjecture, mere opinion and not scientific, empirical truth. It mocks the truly expert opinion that derives from a reasonable degree of scientific certainty.

"Also, it betrays the purpose of a criminal trial, which is the search for truth and the meting out of justice. Instead, the insanity defense gives criminally violent and unpredictable individuals in our community an opportunity to avoid being held accountable for their actions. In effect, they are exonerated not because they have provided a legitimate defense, such as a justification like self-defense, for example, but because their hired-gun psychiatrists are more convincing than the ones testifying for the opposition."

Karp turned and pointed at LeJeune. "The People did not resort to such tactics," he said. "But the defense did, in order to try to pull the wool over your eyes. The victims of crimes, the deceased's families and friends, care precious little for such gamesmanship. They only want to see justice done. The People are asking that you set aside the smoke and mirrors of the insanity defense and find the defendant guilty not just beyond a reasonable doubt but beyond any and all doubt. Thank you."

Looking at the jurors as he took his seat, Karp saw in their faces that he'd won the case. They affirmed that fewer than four hours later when they returned a guilty verdict. But even he was surprised by what happened next.

Mueller suddenly turned to Karp. "I want to talk to you," he said.

Shocked, LeJeune grabbed him by the arm. "Now is not the time, Dean," he said with a tight smile. "We'll appeal. This will never stand. You still have many friends."

"Yeah, friends like that cop, or whoever put him up to it, who want to see me dead," he scoffed. "You're fired, LeJeune. Karp, if you want to talk to me, you better get me out of here now."

Karp turned to Fulton. "Clay, would you please escort Mr. Mueller to my office: I believe he has something he wants to share with us."

16

Six months later

"OYEZ, OYEZ, OYEZ, ALL RISE. ALL THOSE HAVING BUSI-
ness in Supreme Court Part 42, State of New York, New York
County, draw near and ye shall be heard. The Honorable Supreme Court Justice Vince Dermondy presiding."

Chief Administrative Court Clerk Duffy McIntyre stepped
back and nodded to Dermondy, who sat down at his dais. "Be
seated," the judge announced. "We're here in the matter of the
State of New York vs. Wellington Constantine. The defendant is
present with counsel, Mr. Michael Arnold. The People are represented by District Attorney Roger Karp and Assistant District
Attorney Kenneth Katz. The jury is present, so let us proceed."

Dermondy looked over at Karp, who had remained standing

and was looking down at his yellow notepad. "You may call your next witness."

"The People call Dean Mueller." Karp nodded to Fulton, who stood next to a side door leading from the witness waiting room. The detective opened the door and the witness shuffled into the courtroom dressed in a jail jumpsuit.

NEARLY SIX MONTHS after the conviction of Mueller, and three weeks into the trial of Wellington Constantine, Karp was laying out his case with all the attention to detail and structure of a master builder. So far he'd weathered the storm of media attacks and denunciations by politicians, "community organizers," movie stars and musicians, and the liberal establishment, who'd rallied to Constantine's accusations that the charges were politically motivated and untrue.

As predicted by Jaxon, there'd been a lot of threats and even one poorly constructed explosive device that had been found by NYPD bomb squad dogs outside the family loft on Crosby Street. Poorly constructed or not, it had been enough to ship the family off to New Mexico, where Marlene reported that the boys were not missing the start of summer in New York City in exchange for playing cowboy on the ranch.

Alone at night in the weeks leading up to and into the trial, he missed his family, but it allowed him to concentrate on the case. The only other change to his normal schedule was a concession to Fulton to allow extra security outside his building and a promise to let Ewin drive him back and forth to the Criminal Courts Building rather than enjoy his customary walk.

After the opening statements, Karp proceeded to lay the foundation for the prosecution of Constantine much the same as he had with the Mueller case. The crime scene was described with the diagram and photographs, and Assistant ME Gail Manning had ascertained the cause and manner of Swindells's death for this second jury. In every murder case, there are two things that the People have to prove: that the deceased is in fact dead, and that the deceased died as a result of the criminal acts of the defendant.

After the "official" witnesses, Sasha Swindells was called to the stand. She testified that her father had been deeply concerned about something that had occurred during his last tour of duty while stationed in Saudi Arabia. He had not told her about any specifics, she said, but she knew it was connected to a text she received asking her to deliver something to Ariadne Stupenagel.

"Did you know Ms. Stupenagel?"

"I met her once, a few minutes before my father was shot,"

Sasha had testified. Up to that point, the young woman had done her best to present herself as a newly commissioned officer in the U.S. Army, but now she broke down and cried the tears of a daughter.

Wisely, Arnold had not tried to cross-examine her. There was nothing to be gained by grilling the daughter of the deceased.

Sasha Swindells's testimony had been followed by Ariadne Stupenagel, whom Karp eased into her testimony by having her describe how she knew Colonel Swindells, as well as her career as an investigative journalist.

"What prompted you to go to Central Park to speak to Colonel Swindells?" Karp had asked after several preliminary questions to set the stage.

"A source told me about a black ops mission in Syria in which a file, code-named MIRAGE, had been seized," Stupenagel said. "During this mission, several highly placed people connected to the governments of Russia, Syria, and Iran, as well as a leader of the terrorist group ISIS, were killed just prior to U.S. forces arriving."

"Do you know, or were you told, who killed them?" Karp asked.

"I was told they were killed by a Russian assassin named Nadya Malovo," Stupenagel said. "The source also informed me that one other person had been expected at the meeting but wasn't present, a wealthy, well-connected American."

"Did this source tell you the name of this American?"

"No. The source did not have that information."

"Did the source know any details about MIRAGE?"

"Only that it involved powerful people with connections to the governments of these other countries and had something to do with black-market oil."

"In Central Park, did you ask Colonel Swindells about MIRAGE?"

"Yes, I did."

"What was his reaction?"

"He told me to forget about it, that he was looking into it but that it was too dangerous for me. He even voiced concerns over his own safety and mine. He said I would be swimming in shark-infested waters."

"Was there anything else he said to you?"

"Just that I shouldn't contact him again for my own safety."

"Did you take his advice?"

"Not after he was killed," she replied, and described how she, Sasha Swindells, and "a government agent named S. P. Jaxon" came to be in possession of a flash drive that the colonel had secreted in a book at the West Point library.

"Do you know what is on the flash drive?"

"No. Apparently it contains encrypted information. But according to Colonel Swindells's Gold Book I mentioned, it is somehow connected to MIRAGE."

AS HE BUILT his case, Karp knew that the jurors would be waiting for the proverbial smoking gun, that aha moment when it would all be made clear. But this wasn't that sort of case, and the moment of truth wasn't going to arrive until the end, when he could put all the pieces together for them. Following Stupenagel's testimony, the next piece was Dean Mueller, who now took the stand and sat with his head down. The first thing Karp did was establish that the witness was the man who pulled the trigger that killed Colonel Swindells.

"Were you convicted of this heinous murder?" Karp asked.

"Yes. I pulled the trigger."

"Did you know the deceased?"

"Yes. He was my commanding officer."

"Did you know what you were doing when you shot him in the head?"

"I was there to kill him."

Karp let it sink in for a moment before backtracking. "Describe your professional relationship to Colonel Swindells."

"I was assigned to the colonel's staff after we returned from Saudi Arabia."

"And how did that lead to you murdering him?"

"I was contacted by a man who said he represented a wealthy businessman," Mueller said. "He told me that his employer wanted something that the colonel had in his possession."

"Did he say what it was?"

"Yes. A flash drive."

"Did he give it a name?"

"He said to look for anything connected to the word 'mirage.'"

"Were you offered compensation for locating this flash drive?"

"I was told I would receive two million dollars if I returned it."

Karp raised his eyebrows. "That's a lot of money. Did you have any other information?"

"I knew it was connected to a black ops raid conducted by another group and that upon their return to Saudi Arabia they were intercepted by Company D of the 148th, which was the colonel's brigade."

"Is there anything in particular you know about Company D?"

"Yeah, a bunch of cowboys. They don't follow the usual chain of command, and in fact bypassed the colonel who was our commanding officer. They supposedly do a lot of missions no one wants anybody else, especially the public, to know about."

"Were you able to locate the flash drive?"

"I was able to locate a flash drive that was in a file marked MIRAGE. But it was a fake. Apparently the colonel suspected that someone was after the real flash drive. He couldn't prove I took it, but I was forced to resign with an Other Than Honorable discharge to avoid court-martial."

"What was the reaction to this fake flash drive from the man who represented the wealthy businessman?"

"He was pissed off," Mueller said. "He said they weren't paying for nothing. He also said that he'd learned that Colonel Swindells was pursuing charges against me and was going to have me sent to Leavenworth federal penitentiary."

"Did this other man suggest a way to make up for your mistake as well as prevent prosecution?"

Mueller nodded. "Yes. He said I had to kill Colonel Swindells. But the colonel was being real careful. It was hard to find a time when he wasn't on guard. This other man learned he'd be at the picnic."

"Was there anybody else with this man when you met?"

"Yeah, there was a guy he said was a New York City detective and was going to be part of the plan."

"Why did you shoot Colonel Swindells in broad daylight in front of witnesses?"

"It was part of the plan," Mueller said. "I know it sounds idiotic now. But like I said, it was hard to get at the colonel. But the way it was supposed to work was I'd shoot the colonel and then act crazy. Like I was out of my mind. Then the detective guy would take me into custody and back up my story that I appeared to be out of it. The first guy, the big guy, said they'd get me off on an insanity plea. I'd do a couple years in some cushy hospital, but then I'd have four million, twice the initial offer, waiting for me when I got out."

"Did something happen after you shot the colonel that convinced you there was something wrong with the plan?"

"Yes. I heard another gunshot. I looked around, and that detective had just taken a shot at me but hit someone else. I shot back and wounded him."

"What did you do next?"

"I realized it was a setup. So I took off running."

"If you knew it was a setup, what convinced you to go to trial and enter a not guilty by reason of insanity plea?"

"They got to me with their lawyer, Robert LeJeune. He convinced me that the detective was just trying to stop the guy who tried to tackle me after I shot the colonel. That I had misunderstood what was going on. They waved that money in my face, and I went for it."

"After you were convicted, why did you agree to testify in this case for the People?"

Mueller shrugged. "I knew that if I went to prison, they'd kill me. I was a loose end, which that big guy was always talking about. I figured I might stand a chance if I testified."

"Did I offer you any kind of deal to testify?"

"No. You said that if I testified truthfully, you'd note that to the judge when I get sentenced for killing the colonel. You also said that I might be able to serve my time in a minimum security federal penitentiary."

"Did you subsequently reach an agreement with a federal agency regarding your forthcoming incarceration?"

"Yes. Again if I testify truthfully, I will get a new identity and be housed in administrative segregation so that I don't have to be in with the general population. I wouldn't last a day in there."

"Do you have any hope of getting out of prison eventually?"

"It's possible if the judge takes into consideration that I'm telling you the truth now. But I'll be an old man."

Mueller ended his testimony with Karp entering into evidence his photo array lineup identification of Detective Ted Moore as the other shooter in the park, and Shaun Fitzsimmons as the man who represented the wealthy businessman.

"One last question, Mr. Mueller," Karp said. "Was there another reason you decided to testify today for the People?"

"Yeah," Mueller said, looking over at Constantine. "These guys with money, they get away with everything. They start the wars so that they can make a profit selling oil or guns. Guys like me, the soldiers, as well as a lot of innocent people, die because of them. Then if they need some dirty work done to clean up their messes, they wave the cash around and get guys like me to do it. But guys like me, we end up in prison or dead while they're having dinner at the White House and golfing with the president. I figured if I was going down for this, so was he."

Karp followed his glare over to the defense bench, where Arnold smirked and Constantine looked up at the ceiling as if bored. "Thank you, no further questions."

17

"THE PEOPLE CALL SHAUN FITZSIMMONS."

Waiting for Constantine's former bodyguard and henchman to enter the courtroom, Karp went over in his mind how the previous day in court had ended.

AS ANTICIPATED, THE defense attorney, Mike Arnold, a white-shoe hot-shot aggressive young Harvard Law type who liked to hear himself talk, had hammered away at Mueller during cross-examination. Arnold was the prototype big-reputation Wall Street litigator whose comfort zone was securities-fraud-type cases. But an overriding ego inexorably led him to the unfamiliar and, in his warped sense of superiority, the pedestrian state court. Defending the proverbial big guy in a steamy major media case, Arnold craved the elixir of celebrity.

The gist of his attack was that Mueller had killed Swindells because the colonel had run him out of the Army. "And now you're trying to get a sweetheart deal by going along with the fantastical story invented by the prosecution," Arnold accused.

Listening passively to Arnold's vitriol, Karp knew that even some members of the jury had to be questioning Mueller's account. Taken on its own it would be hard to believe. However, the case didn't rely on the testimony of any one witness or lack of corroboration.

Whatever the jury thought of Mueller and his "fantastical" testimony, they were in rapt attention when Karp next called Ted Moore Sr. to the stand. The former police officer began by testifying that he and his wife had identified Shaun Fitzsimmons in a lineup, which contained five stand-ins, as the man who visited their son.

"What happened immediately following that visit?" Karp asked after he entered into evidence a lineup photograph of Fitzsimmons holding the number 6 against his chest.

"My son . . ." the old man started to say, then broke down and had to pull himself together. "My son killed himself."

Karp questioned Moore about bank statements he and his wife had located in their son's room after he shot himself. "Would you tell the jury what bank these statements were issued by?"

"Grand Cayman National Bank."

"And what is the balance on the last statement issued, I believe, two weeks before your son died?"

"It says $579,283."

"What does that say to you?"

"That my son was on the take," said Moore, his voice grim. "Thirty-five years on the force, I know a dirty cop when I see something like this."

"Was your son a dirty cop?"

Moore hung his head and his shoulders shook. But when he looked up, his face was hard in spite of the tears on his cheeks. "Yes, he was a dirty cop."

As the old man left the witness stand, Karp reflected on the orchestration of the People's case. He sometimes saw himself as moving the pieces of his cases around like playing chess, a game he'd learned from his mother. She'd taught him that it wasn't all about a frontal attack and a war of attrition, trading pieces with an opponent. "With a true grandmaster," she said, "you can't see the strategy until it's too late and you're in checkmate."

• • •

KARP APPROACHED PROSECUTING criminals the same way and was prepared to move another piece as the hulking presence of Fitzsimmons entered the courtroom. Just getting Constantine's bodyguard on the theoretical game board had required moving a lot of pieces to put him into check.

Pretending to be irritated but secretly pleased, he'd gone along with motions by Fitzsimmons's attorney to delay the trials for murdering Clare Dune and Jim Hughes. Then after Mueller's conviction, he asked to meet with Fitzsimmons and his attorney, Stephanie Clagel.

"Maybe you heard," Karp said to Fitzsimmons when they were seated with Fulton and a stenographer present but waiting for the go-ahead to record, "that Mueller's talking and he's pointing the finger at you as the guy who set up the murder of Colonel Michael Swindells. And I want to talk to you about that."

Fitzsimmons gave him a bored look. "Snitches end up in ditches," he said. "You just don't get 'fuck off,' do you, Karp? You think a different month is going to change anything?"

"Mr. Karp, you're wasting our time," Clagel said.

"Well, then, let me get to the point," Karp said. "You've also been identified as having visited Detective Ted Moore shortly before he committed suicide."

"Don't know the man," Fitzsimmons said. "Wasn't my finger on the trigger."

"How'd you know he pulled a trigger?" Karp asked.

"Mr. Fitzsimmons, I'd advise you not answer any more of the DA's questions," Clagel cautioned.

Fitzsimmons shrugged. "It's boring in jail. I want to hear what this clown has to say. Maybe his bullshit will be entertaining."

"Well, that identification connects you to Moore," Karp said. "Mueller also picked you and Moore out of lineups as the men who put him up to murdering Swindells."

"I must have a doppelgänger out there," Fitzsimmons said with a smirk. "Somebody who looks like me."

"Go ahead and play stupid," Karp said. "But now the feds are interested. You do know that conspiring to murder an active-duty Army officer during the performance of his duty, while acting in concert with agents of foreign governments, is a federal crime. There's one other person involved in this, a Russian, and she can put you in Istanbul."

"Big deal," Fitzsimmons said. "I'll beat these two you have lined up against me. And I'll beat that one, too."

"Maybe you will, and maybe you won't," Karp said. "And

maybe the thought of hard time in a New York prison doesn't faze you. But the federal murder beef is a death penalty case, and I have reason to believe they'll be trying to send you to the federal prison in Terre Haute, Indiana, where they'll strap you to a gurney and put you down like the junkyard dog you are."

Fitzsimmons's eyes narrowed as his lawyer spoke up. "I think we've heard enough of your threats, Karp. We'll be leaving—"

"Shut up, you worthless twat," Fitzsimmons said. He leaned forward. "What do I get if I testify?"

Karp smiled. "I believe I can talk the feds into suspending their case against you. You plead guilty to the murder of Clare Dune, and I suspend the cases against you for Hughes and Swindells. That's *if* you testify truthfully. Lie, and the feds and I will be fighting over your bones like a pack of wolves. On the other hand, testify truthfully, and you stand a slight chance of getting out of prison as an old man instead of in a wooden box."

WITH THAT IMAGE in mind, Fitzsimmons had caved and told his side of the story as the stenographer took it down. Now, seated on the witness stand, he glared about as he took in the packed gallery and men sitting at the defense and prosecution tables. His lip curled and he shook his head when he looked at Constantine, who pretended to stifle a yawn and looked away.

Two hours later, Fitzsimmons had laid it all out for the jury. Admitting to the murder of Clare Dune, he said he'd been ordered to kill her because "she'd been having an affair with her kid's basketball coach, Richie Bryers. And Mr. Constantine wanted her dead." Only later, when Bryers called pretending to blackmail Constantine, did they learn that Dune had taken a photograph of one of his boss's journals that discussed the MIRAGE file.

"He was writing in those damn things all the time," Fitzsimmons testified. "I told him it would come back to haunt him, but he wouldn't listen. The arrogant son of a bitch thought he was untouchable."

Karp also questioned Fitzsimmons about telephone conversations Constantine had on the day of Swindells's murder in which he discussed both Mueller and, in a separate conversation, "the MIRAGE plan with someone in the White House."

Fitzsimmons said he didn't know the details of MIRAGE, "except it has something to do with black-market oil and Mr. Constantine's facilities in Iraq." He described his meeting with a Russian woman named Ajmaani in Istanbul to arrange the subsequent meeting with the Russians, Syrians, Iranians, and ISIS.

"Did the defendant end up attending that meeting?" Karp asked.

"No," Fitzsimmons said. "He was warned that there might be trouble and decided not to go."

Fitzsimmons detailed how he'd been instructed by Constantine to get the MIRAGE file back after it was seized in the Syrian raid. "We learned that Swindells was trying to get the file deciphered. That's when Constantine decided that the colonel had to go. He figured if Swindells was out of the picture, the problem would go away and he could move forward with his plan."

"What was supposed to happen to Dean Mueller after he shot Swindells?" Karp asked.

"Moore was supposed to shoot him," Fitzsimmons said. "Mueller would be just another crazy vet with a bone to pick with his commanding officer, and Moore would be the hero. But he fucked up. The whole thing was a fucked-up idea from the get-go, but you couldn't say that to Mr. Constantine. He had it all figured out. He gets off thinking he's smarter than everybody else."

After Karp finished questioning Fitzsimmons, there were still blank spaces in the mosaic. He'd carefully avoided questioning him about Constantine's connections with the administration in Washington. There was a piece on the chessboard he wanted even more than Constantine, but it required laying a trap for his opponents to fall into.

Again during cross-examination, Arnold had to attempt to discredit Fitzsimmons as "an admitted murderer" who was trying to pass the blame onto Karp's political enemy in exchange for leniency. "You and Mueller and Karp made up this whole implausible plot, didn't you," he demanded.

"Nope," Fitzsimmons said. "If I was going to make up something, it would have been airtight. But I wasn't in charge." He pointed at Constantine. "That arrogant son of a bitch was, and now we're all going down."

With nothing else to go on, Arnold continued trying to say the same thing in different ways until Fitzsimmons said, "What is it about 'fuck off' you don't get, Arnold?"

Karp had to suppress a smile when Arnold complained, but Judge Dermondy said, "In spite of the witness's crude remark, I have to agree that you've asked your question and had it answered, Mr. Arnold. Let's move on."

"No further questions," he said in disgust.

As Fitzsimmons left the courtroom with one last glare at Constantine, Dermondy looked at Karp. "Do you have another witness?"

"One more, Your Honor. The People call Richie Bryers."

18

RICHIE BRYERS SAT ON THE WITNESS STAND WITH HIS head down and tears streaming down his cheeks. When he'd met with Karp that morning before court, his old friend had warned him about what to expect. "I won't kid you, Richie, it's not going to be easy. It will be tough enough answering my questions, but I expect the defense attorney will come after you with both barrels."

Bryers had nodded. "I understand. I guess in some ways I deserve what's coming. I fell in love, but I should have done the right thing and waited until she was divorced."

"I'm not going to second-guess you there," Karp had countered. "But you didn't kill Clare. Fitzsimmons did, under orders from her husband. They're the ones guilty of her murder, not you. This will be your chance to see that justice is done. Just remember that when the questioning gets tough."

"MR. BRYERS, HOW do you know the defendant in this case?" Karp began.

"I teach, or I taught, at the private school his son attended," Bryers replied. "I was also the basketball coach. Mr. Constantine's son, Tommy, was on the middle school team and I was asked if I would work one-on-one with him."

"By Mr. Constantine?"

"Yes. We met at his home, and he offered me the job."

"Did it pay well?"

"Yes, in fact, several times my going rate for private lessons."

"And you accepted the terms and money?"

"Yes. He insisted and obviously he could afford it. I'm a teacher, and it was a lot of money to me."

"And during your tenure, did you have occasion to meet Mr. Constantine's wife, Clare Dune?"

Bryers nodded. "Yes, I met Clare."

"In addition to the pay, were you offered other perks?"

"Yes. I was invited to use the guesthouse at their Long Island property in Suffolk County," Bryers said. "I stayed there some weekends."

"In a sense you became a family friend."

"Yes."

"At some point did that friendship evolve into a romantic relationship with Clare Dune?"

"Yes. A couple of months after I began working there, Clare and I became romantically involved," Bryers admitted.

"Is it fair to say that the relationship between Clare Dune and the defendant was strained?" Karp asked. At a pretrial hearing, Arnold had won a motion precluding Karp from discussing Constantine's domestic violence against his wife.

"It was not a happy marriage."

"Did the two of you plan a future together?"

"I'd asked her several times to leave her husband." Bryers looked over at Constantine, who stared back at him as if he smelled bad. "But she was afraid she would lose custody of her son, Tommy. She also believed that her husband was preparing to divorce her, and she wanted to wait for him to make the first move."

With that out of the way, Karp moved on to the crux of Bryers's testimony. "Have you ever heard of something called MIRAGE in relation to the defendant and this case?"

"Yes."

"Would you tell the jury under what circumstances?"

"I was staying at the cottage when I saw a page in a journal Mr. Constantine was writing."

"What, if anything, could you read?"

"Well, it's been a while, but it mentioned a raid and that something called the MIRAGE files ended up in the wrong hands," Bryers said. "I remember specifically because of a comment that stated that 'Col. S and the Russian bitch need to be eliminated.'"

"What was your initial impression of what you read?"

"I asked Clare if her husband was writing a book. It read like a wanna-be author's first stab at a thriller."

"Did something happen to make you question your belief that Mr. Constantine was writing fiction?"

"Yes. A couple of minutes later, I went inside the main house to wash my hands for lunch. I was passing Mr. Constantine's library when I heard his voice. He was angry and yelling at somebody."

"What did he say?"

"He told whoever it was to make sure that someone named Mueller kept his mouth shut."

"Was there anything else?"

"Yes. Fitzsimmons told him there was a call from the White House. He asked if Mr. Constantine wanted to take the call."

"Do you know if the caller was a man or a woman?"

"I believe a woman, because he called the person a bitch."

"Was there anything else?"

"Yes. He told this person that because of a raid, MIRAGE was, and I quote, 'fucked up.' He seemed to think it was her fault."

"What did you do after you overheard this conversation?"

"I went back outside and told Clare what I heard. She didn't think much of it at the time."

"You said you read a comment about a 'Col. S and a Russian bitch' needing to be eliminated. Did you later have reason to attach any special significance to that statement?"

"Yes. As I found out later, that was the day Colonel Swindells was shot in Central Park. Given that phone call, I wondered if there was a connection."

"Did you go to the police with your suspicions?"

Bryers shook his head. "It still seemed pretty far-fetched that Mr. Constantine would be mixed up in something like that. I wanted to get another look at his journal first."

"Did you discuss that with Clare Dune?"

"Yes."

"Did she act on it?"

"I didn't want her to, at least not alone, but yes. Sometime later, I got a call from her. Her husband had gone to Washington, and she was alone. She wanted to see what she could find in the journal."

"Did she sound drunk or like she was doing drugs when she called?"

"No. She was perfectly lucid."

"Did she then send you something from her cell phone?"

"Yes. She'd taken a photograph of one of the pages in Mr. Constantine's journal."

Karp walked over to the prosecution table, where Katz handed him two clear envelopes, one of which he handed to Bryers. "You have what has been marked for identification People's Exhibit 60. Do you recognize it?"

"Yes, it's the journal photograph she sent to me."

"Your Honor, I move that People's Exhibit 60 be received in evidence."

Dermondy looked at Arnold, who rose from his seat. "Your Honor, the defense objected to this and other exhibits tendered by the prosecution at a pretrial hearing. We have the same objection."

"Duly noted," Dermondy replied. "Overruled. You may continue, Mr. Karp."

Karp turned back to Bryers. "Would you please read what is on the photograph to the jury and the court."

"Yes. It says, 'MIRAGE is moving forward at last. All the players have been replaced. Just movable pieces. The refineries are back at full capacity and deliveries are being made. One problem has been eliminated but another remains. She's the weak link and has to go.'" Bryers looked up. "That's all."

Karp handed him the other clear envelope. "I'm handing you what has been marked for identification People's Exhibit 61. Can you identify it?"

"Yes. It's a copy of the text Clare sent me after the photograph from the journal."

"And what does it say?"

"That she thought someone was in the house."

"Was Clare able to contact you again after that?"

Bryers shook his head. "No. That was the last time I heard from her," he said, his voice catching at the end.

"Did you attempt to reach her?"

"Yes. I texted her and asked if she was okay. She didn't answer. I thought maybe her husband had come home unexpectedly and she wasn't able to text me back."

"Do you now know why she wasn't able to?"

"She was murdered by Shaun Fitzsimmons," Bryers said, and buried his face in his hands. "Because of me."

"No further questions," Karp said softly.

Arnold's cross-examination was as harsh as Karp had predicted. He painted Bryers as a gigolo who'd taken advantage of "a lonely wife, whose husband's work took him away from her too often."

"You were happy to take his money and his wife's affection, weren't you, Mr. Bryers?"

"I did both," Bryers admitted.

"Did you also hope to talk her into a divorce so that you could live off of whatever settlement she got?"

"I didn't want his money."

"No. But you tried to blackmail him by sending those text messages and that photograph of a private journal. You asked for four million dollars for your silence."

"I did that with District Attorney Karp present."

"Yes, you did, didn't you?" Arnold said with a sneer. "Just one more pawn in the prosecution's witch hunt."

"Objection, Your Honor!" Karp said, rising to his feet. "If Mr. Arnold has any proof pertaining to any witch hunt, we'd like to see it. Otherwise it's just sheer self-serving speculation and objectionable."

"Mr. Arnold, you wish to respond?" Dermondy asked.

"I'll rely on my cross-examination to demonstrate Mr. Karp's bad faith," Arnold said.

"Very well, Mr. Karp's objection is sustained. The jury is instructed to disregard Mr. Arnold's last statements."

Arnold gave Bryers and then Karp one more disdainful look and shook his head. "No more questions, Your Honor."

After Bryers left the courtroom, Karp turned to Judge Dermondy and addressed the court. "Your Honor, that concludes the People's case."

The gallery was silent for a moment, and then began buzzing. It was obvious they'd expected more from the prosecution. "Very well," Dermondy said, and turned to the jurors. "Ladies and gentlemen, it's now late in the afternoon and so I'm going to send you home with the same admonition to avoid watching or reading any information or material having to do with this case, and please use caution when viewing social media. Please do not discuss the case among yourselves, or with anyone else. We will see you in the morning, and now we stand adjourned until nine a.m. tomorrow."

After the jury was escorted out of the courtroom, Dermondy turned his attention to Constantine and Arnold, who were engaged in a whispered conversation at the defense table. "Will you be calling any witnesses, Mr. Arnold?"

Arnold stood and glanced at his client, who nodded. "Just one, Your Honor. Mr. Constantine will take the stand."

This time the spectators in the gallery responded with excitement. Tomorrow morning was bound to have more fireworks.

"Very well," Dermondy said.

After the judge and all but a few members of the press had left, Constantine stood and faced Karp. "Is that all you got?" he said contemptuously, catching everybody, including his own attorney, by surprise.

"Excuse me?" Karp replied.

"Is that all you got?" Constantine's face was contorted and red with anger. "I thought you were supposed to be the top dog prosecutor. More like a mutt nipping at my heels."

"Wellington, this isn't the—" Arnold placed a hand on his client's shoulder.

Constantine shrugged him off. "Get your hands off me, Mike," he snarled. "Drop the charges now, Karp, and maybe I won't sue you personally for wrongful prosecution."

Karp looked Constantine in the eye. "I hope you got your toothbrush with you," he said matter-of-factly.

"What's that supposed to mean?" Constantine shot right back.

"Just that you're never going home again after the jury convicts you," Karp said with a laugh.

With that, Karp walked out of the courtroom and into the

hallway, where Katz and Fulton waited for him. He could hear Constantine screaming obscenities at him.

"Hear that, gentlemen? Sounds like Dean Wormer in *Animal House* berating John Belushi and his frat brothers at Delta Tau Chi. But on to more serious business, is everything ready for tonight?"

"Oh, yeah," Fulton replied. "There will be a direct feed into the office."

"Could be a late night," Karp noted.

"I ordered pizza, sodas, and coffee," Katz said.

"You're a good man, Kenny Katz," Karp said with a laugh. "I hope you told them extra pepperoni."

19

WELLINGTON CONSTANTINE TOOK A MOMENT TO STRAIGHTEN his light gray Italian designer pashmina suit coat and settled into the chair on the witness stand before looking at the jurors with a smile. He was feeling confident as he turned to his attorney, who stood behind the defense table gazing down at his legal pad.

At the start of the morning session before the jury was brought back into the courtroom, he and Arnold had conferred quietly.

"I still recommend against this," his lawyer had whispered. "It's a weak case at best. Why expose yourself? You don't have to take the stand. I think we can win without presenting anything. I'll tear their witnesses apart in summation."

"No. I told you last night I want to personally humiliate that asshole Karp," Constantine insisted. "We've been over every-thing. They don't have anything that I can't explain away, and I'm not leaving any of it to chance. I didn't get where I am by backing off when someone gets in my business."

"What if they call you-know-who to the stand?"

"We had a long talk last night after she got back from the the-ater," Constantine said. "She knows the drill. They want Karp's hide on the wall down in D.C. as much as I do. We'll see who's the last man standing when I'm done kicking his ass."

After he was called to the stand, Judge Dermondy had quizzed him about his decision. "You are not obligated to testify on your own behalf," he said.

"I understand, Your Honor," Constantine replied.

"Are you making this decision of your own free will after con-ferring with your attorney?"

"Yes." He knew that Dermondy was questioning him so that he couldn't come back later on appeal and say that he didn't understand or had been talked into it by Arnold. *There isn't going to be any need for an appeal*, he thought as Arnold fin-ished jotting notes and walked confidently into the well of the courtroom.

"Good morning, Mr. Constantine. Would you please state your name and spell the last."

"Good morning, Mr. Arnold, I'd be happy to. It's Wellington Constantine. C-O-N-S-T-A-N-T-I-N-E."

Arnold smiled and almost apologetically asked his first question. "I'm sure most everyone in this courtroom has heard about your business and philanthropic efforts, so I'm sorry if this seems a little unnecessary, but tell us a bit about your background."

Constantine laughed lightly. "Well, I guess I could start by noting that I'm the son of a British mother and a Greek-American father, thus the name they gave me, their only child. My mom stayed at home to raise me, Dad was into shipping. It was a happy childhood."

"Your father was a self-made man?"

"Yes, a real American success story. Second generation. Started off as the captain of an old cargo transport, saved his money and bought the ship, then another and another."

"I take it he did well?"

"Yes. By the time he retired he owned one of the largest shipping companies in the world. Constantine Shipping."

"And you inherited that wealth."

"Yes, though I like to think I've done okay on my own. Constantine Shipping is just one of more than a dozen subsidiaries of Well-Con Industries."

Arnold continued, "Didn't *Wealth* magazine name you one of the five richest men in the world?"

Constantine nodded. "I've heard that, but I really don't pay attention to those sorts of things. I will say I'm a good businessman, and lucky. I was also fortunate that I had a hardworking father as a role model whose efforts set me up with certain advantages. I've also worked hard and seem to have a knack for making money."

"The Midas touch, right?"

Making a face as if he was embarrassed by the line of questioning, Constantine shrugged. "I suppose you could say that."

Arnold turned to the jury. "But it's not all about the money to you, is it?"

Constantine frowned. "What do you mean?"

"Well, tell us about Clare's Legacy."

Constantine bowed his head and sat quietly for a moment before looking up at the jurors. "Clare's Legacy is a charitable foundation I started in honor of my wife . . ." His voice faltered. "My wife, Clare."

Arnold shook his head sadly before looking back at his client. "I know this is tough, especially after the lies—"

"Objection," Karp said. "Counsel is free to characterize statements made by the People's witnesses during his summations, but not when asking questions."

"Sustained," Dermondy said. "Mr. Arnold, try to avoid the editorializing."

Arnold nodded and continued. "I know this is tough for you to talk about, but what exactly is Clare's Legacy?"

Constantine smiled sadly. "Clare was involved in a number of charitable causes—everything from saving elephants in Kenya to providing health care on Native American reservations. She channeled literally millions of dollars of our money into these during the eighteen wonderful years of our marriage. After she . . . she was murdered . . . I decided to create a single foundation where these groups can apply for funding. I wanted her life to mean something even though she's gone."

"And what was your initial endowment for the foundation?"

"Forty million dollars."

Glancing at the jurors to see how they reacted to that number, Arnold spoke softly. "These fine people have heard a lot about your relationship with your wife and her alleged relationships with others. But first, tell us about Clare through your eyes."

Sighing, Constantine turned to look at the jurors as well. "She was beautiful, both inside and out. I fell in love the first time I saw her, and the day we got married was the best day of my life. Except, perhaps, the morning she gave me our son, Tommy."

"You loved her?"

"Very much." Another sigh for the jurors. "I still do."

"What sort of an effect did she have on you?"

Constantine cleared his throat. They'd been over this so many times the night before that he felt like he was reading lines from a script. "To be honest, I used to get so caught up in running my company, I would forget to stop and 'smell the roses,' or think about what other people might be going through. She taught me that there were more important things in life than money and running companies, like a family life, and love. She was also my moral compass."

"Tell us about that," Arnold said. "What do you mean by 'moral compass' when you're talking about your relationship with Clare?"

"Well, I wouldn't say that I was uncaring before I met her," Constantine explained. "My mother and father saw to it that I knew right from wrong, and that we should help those less fortunate than ourselves. And I used to donate quite a large sum to charitable organizations, such as the Red Cross. But I was never really involved, you know; I just wrote checks and went about my business. I'm something of an introvert by nature anyway." He looked off to the side and chuckled, as if recalling a funny memory. "But Clare would have none of it. She brought me out of my shell, both socially and as an ethical human being. I'm a better man today because of her."

Constantine stopped and reached for the box of tissues on the witness stand. He methodically removed one and wiped at the corners of his eyes. "I'm sorry. I got caught up in the moment a little bit. Please continue."

"I apologize that I have to pull up painful testimony by the prosecution witnesses," Arnold said. "But the jurors heard two witnesses describe acts of infidelity between your wife and the prosecutor's witness, Richie Bryers. How did you react when you learned about the affair?"

Constantine's face and voice hardened. "At first I didn't believe it. Then I saw the photographs and was angry."

"When were you shown the photographs?"

"They arrived anonymously in the mail a few days before Clare drowned . . . was murdered."

"Then what happened?"

"I got a telephone call threatening to send them to the media if I didn't pay two million dollars."

"Did you recognize the voice?"

"No. Just a male."

"Did you pay?"

Constantine hung his head. "No, though now I wish I had." He looked up with tears in his eyes. "You have to understand that a man with my assets is constantly threatened with lawsuits and blackmail. That's why I had someone like Fitzsimmons on my payroll."

"Did you go to the police?"

"No. There would have been an investigation, and you know how cops are; one of them would have smelled a payday and sold the story and photographs to the press."

"What did you do?"

"I told Fitzsimmons to look into it," Constantine said. "I never thought he was the one betraying me . . . him and Bryers."

"So you didn't tell Fitzsimmons to spy on your wife?"

"No. Never. I trusted her implicitly. But he knew I would do anything to protect her reputation."

"What happened after that?"

"I got another call. Fitzsimmons was there with me. I told the caller I wasn't going to pay. He said I'd regret it."

"And then?"

Constantine took a deep breath and then let it out dramatically. "Three days later, she was dead. I thought it was an accident until I got the toxicology report. Then I thought suicide. I was stunned when I learned Fitzsimmons had admitted to murdering her."

"Again, I'm sorry, but we need to get to the bottom of this for the jury," Arnold apologized. "What about Clare? She cheated on you and put you in a situation where you could be blackmailed."

Rubbing his face with his hand, Constantine made it appear that he was struggling with his answer. "I guess," he said at last, "like any husband I wasn't happy to hear that my wife was unfaithful, particularly with someone I considered a friend. But I've had some time to digest this and realize that I have to assume part of the blame as well. I was gone a lot, and when I was home I wasn't all there, if you know what I mean. Also . . ." He hesitated. "This is rather embarrassing, but also there was quite an age difference between us and I may not have been as attentive to her physical needs as she might have wanted. I guess she decided to do something about it. I just have to accept that."

"Did you ever confront her about the affair?"

Constantine shook his head. "No. I thought she'd leave me if I did. I made up my mind to be a better husband and see if we could fix this thing. I didn't realize we didn't have much time left."

"What about the testimony that you abused your wife physically and emotionally?"

"I never laid a hand on her," Constantine spat out.

"Have you considered that your wife might have been helping Bryers and Fitzsimmons with their blackmail scheme?"

Constantine shook his head violently. "No. I refuse to believe that she was capable of that sort of deceit. I gave her everything she could want."

"Unless she wanted to leave you for her lover," Arnold said. "Wasn't there a prenuptial agreement that would have prevented her from getting support if she divorced you?"

"STOP IT!" Constantine demanded, partly rising from his seat. "Infidelity, yes, she was young, I was less than she needed. But blackmail . . . NEVER!" He slumped back down in his chair, satisfied that he'd played the scene well.

Arnold held up his hands. "It's okay. I'm sorry that I had to do that, but sometimes the truth is ugly, and this jury deserves to consider all the possibilities."

All the possibilities except that I told Fitzsimmons to kill the bitch, Constantine thought. "Of course," he said, "please excuse my outburst. It's all still a little bit raw."

"We understand," Arnold replied, looking at the jury. "Let's move on and talk for a few minutes about your professional relationship with Mr. Fitzsimmons and Mr. Bryers. The jury heard that you contracted with Mr. Fitzsimmons to provide security for Well-Con Industries and for yourself personally. They also heard that he was dishonorably discharged from the Army for what were essentially war crimes—he was suspected, though never convicted, of killing innocent Iraqi citizens—"

"Yes, though I didn't know that when I hired him," Constantine interjected.

"Obviously," Arnold agreed. "And there was testimony that he was recommended to you by some unknown government official in Washington, D.C."

"To be quite honest, I don't remember who recommended him. I left security details to my assistants and they sent him to me. I was told that he was a former Special Forces soldier who'd served in Iraq. It's true I interviewed him and hired him after that; he talked a good game and seemed a stand-up guy. I have a lot of respect for our veterans. I guess I should have vetted him more carefully myself."

"You couldn't have known," Arnold said, as he walked over to the witness stand and stood looking up at his client with his hands on his hips. "And what about Richie Bryers?"

"What about him?" Constantine retorted. "He took my money and had sex with my wife. I think that pretty much defines his character."

"What about his claim that he read a page in your journal on the day Colonel Swindells was murdered by Dean Mueller that seemed to indicate you knew about an alleged black ops raid and someone named al Taizi?"

"I never wrote anything like that in my journal," Constantine replied.

"What about something called the MIRAGE files?"

"I know about Operation MIRAGE, but it has nothing to do—to my knowledge—with any black ops raid," Constantine said, shaking his head.

"We'll get into what you know about MIRAGE in a moment," Arnold said, "but what about Bryers's testimony regarding a notation that, and I quote, 'Col. S and the Russian bitch' needed to be eliminated?"

"Lies. Just like all the rest of what they said. Lies."

"And what about the alleged telephone call Bryers and Fitzsimmons testified to?"

"Never happened."

"Nothing about needing to keep Mueller quiet?"

"Nothing."

"Do you know Mr. Mueller?"

"I read about him in the newspapers after he murdered Colonel Swindells, just like everyone else. But I've never met the man, or seen him until a few days ago in court."

"What about the allegations that he was hired by Fitzsimmons to murder the colonel, presumably at your behest, to prevent Swindells from revealing the true nature of MIRAGE?"

"I think Mueller's a very disturbed young man," Constantine said. "It's a shame that someone like Fitzsimmons would use a former soldier with mental health issues for his own devious gains."

"But what could he hope to gain by the death of Colonel Swindells?" Arnold asked, perplexed.

This was the trickiest part of his testimony, but as Arnold had said, what they couldn't explain away, they'd obfuscate. "I don't really know what game Fitzsimmons was playing," Constantine said. "The man is obviously capable of anything, including murdering an innocent woman to get at me. But everyone knows that I am friends with the president, and I have to think that somehow this was an attempt to get at the administration by attacking me."

"And the blackmail attempt over your wife's affair with Mr. Bryers?"

Constantine shrugged. "I don't know. Maybe Fitzsimmons picked up on that and was working a side deal to make money with Bryers. Or maybe it was just part of a plan to bring me down, embarrass me, and at the same time discredit the president's foreign policy in Iraq and his dealing with ISIS. I just don't know. But what I do know is that the president has a lot of enemies, including this district attorney."

"Objection, Your Honor," Karp said, rising to address to the court. "Counsel is trying to elicit opinions from the defendant that are based on rank speculation. He and the defendant have done violence to the basic rules of evidence."

"Sustained," Dermondy ruled. "Be careful, Mr. Arnold, you're on thin ice. Please proceed."

Arnold nodded and continued. "The jury also heard testimony from the prosecution witnesses about a telephone call Bryers allegedly overheard between yourself and someone in the White House?"

"Never happened. At least not what he said. I talk to the president fairly often."

"You didn't call someone a bitch? Or ask who conducted a raid in Syria?"

"I don't refer to people in the White House as bitches. Nor do I get involved in foreign policy."

"Did you make a remark about this purported raid 'fucking up' MIRAGE?"

"I did not."

"Mr. Constantine, were you ever aware of some alleged conspiracy called MIRAGE between Well-Con Industries and what could best be described as criminals from Russia, Syria, and Iran?"

"Absolutely not."

"And no playing footsie with ISIS?"

Constantine rolled his eyes. "Who'd ever even dream up such a fantasy? No, there were no dealings between Well-Con and any of those people."

Arnold wandered over to the evidence table and picked up one of the exhibits. "Mr. Constantine, you said you're aware of something called MIRAGE. Can you tell us what you meant by that?"

"Yes. As you know, Well-Con Industries has operations all over the world, one of which includes oil refineries in Iraq that we operate in conjunction with Iraqi Oil. Or I should say *operated* until ISIS took over that part of the country. They murdered a number of our people and have forced others to work for them."

"And what does that have to do with MIRAGE?"

"About a year ago, I was asked to speak to the president's national security adviser, Sylvia Hamm, regarding U.S. operations against ISIS."

"And why would Ms. Hamm want to talk to you about a national security issue?"

Constantine frowned. "I have to be a little careful here, as I was asked during that initial conversation to keep the details confidential, since they involved the U.S. military. But in general it was something of a courtesy call. ISIS was selling oil on the black market to fund its operations, and the president was considering ordering air strikes against the refineries and transportation under ISIS control. Ms. Hamm was essentially informing me that some Well-Con operations would be among the targets. She called it Operation MIRAGE."

"And what was your reaction?"

Constantine laughed grimly. "Well, no businessman wants to hear that he's about to have tens of millions of dollars in equipment and product destroyed," he said, then allowed his face to grow hard. "But some of the people who worked for me were murdered by ISIS. If that's what it took to fry those bloody bastards and put an end to their reign of terror, then I was all for it."

"And what has been the result of Operation MIRAGE? At least those details you can share with us."

"Essentially, Well-Con Industries' oil refineries and transportation no longer exist in northern Iraq."

"And this damaged you financially?"

"As I said, tens of millions of dollars, as well as thousands of jobs for our Iraqi employees. We've started a fund to try to help them until we can rebuild, though we've lost touch with many of them, who are feared dead."

Arnold held up the exhibit. "I have here People's Exhibit 60, a photograph purportedly taken by your wife, Clare, using her cell phone and sent to Mr. Bryers, on the day she was murdered. As the prosecution's handwriting expert testified, it's from a page in one of your journals. But let me backtrack a moment . . . tell the jury about your journals."

Constantine nodded and turned to the jury. "I said that I had a happy childhood, and that's true. But it was also often a lonely one. My father was frequently absent, and Mom had a lot on her plate. Because we were wealthy and lived on a large estate in Mount Vernon, I didn't have a lot of playmates. But I liked to read and I guess that led to writing my journals, which I did and still do nearly every day. It was a way to pass the time. I even dreamed of being an author at one point."

"What would you journal about?"

Constantine shrugged. "Same sort of things anybody would, I guess. When I was young it could be about a new puppy or a girl I liked. Sometimes I wrote about missing my father or a vacation we took. As I got older, and into my career, I wrote about some of my business ventures as well . . . private thoughts, sort of a chronicle of my day . . . though such things might be inter-spersed with something I was doing with Clare and Tommy."

"Okay, let's talk about People's Exhibit 60 and walk through it sentence by sentence. First, what did you mean by 'MIRAGE is moving forward at last'?"

"I think it's pretty clear. The air strikes had begun."

"What about 'All the players have been replaced. Just mov-able pieces'?"

"We had a way to contact our people on the ground and, with-out being specific, warn those we trusted to leave the area. ISIS replaced them with others to keep the refineries and trucks going."

"And that's what you meant by 'the refineries are back at full capacity and deliveries are being made'?"

"Yes. ISIS had quite a black-market oil operation going."

"Do you know who they were selling to?"

Constantine shrugged. "I can guess, but I have no firsthand knowledge."

"What about 'one problem has been eliminated but another remains. She's the weak link and has to go'? Explain these statements, please."

Constantine grimaced. "This is where I have to be care-ful, as I may have been speaking out of turn regarding international affairs that are none of my business. But my understanding was that two of my competitors, one of them a woman CEO of another oil company, were opposed to the air strikes and tried to bring heat on the White House to stop them. I was asked to reach out to both of them, which I did; one agreed to the president's plan, the other—the woman—remained opposed."

"What did you mean by she has to go?"

"That I intended to speak to the owner of the company, an old friend of mine, and ask him to intercede."

"Nothing about a Russian bitch?"

Constantine smiled. "I don't know any Russian bitches."

"One last question, Mr. Constantine. What happened to the journal that page was taken from?"

"I don't know," Constantine replied. "It's gone. Because of what happened to Clare, I didn't notice it for some time, but when I went to look for it, it was missing from its place on my bookshelf. I suspect that Mr. Fitzsimmons didn't want the entire story told."

"Thank you, Mr. Constantine," Arnold said. "No further questions."

Judge Dermondy looked at his watch. "Very well. We are approaching noon, so I'm going to recess for our lunch break. We'll reconvene at one fifteen this afternoon."

Constantine looked over at Karp, expecting some anxiety since in his mind he had convincingly won the day. But Karp was smiling at him, sending a chill down his spine.

20

As Karp walked into the waiting area outside his office, his receptionist, Darla Milquetost, nodded toward the conference room. "They're all in there," she said. "I have to say that one man looks a lot like you. Are you related?"

"Thanks, Darla," Karp replied, and opened the door.

Clay Fulton stood leaning against a wall talking to Kenny Katz, Espey Jaxon, and the tall man Darla had referred to who, in actuality, was his cousin, Ivgeny Karchovski. Except for the patch over one of his eyes and scars on the side of his face he'd received as a colonel in the Russian army fighting in Afghanistan, there was a strong family resemblance. They kept the relationship on the down-low, seeing as how Karchovski was a Russian gangster in Brooklyn, though he sometimes helped Jaxon's group of antiterrorism agents. But the respect was mutual.

A woman was seated at the table reading a copy of the *New York Post* with the front page headline blaring: CONSTAN-TINE THREATENS KARP WITH LAWSUIT! Nadya Malovo looked up when Karp entered the room and smiled as she put the newspaper down. "Butch, darling, is so good to see you," she purred in heavily accented English.

"Good morning, Nadya. How was the show last night?" As always, Karp was impressed by the woman's beauty and animal magnetism. She had cat-like jade-green eyes set in an oval face. *Beautiful and deadly*, he thought. *A cold-blooded killer with the body and face of an angel. And yet on several occasions she'd shown that somewhere inside the assassin a conscience existed.*

"It was good," Malovo replied. "This Hamilton was an interesting man in American history, no? I am not so sure about the hip-hop songs, it was difficult for me to follow, or black actors playing the main characters, who were white in real life, no?"

"Actually, yes to both," Karp said. "As one of our Founding Fathers, Hamilton was a real champion of the U.S. Constitution and a strong central government. He created our financial system and, as a matter of fact, founded that newspaper you're reading."

Malovo glanced down at the *Post*. "Ah, yes, the newspaper," she said. "Apparently, you have failed to strike fear in the hearts of the opposition, and even the journalists are saying the defendant will walk away from this."

"We got them right where we want them, overconfident and careless," Karp replied. "Arrogance comes with the territory for these people. But that's where you and Espey come in, too."

"Ah, yes, did you enjoy my performance last night?"

"It was worthy of an Oscar," Karp replied as he sat down across the table from her. "Now let's spend a few minutes going over your testimony one last time."

"Anything for you, Butch."

Some forty minutes later, Karp stood up. "I think we're good," he said, then paused before adding, "You know that after your testimony, you will be taken into custody by federal authorities to be driven to Fort Dix in New Jersey, where they'll hand you over to Russian law enforcement."

"That was the arrangement, yes."

Giving her a long look, Karp asked, "Why did you agree to this? Aren't you in danger going back to Russia? The only thing you asked was to meet with Ivgeny."

The smile disappeared from Malovo's face. "Yes, I would be at risk in Russia, even though Ivgeny still has powerful friends there. But maybe I'm getting soft in my . . . middle age." She looked at Fulton. "Perhaps I have a few debts on my account to repay as best I can. And perhaps I have an issue with ISIS, the murderers of children and women, though I have done both and am haunted by it, and with governments that pretend to be moral and just but in actuality are in the control of entities that thrive on chaos, war, and suffering."

Malovo stopped talking for a moment, then looked up at Ivgeny, her former lover. "And perhaps the girl in me who has been buried for so long is tired of being hunted and longs for peace." She turned back to Karp. "You and I are through after this?"

"As long as you stay out of New York County," Karp replied.

"Oh, but I will miss Broadway," Malovo said with a laugh. "But it is a deal."

"Good. I hope never to see you again and, though I shouldn't, I wish you good luck finding that peace." Karp looked at his watch. "Time to get back to court."

A HALF HOUR later, with the jury seated, Constantine was recalled to the stand as Karp stood directly in front of him holding a manila folder. "Mr. Constantine, was it your testimony this morning that during your marriage to your wife, you were never physically violent with her?"

"That's correct. I never raised a hand to her."

"So then the testimony of Mr. Bryers and Mr. Fitzsimmons that you physically abused your wife was . . ."

"Lies. All lies."

Karp stepped forward and handed the folder to the witness. "Mr. Constantine, I'd direct your attention to the contents of this folder."

Opening the folder, Constantine's eyes widened for a moment and his face grew grim as he leafed through several photographs. He slammed the folder shut and handed it back to Karp.

Walking over to the defense table, Karp handed the folder to Arnold. "Mr. Constantine, as you saw, the folder contains several photographs as well as a copy of a text message sent from your wife's cell phone to the cell phone of Richie Bryers. Can you identify the person in the photographs—?"

Before he could answer, Arnold jumped up. "Your Honor, I object to the contents of this folder, as well as this line of questioning. May we approach the bench?"

"Please do," Dermondy replied.

With Karp present with him at the judge's dais and out of earshot of the jury, Arnold spoke in quiet angry tones. "Your Honor, we've never seen these photographs, which appear to show my client's wife with what looks to be bruising on her arms, breast, and legs. Not only do we have no idea when these photographs were taken or in what context, we also object to the relevancy of this line of questioning. Mr. Constantine is not on trial here for physically assaulting his wife, or the further implication that he was involved in her death."

"Maybe he should be," Karp said, "though Long Island is not within my jurisdiction. However, these photographs were taken by the same cell phone our expert identified in earlier testimony. They were received by the cell phone belonging to Richie Bryers. There is also a verified copy of a text message sent and received by the same telephones immediately before the photographs were sent."

"What about the objection on grounds of relevancy?" Dermondy asked Karp.

"Your Honor, the defendant has stated unequivocally that he has never physically abused his wife, and counsel has used that testimony to impeach the prosecution witnesses as liars," Karp said. "These photographs and the text go toward who is being truthful."

Dermondy nodded. "I'm going to allow it. You opened the door for this rebuttal, Mr. Arnold. Objection overruled."

With Arnold returned to his seat, Karp again handed the

folder to Constantine and asked him to identify the person in the photographs.

"It's my wife."

"Does she appear to have any discolorations on her arms, left breast, and legs that would indicate bruising?"

"Clare was a good athlete," Constantine answered weakly, "but she was always running into something or hurting herself when she was working out. We used to laugh about what a klutz she was."

"Is that a yes?" Karp asked.

Constantine's jaw tightened. "It would appear that she has bruises on her body."

"There is also a photograph attached to a text sent by your wife to Mr. Bryers, and one return text from Mr. Bryers to your wife. It shows that it was sent a few minutes before the photographs. Would you please read the text."

Constantine's eyes narrowed, but he looked down at the document. "'This is what he did to me this time. I'm so tired of him hitting me.'"

"And the response?"

"'Leave him. Marry me. If he does this again, I'm going to the police if you won't.'"

Karp retrieved the folder again. "Your Honor, I move that People's Exhibit 49 previously marked for identification be received in evidence."

"Same objection made previously," Arnold said in a perfunctory manner.

"Overruled, Mr. Arnold."

Returning to his spot in front of the witness stand, Karp asked, "So would you care to revise your earlier statement that you didn't physically abuse your wife and that Mr. Bryers and Mr. Fitzsimmons were lying about that?"

"I do not know who did that to her."

"So the text was not referring to you?"

"No. I told you I never hit my wife."

"Any idea who would?"

"I don't know. Maybe Fitzsimmons. Maybe she was also having an affair with Fitzsimmons and he was hitting her."

Karp looked at the jurors. They weren't buying it.

"So were Bryers and Fitzsimmons also lying about the telephone calls on the day Colonel Swindells was murdered?" Karp asked as he walked over to the prosecution table, where Katz handed him a document.

"Yes."

Karp held up the document. "I have here a verified copy

of your telephone records from that day, Mr. Constantine, on which two numbers, one right after the other, have been highlighted in yellow. One of them has a New York area code; the other is a Washington, D.C., area code." He handed the document to Constantine. "Do you recognize either of those numbers?"

Constantine looked at the document and shrugged. "Not offhand. I call a lot of people."

"Would it surprise you that the first number, the New York area code, is the law office of Robert LeJeune, the attorney for Dean Mueller in his murder trial?"

"I know Mr. LeJeune. I've used his law office on several occasions."

"And you happened to call him on the day Mr. Mueller was arrested for the murder of Colonel Swindells?"

"I may have."

"So Mr. Bryers could have heard you talking to him?"

"Not in the context or with the words he claims."

"He just happened to overhear you talking business with the attorney who would volunteer to represent Mr. Mueller?"

"It's possible."

"Yes, possible. But is it probable? And what about the other number, the D.C. area code. Do you recognize that number?"

Constantine looked over at his attorney and then back at Karp. "I believe that number is the home residence of the president's national security adviser, Sylvia Hamm. This was about the time I was conferring regarding Operation MIRAGE."

"So Mr. Bryers could have overheard this conversation?"

"I suppose, but once again, he's lying about what was said, or misinterpreted it."

"You didn't refer to Ms. Hamm as a bitch?"

"Of course not."

"Or wonder what agency raided the compound in Iraq and, using your words, quote, 'nearly fucked up the MIRAGE deal'?"

"No. I might have said something about MIRAGE, but not in that context."

"It is your testimony today that Mr. Fitzsimmons was lying when he said that MIRAGE had something to do with Well-Con working out a deal for black-market oil under the control of ISIS?"

"That's a lie!"

Karp walked over and leaned against the jury box rail. "Mr. Constantine, where were you in November two years ago?"

"I have no idea."

"Well, Mr. Fitzsimmons said he traveled with you to Istanbul, Tehran, and Damascus. Are you denying that?"

"It's possible. I travel a lot for business."

"At the same time this raid occurred and the MIRAGE files were seized?"

"I was unaware of any raid or files."

"Just a coincidence?"

"If I remember correctly, Mr. Fitzsimmons suggested the timing of that trip. Maybe he had an ulterior motive. He's former Special Forces, you know."

"So I've heard," Karp replied. "He's also a murderer and your right-hand man." He pushed off the railing and went to stand directly in front of the witness, where he and Constantine glared at each other over the space of a few feet. "Mr. Constantine, your testimony is that the only knowledge you have of something known as MIRAGE is that it is a military operation to attack oil-producing facilities and oil transportation under the control of the Islamic State, otherwise known as ISIS?"

"That's correct, Karp," Constantine shot back.

"It has nothing to do with your attempt to protect Well-Con facilities and equipment from an attack by the U.S. military and its allies, while selling oil on the black market to Syria, Russia, and Iran, in exchange for funding and arms for the Islamic State?"

"That's a lie, Karp, and you know it," Constantine snarled.

"This is just more of your right-wing politics trying to damage the president and anyone associated with him, including me."

"That's where you're wrong, Mr. Constantine," Karp retorted. "This is a search for the truth about who killed Colonel Michael Swindells and why." Karp turned to Dermondy. "Your Honor, may we approach the bench at sidebar on the record?"

The judge furrowed his brow but motioned to the sidebar next to his dais. "By all means, Mr. Karp."

When Arnold joined him, Karp looked up at the judge. "Your Honor, defense counsel indicated that they would be presenting only one witness, the defendant. We'd like to inquire if this is still true."

Dermondy looked at Arnold, who seemed shaken but nodded. "That's, uh . . . all we're prepared for."

Karp nodded. "In that case, the People would like to suspend the cross-examination of the defendant to present several rebuttal witnesses, and ask that the defendant step down subject to recall."

"This is rather unusual, Mr. Karp," Dermondy said.

"We believe that it's a matter of grave national security, and goes to the very heart of this case. In fact, I will be making an application to treat this person as a hostile witness with interests contrary to the People's case, which will become apparent very quickly when I begin my examination. Therefore, my questions may be more leading than is usually allowed."

"Very well, Mr. Karp, but we'll be watching, and if deemed inappropriate, the questions and responses will be stricken from the record," Dermondy responded.

"I understand, Your Honor."

"Very well, return to your places, gentlemen." Dermondy looked at Constantine and announced, "You may step down, but you are still under oath and are subject to recall."

The judge turned to the jurors. "Ladies and gentlemen of the jury, the defense has indicated that the defendant, Mr. Constantine, will be their only witness, which concludes their case. At this time, the People are allowed to call rebuttal witnesses to refute evidence or testimony presented by the defense. Mr. Karp, you may call your first witness."

"The People call Sylvia Hamm."

21

A MOMENT OF SHOCKED SILENCE ENVELOPED THE COURT-
room. Members of the media looked at one another and
mouthed the words, "Sylvia Hamm? The president's national
security adviser? Holy . . . !"

As the room began to buzz like a beehive that had just been
kicked, several members of the press stood and tried to push
their way between the pews as they rushed for the exit. The appearance of one of the most influential people in the country
was a shocking turn of events, and their bosses were going to
want to know.

With the spectator section beginning to devolve into bedlam,
Judge Dermondy banged his gavel. "Order in the court. If you

can't control yourselves, you'll be removed," he threatened, which had the desired effect of silencing the spectators in the gallery.

All eyes turned to the side door leading from the witness waiting room. It opened to reveal the short, blockish national security adviser, Sylvia "Sukie" Hamm. She looked like an angry badger in a purple pantsuit.

"Madam, would you please step forward to be sworn in," Dermondy said.

Hamm stalked into the courtroom and toward the witness stand, glowering at Karp as she advanced. She continued to stare him down as she was sworn in and took a seat.

"Good morning, Ms. Hamm," Karp said as he walked out into the well of the court.

She didn't reply, but he'd expected the chilly reception. Jaxon told him that three days earlier, when federal marshals served her with the subpoena to appear, she'd laughed it off. But her federal lawyers were unable to quash the subpoena, and now she feared that the "chickens may have come home to roost." In any event, Karp had an ace up his sleeve to get her to New York City that had worked like a charm, though Hamm didn't yet realize she'd fallen into a trap.

"Ms. Hamm, would you please tell the jury what you do for a living?" Karp asked.

Hamm rolled her eyes. "Really, Mr. Karp? Is this charade necessary?"

Annoyed with her arrogance, Judge Dermondy admonished the witness's hubris. "While you're in this courtroom, you'll answer the questions posed by the prosecution, unless I rule otherwise. Is that clear, Ms. Hamm?" Hamm stared at Dermondy, but then nodded. The judge told Karp to proceed.

Hamm answered, "I'm currently the assistant to the president for national security affairs, sometimes referred to as the national security adviser."

"And who do you work for?"

"I serve at the pleasure of the president of the United States."

"You work for the president."

"Yes, that's what I said."

"And what does that job entail?"

"I'm the chief in-house adviser to the president on national security issues. I also participate in meetings of the National Security Council, as well as committee meetings with the secretary of state and the secretary of defense."

"And how often do you meet with the president?"

"At least once a day—almost every morning to brief him on national security issues and offer my advice. However, it may be more often; for instance, during times of crisis, I keep him updated on important developments as they occur."

"You mentioned that you attend meetings with the secretaries of state and defense," Karp said. "Do you also confer regularly with U.S. intelligence agencies, such as the CIA and Federal Bureau of Investigation?"

"Yes, those and others. It's part of my job to assimilate the information these various groups provide, put it together as an overview, and present it to the president."

"So it's fair to say you have your finger on the pulse of those issues that affect the security of the United States and its citizens?"

"That's one way to put it."

Karp strolled over toward the defense table, where Constantine looked bored while his attorney jotted down notes on a legal pad. Looking down at the accused billionaire, Karp asked, "Do you know the defendant, Wellington Constantine?"

Hamm looked up at the ceiling as if she couldn't believe she had to endure such vapid questions. "Of course I know Mr. Constantine," she said, "and consider him a friend, as does the president, I might add."

"And how do you know the defendant?"

"Oh, come on, Karp," Hamm said tersely.

Karp looked at Dermondy. "Your Honor, would you direct the witness to just answer my questions, please."

The judge looked at Hamm and raised an eyebrow. She sighed.

"I believe I met Mr. Constantine during the president's first presidential campaign."

"In fact, he's been a major contributor to both of the president's campaigns, isn't that true?"

"Objection," Arnold said, rising to his feet. "Your Honor, what is the relevance of this line of questioning? Mr. Constantine's relationship to Ms. Hamm and the president isn't on trial here."

"Mr. Karp?" Dermondy asked.

Karp crossed his arms and walked back over to the jury box, where he leaned against the rail. "Subject to connection, Your Honor. The rebuttal case will reflect the linkage among what I'm asking Ms. Hamm, the testimony of Mr. Jaxon, and the defendant's substantial financial influence at the highest echelons of the executive branch of the U.S. government. And the chain reaction that influence has on the sale of black-market oil, collusion with rogue governments, the arming of terrorists, subterfuge meant to dupe the American public, and the murder of the victim in this case, Colonel Michael Swindells."

As he spoke, Karp glanced at Hamm and saw her face tighten. *Surprised her with what we know*, he thought. *That's what arrogance will do for you.*

Dermondy nodded. "I'll overrule the objection, subject to connection. The witness will answer the question."

Hamm shot the judge a hard look. She shook her head but answered. "Yes, he, like many other people and organizations in this great country, believed in the president and contributed to his first and second election campaigns."

"And, in fact," Karp pointed out, "contributed the maximum amount allowed by individuals, is that true?"

"I believe that's true . . . as did many other people," Hamm said. "He's a wealthy man, and I believe he supports many candidates who share his views."

"The maximum personal contribution is twenty-five hundred dollars, barely a drop in the bucket for a man whose net worth according to *Wealth* magazine makes him one of the richest men in the world."

"I wouldn't know Mr. Constantine's net worth. But his contribution was what the law allowed."

"But that's just the personal contribution," Karp said. "There are other ways to contribute to political campaigns and causes, aren't there? Such as the so-called Super PACs that allow well-heeled special-interest groups, corporations, and unions to contribute millions of dollars to candidates and causes, correct?"

"It is all within the law, Mr. Karp."

"It is," Karp agreed. "But nevertheless, it allows an individual, such as the defendant, to contribute millions of dollars through these political action committees."

"It allows people associated with these committees to support candidates and causes they believe in. Campaigns are expensive these days."

"Indeed they are," Karp replied. "I believe the current president's last campaign spent more than seven hundred million dollars."

"I wouldn't know."

"No?" Karp responded rhetorically. "And these millions of dollars that go into campaigns are intended to buy influence, are they not?"

"Your term 'buy influence' has a negative connotation that I suggest resides more in your mind than in reality. As I said, these committees use the money to support candidates and causes they agree with, and it's not illegal."

"No, but would you agree that attempting to buy or sell political influence is immoral?"

"OBJECTION!" Arnold shouted. "The prosecutor is making political speeches."

"I'll withdraw the question," Karp responded. "Would it surprise you to know that the defendant is nearly the sole source of money for the Super PAC known as Americans for Change and Progress, which contributed nearly eighty-five million dollars to your employer's last campaign?"

"I know AFCP contributed to the campaign, as well as to other campaigns and causes. I don't know the amount. I have no idea what Mr. Constantine does with his money," Hamm replied. "I know that he is a big contributor to the president's party, as well as many candidates, and that AFCP is a well-funded Super PAC. But I'm a foreign policy wonk, Mr. Karp; I don't get involved in politics and wasn't expecting to debate campaign finance reform today."

"A foreign policy wonk," Karp repeated. "Still, you're aware that the defendant is, as you said, a big contributor. Would you say he spends millions of dollars to buy influence with the president?"

"OBJECTION!" Arnold shouted.

"Sustained," Dermondy said. "You've made your point. Move on, please."

Karp nodded. "Ms. Hamm, are you aware of whether the defendant attends White House social functions, such as state dinners?"

"Yes. I have seen him at such events on occasion. It's not unusual for business leaders, as well as politicians, and even entertainers, to attend these functions."

"And are you aware if the defendant ever meets privately with the president?"

"Again, as I pointed out before, the president considers Mr. Constantine a personal friend. He also welcomes his advice on the economy as an astute and successful businessman."

"Would this include foreign business ventures?"

"Quite possibly. Mr. Constantine's company, Well-Con Industries, has interests and facilities all over the world."

"Including oil refineries in the Middle East?"

"I believe that's true."

"Including Iraq."

Hamm frowned. "If I remember correctly, his assets in Iraq are in the hands of the terrorist organization Islamic State of Iraq and Syria, or ISIS. Some of those facilities are now destroyed to prevent ISIS from refining or transporting oil due to coordinated U.S., Syrian, and Russian air strikes, which are a testament to the president's persuasive diplomacy."

"And how do we know these facilities have been destroyed?" Karp asked.

"We have satellite and military surveillance imagery, as well as assets on the ground who report on the damage."

"And some of these strikes have been directed at Well-Con assets?"

"Yes, unfortunately for Mr. Constantine."

"Was he told of these impending strikes?"

"As a courtesy, yes."

"And he approved?"

Hamm smiled over at Constantine, who smiled back. "I don't know if he approved, but he certainly understood the necessity and, I must say, has been asked to accept an enormous financial blow on behalf of national security."

"Does the defendant regularly discuss national security issues with you or the president?"

"Of course not," Hamm scoffed. "We may ask him a question about the political or business situation in a part of the world where he has assets, including people on the ground. But he is not privy to discussions and decisions regarding national security issues."

Karp walked over to the evidence table and picked up a sheet of paper in a plastic sleeve. "Ms. Hamm, I am handing you People's Exhibit 38, a single page from a journal kept by the defendant."

Hamm accepted the exhibit and studied it. She shot the defendant a look, then turned to Karp. "I've read it."

"What do you believe the defendant meant by the statement 'MIRAGE is moving forward at last'?"

"I believe he's referring to the air strikes on his facilities. The program is called Operation MIRAGE."

"Why is it called MIRAGE?"

"Because it's in the desert, Mr. Karp, and seemed to fit."

"What about the statement 'All the players have been replaced. Just movable pieces'?"

"I have no idea what he meant by that. An editorial comment, perhaps?"

"And the statement 'The refineries are back at full capacity and deliveries are being made'?"

"Mr. Constantine had been informed that ISIS, either through forced participation or their own experts, were running his refineries at full capacity until destroyed by the air strikes."

"He doesn't say anything about the facilities being destroyed. Just that MIRAGE is moving forward at last. Wouldn't he have noted that?"

"I don't know the date of that journal entry," Hamm said. "Perhaps he had not yet been informed about the destruction caused by the air strikes. But really, Mr. Karp, I have no idea what Mr. Constantine chose to include in his journal."

"The air strikes that were confirmed by satellite and military surveillance imagery?"

"Yes, that's right. As well as people on the ground reporting in."

"Do you know who ISIS was selling this black-market oil to?"

"We have reason to believe they were selling the oil to Iran and North Korea."

"Which U.S. oil companies are not allowed to do business with because of economic sanctions, correct?"

"That's correct, which is why they'd been happy to deal with ISIS."

"Ms. Hamm, in the defendant's journal, he also wrote, 'One problem has been eliminated but another remains. She's the weak link and has to go.' Any idea what he meant by that?"

Hamm frowned and shook her head. "I'm not sure. I know there were some high-level meetings with executives from other oil companies that stood to lose their Iraqi assets during Operation MIRAGE. They weren't happy about it, and the president asked Mr. Constantine to attempt to persuade them of the national interest in this matter. I think these meetings were sometimes rancorous."

"Can you provide us with the names of these other oil company executives, so that we can interview them and possibly bring them to court to testify about these matters?"

Hamm's face went blank. "Not offhand. I wasn't present at that particular discussion. I believe it was between the president and Mr. Constantine."

"And so you, the national security adviser, weren't privy to the details."

"Only that it existed as an issue. I have a lot on my plate as the NSA, and the president is quite capable of handling his own business."

Karp walked over in front of the witness stand and looked directly at Hamm. "Is it your testimony today that Operation MIRAGE was the name given to U.S., Russian, and Syrian air strikes against oil refineries and other affiliated assets controlled by ISIS?"

"Yes."

"You're saying that it's not a conspiracy among the defendant, the administration, and the representatives of foreign governments to protect his oil assets in Iraq, as well as sell oil on the black market, while in fact supporting ISIS?"

Hamm's face scrunched into a sneer. "Absolutely not, Mr. Karp! What piece of fiction have you been reading in your little right-wing rags?"

Karp didn't respond except to change the direction of his questions. "Do you know a woman named Ajmaani?"

A small twitch registered on Hamm's face, but she shook her head. "I don't know anyone by that name."

"How about Nadya Malovo?"

"No. Should I?"

Karp nodded to Fulton, who was seated at the prosecution table. The big detective got up and walked over to the door leading from the witness rooms. He opened the door and said something to someone on the other side. He then stepped back as Nadya Malovo entered the courtroom and stopped.

"Do you recognize this woman?"

Hamm glanced at Malovo and shook her head. "I don't believe . . . no, I've never seen her before that I can recall. I do meet a lot of people."

"A little over a year ago, did you have occasion to be in Istanbul, Turkey?"

Acting as though she had to think about it, Hamm hesitated. Then she nodded. "Yes, I believe I was there attending a NATO meeting."

"Did you also meet with the representative of a man named Ivan Nikitin?"

"I'm not familiar with that name."

"He is, or was, a general in the Russian army and a gangster with ties to the Kremlin."

Hamm looked bemused. "I'd have no reason to meet with someone representing such a person."

Karp walked over to the prosecution table, where Katz handed him a photograph. He returned to the witness stand and handed it to Hamm. She looked down and was visibly shaken.

"I've handed you People's Exhibit 75 marked for identification. Do you recognize the two women in the photograph?" Karp asked.

With her hands shaking, Hamm didn't answer. "Do you recognize the two women in the photograph?" he asked again.

"This is an outrage," Hamm hissed. "A setup."

"Whatever you want to call it," Karp said, "would you please tell the jury if you recognize anyone in this photograph?"

"I was sitting at a sidewalk café in Istanbul when a woman I didn't know came up and sat down at my table . . ." Hamm tried.

"Would you just answer the question," Karp said.

"I'm trying to explain how this happ—"

"Your Honor," Karp said, looking at Dermondy.

The judge leaned across his dais. "Ms. Hamm, I direct you to answer the district attorney's questions directly, as I previously admonished you."

"Yes, Your Honor," Hamm answered meekly. "I'm in the photograph. I don't know the other woman."

"You don't know the identity of the woman?" Karp said. He pointed at Malovo. "Does that woman refresh your recollection?"

Arnold shot to his feet. "Objection, Your Honor! This is improper examination!"

Karp held out his hands. "Your Honor, any first-year law student knows that you can use a shoe to refresh someone's recollection. I can assure you, this woman's presence is much more meaningful than a shoe."

"Overruled. Ms. Hamm, answer the question."

Hamm looked again at Malovo. "I suppose it could be her."

Karp's eyes narrowed. "We're not in some back room at the White House; it's just you and me, the judge, and the jury now, and you're under oath," he said, allowing his voice to rise. "Tell us about your meeting with a woman you know as Ajmaani, also known as Nadya Malovo. That woman," he said, pointing again, "standing right there!"

"I don't know this woman," Hamm protested. "She could be the woman in the photograph, but like I said, she came over and sat down, then left."

"And this same woman just happens to be standing in this courtroom?"

"It's obviously a setup, Karp! A cheap setup by you and your cronies to attack me and this administration, as well as an innocent businessman, Mr. Constantine, because he supports the president. Well, you won't win this one, Karp!"

Karp listened to her tirade with his arms folded over his chest. When she finished, he shook his head. "The sad thing is, no one will win this one, particularly the American people."

He looked at the jury as he asked his next question. "Ms. Hamm, did you attend the theater production of *Hamilton* last night on Broadway?"

"It was in all the newspapers, Karp," she replied.

"And did you have the opportunity at the end of the play to go backstage?"

Hamm frowned. "I was invited by the director to meet the cast."

"The cast?" Karp replied, raising an eyebrow. "Who else did you meet other than the cast?"

Hamm's eyes shot to Malovo. *She's counting on the little deal they made last night*, Karp thought.

"I met a lot of people," Hamm replied. "There were a lot of people backstage."

"Did you meet with Ajmaani, aka Nadya Malovo?"

"Not that I recall."

"You don't recall meeting with her and instructing her not to cooperate as a witness for the People?"

"I certainly did nothing of the kind," Hamm scoffed. "You ought to write thrillers, Karp. You have quite the imagination."

"You didn't discuss the MIRAGE files?"

"More fiction."

"Or the complicity of your office and the administration in protecting the oil interests of the defendant, as well as the sale of black-market oil produced and controlled by ISIS?"

Hamm rolled her eyes and looked at the judge. "Your Honor, do I have to endure this nonsense?"

"Try your best," Dermondy said.

"You're making it all up, Karp," Hamm shot back. "You don't have anything to back up these wild fabrications."

"No?" Karp smiled and walked over to the prosecution table and picked up two photographs, one of which he handed to Hamm.

"Do you recognize this man?"

Hamm looked at the photograph and shrugged. "It looks like one of the actors from the show last night. It was an all-black cast and they were dressed up in eighteenth-century costumes."

"Well, look around the courtroom and see if you can spot the man in the photograph," Karp said.

Confused, Hamm did as told until her eyes came to rest on Detective Fulton. Her jaw dropped.

"You seem to be looking at Detective Clay Fulton. Is he the man in the photograph?"

Hamm nodded dumbly. "Yes."

"You'll notice that he's carrying an eighteenth-century-style walking stick. But this stick has a directional microphone."

"So what?" Hamm said.

Karp handed her the second photograph. "This is the same photograph only not cropped so tightly. It now includes two women who appear to be speaking to each other. Do you recognize them?"

"Is this how you do it, Karp?" Hamm said angrily. "You set people up and frame them? Obviously one of the women is me, and the other is that woman." She pointed at Malovo. "But I didn't recognize her from Istanbul when she came up to me backstage. She was just one of many people I met."

Nodding to Malovo, who stepped back out of the courtroom while Fulton closed the door behind her, Karp then turned to Dermondy. "Your Honor, the People would now like to play an audiotape recorded last night backstage at the Richard Rodgers Theatre."

"Go ahead."

Karp gave a signal to Katz, who had taken up a position near a tape machine. The assistant district attorney pressed a button, and immediately a heavily accented Russian female's voice filled the courtroom.

"You have not changed since Istanbul," said the first voice.

"I'm not here to talk about Istanbul," said the second.

Karp nodded to Katz to stop the tape. "Do you recognize that second voice?" he asked Hamm.

When Hamm didn't reply, Karp shrugged and nodded to Katz, who again pressed the button.

"No, you are here about the MIRAGE files and how you were willing to go along with the murder of the colonel to prevent knowledge of your little deal with Well-Con from getting out. The black-market oil. The deal with the Russians, the Syrians, the Iranians, and ISIS."

"What do you want, Ajmaani?"

"As I told you on the telephone, I want ten million dollars in a Swiss bank account for which I can provide a number. You will also get me out of custody in New York and transport me to the place of my choosing. And just so I don't have an 'accident,' I have an accomplice, a Brooklyn gangster named Ivgeny Karchovski—look him up—who will release the deciphered MIRAGE files to the press and FBI if something happens to me."

"That's a lot of money."

"It's worth it, no?"

"We'll want you to testify that Karp put you up to all of this. And that Mueller and Fitzsimmons were part of the conspiracy when your efforts to blackmail Mr. Constantine fell through."

"Whatever you want. But I will need a telephone call from Mr. Karchovski telling me that the money is in the account number on this card, or I will tell the truth about MIRAGE. Do we have a deal?"

"You do what I said, and you'll get your money and we'll get you out of the country. But fuck with me, and we'll feed you to the pigs on a little farm the Agency has in New Jersey."

Karp turned to Hamm, whose face was the color of a tomato. "Do you recognize your voice there, Ms. Hamm? Were you attempting to obstruct justice? Threatening murder? Possibly treason? You've certainly lied under oath."

Slowly, Hamm's lips drew back from her teeth and her eyes stared daggers at Karp. "I'm not answering any more of your questions, you bastard," she snarled. "Executive privilege!"

"Your Honor?" Karp asked, looking at Dermondy.

The judge leaned forward and pointed his finger at Hamm. "While you're in my courtroom, you are ordered to answer relevant questions or be held in contempt."

"I work for the president," Hamm replied, "and answer to no one but him."

"Then I will direct the prosecution to proceed with a grand jury indictment against you for perjury and contempt," Dermondy said, his voice icy. "Mr. McIntyre, I'm directing you as the court clerk to place Ms. Hamm in custody."

As the gallery gasped collectively and Hamm was led from the courtroom, Dermondy turned to Karp. "I'm almost afraid to ask, but call your next witness."

Karp smiled. "With pleasure, Your Honor. The People call Nadya Malovo."

22

ONE LAST TIME, FULTON OPENED THE SIDE DOOR, AND Nadya Malovo sauntered through. Dressed in a gray federal prisoner jumpsuit that failed to hide her lithe, curvaceous body, she still walked like she was the one in control of the situation. Even Court Clerk Duffy McIntyre, who thought he'd seen almost everything in his long service to the court, turned beet red as she approached to be sworn in, and then stumbled over his words as she transfixed him with her eyes.

Malovo gave McIntyre a smile, then stepped onto the stand and took her seat like an Oscar-winning actress aware that all eyes were upon her. She gazed at Karp, who had positioned himself in front of the witness.

"Good afternoon," Karp said. "Please state your full name and spell your last name."

"Good afternoon. I am Nadya Malovo," she purred, "M-A-L-O-V-O."

"Do you also sometimes go by the name Ajmaani?"

"I am known in some parts of the world as Ajmaani, yes."

"And why the alias?"

"I guess you could call it my nom de guerre," Malovo replied with a shrug. "I sometimes find it necessary to pass myself off as a Chechen jihadi."

"An Islamic terrorist?"

"That's accurate."

"Ms. Malovo, let me back up a bit and have you give the jurors a little history about yourself."

Malovo laughed. "A little history," she said with a smile at the jurors. "I have a long and varied history, but I will try to keep this short. I was born in Moscow and raised in an orphanage. I'll skip the horrors of that place and how I was able to escape and rise above it, but eventually I was trained by what was then known as the KGB, the Soviet intelligence agency," she said. "As a KGB agent, I traveled to many places in the world on the orders of my superiors, who in turn reported to whoever was in power in the Kremlin. With the fall of the Soviet Union in 1991, I decided to follow my comrades in the brave new world of capitalism and resigned from the intelligence service and began freelancing for whoever paid for my services, which sometimes included the Russian government, or those who collaborate with the regime."

"You worked for the KGB, but you were not just a spy, were you?" Karp asked.

Malovo shook her head. "Actually, I was trained to be an assassin."

"An assassin. As such, have you killed people?"

"Many."

"Sometimes because you were ordered to by your government, and after that for money?"

"Both. Yes. And sometimes just to survive."

Karp held up a folder, which he handed to her. "Ms. Malovo, I'm handing you legal documents marked for identification as People's Exhibits 54 to 58. Would you please look these over and describe them to the jury?"

Malovo leafed through the papers. She then nodded and closed the folder, handing it back to Karp. "These are indictment papers charging me with six counts of murder in the County of New York."

"You've been charged by my office, is that correct?"

"Yes."

"Have you been offered any deal by my office in regard to those charges in exchange for your truthful testimony today?"

"No."

"Are you aware of what will occur after you testify here today?"

"Yes. I will be handed over to U.S. law enforcement, who also have indicted me for I believe a dozen murders."

"Will you be tried in federal court and then returned to New York to stand trial for murder here?"

"Perhaps someday," Malovo said, "but first I am to be handed over to Russian authorities at Fort Dix in New Jersey. I will then be transported back to Russia, where I am accused of murder and treason. I am so popular, I doubt I will be able to return to New York anytime soon, if ever."

"And yet your testimony today is voluntary?"

"Indeed, my testimony here today would not have happened if I had not arranged for it to happen."

"Why did you agree to testify today without a deal, such as a lesser charge, from my office, perhaps, or the federal government, or the Russian government?"

Malovo looked over at the jurors and studied their faces for a moment before she smiled sadly. "I've asked myself that, too, for some time now, and I don't have a complete answer. But the closest I can come is that I am testifying today to take a little bit off the mountain of debt I owe for the life I've led and the things I've done."

"Are you saying you have a guilty conscience?"

"That's part of it," she replied. "But I am also trying to learn to forgive myself. I take full responsibility for who I am, but I was also shaped by others. I didn't grow up wanting to kill other human beings to make a living. When I was a child, I just wanted a family. And when I was a young woman, even after my training with the KGB, I still dreamed of falling in love and having a home of my own, a safe warm place where my man would be waiting at the end of a day. I confess I never wanted to bring children into a world such as this, but I wanted all the rest."

"Do you still want that?"

The question seemed to catch Malovo by surprise. She was quiet for a moment as she looked out into space at nothing in particular. "I suppose deep inside of me that young woman, who dreams of the soldier she once loved, still exists. But the debt weighs on me, and too many people want me to account for it, for me to ever find that kind of peace. We shall see."

"Are you in danger by testifying today?"

"Extreme danger," Malovo said. "I am making accusations against powerful people both here and in Russia, not to overlook that ISIS will not be happy with Ajmaani's role in wrecking the MIRAGE conspiracy."

"You mentioned that in a sense you 'arranged' to testify today. Can you explain what you meant by that?" Karp asked.

As he spoke, Karp stood firm against the jury rail. The jurors were about to hear a fascinating tale straight out of a Bogart mystery movie, and he recalled how he'd first heard it that day after Jaxon and Fulton got her out of federal custody and transferred to his. She got her meeting alone with Ivgeny, which neither had ever explained to him and he didn't want to know, and then she'd told him the whole story.

"Some eighteen months ago I returned to Moscow from a mission in which I'd nearly lost my life," Malovo began. "It certainly wasn't the first time, nor was it the first time I'd had thoughts that it was time to get out of the business. I was tired of the danger, and the killing, but I was also tired of being a pawn of governments and powerful men who pretend to work for peace and prosperity yet all the while they thrive on chaos, poverty, and death. But in reality they are guilty of worse than anything I've ever done, and on a far greater scale, sometimes even duplicitously claiming it's for 'the greater good' when really it's only about power and wealth."

"How did your . . . I guess we could call it your crisis of conscience eventually lead you to the witness chair in a New York County Supreme Court?"

"I have many enemies in Russia, but I also have very powerful friends," Malovo said. "Some of them are involved in the acquisition and sale of black-market oil. The Russian economy relies on cheap oil. I believe it was your Senator John McCain who said that Russia is a 'gas station masquerading as a country,' and that is not far from the truth. Through them I learned of a complicated plan in which they, and their friends in the Kremlin, would have access to cheap refined oil that would not be otherwise available to them. I knew that the plan would benefit Russian, Syrian, and Iranian interests, as well as those of a well-connected, wealthy American, though I did not have details of the plan or names, except one. I learned that a former Red Army general and organized crime figure, Ivan Nikitin, was involved. We went way back—to the time of the Russian incursion into Afghanistan—and I knew he was enamored of me. I met with him and talked him into a job as his bodyguard and go-between."

"Did this plan also involve the terrorist group known as ISIS?" Karp asked.

"Yes. You could say it was the—what is the American expression?—straw that breaks the camel's back? But when I learned that the plan also involved those murderous monsters of ISIS, I knew I would attempt to stop it."

"Why?"

"Again, there was something that rankled me about these countries and businessmen who publicly rattle their sabers and complain about the horrific abuses committed by ISIS and yet were ready to deal with the devil for money and power."

"Yet you just admitted to these jurors that you kill people following orders and for money?"

Malovo nodded. "Yes, I know . . . What is the other expression, 'Pot calls the kettle black'? I understand my own duplicity. But it is governments and people like these who create monsters like me and ISIS. You can kill me and bomb Islamic fanatics into oblivion. But we will be replaced until you stop the people at the top whose only desire is for power and money."

"So how did you plan to stop this conspiracy?"

"I knew that I was being hunted by a U.S. counterterrorism agency headed by an agent named S. P. Jaxon," Malovo said. "I knew he was a good man, incorruptible, and that if I could get him the information, he would know what to do with it. So I left a trail, so to speak, for him and his operatives to follow. I made my association with Nikitin known and appeared with him in public. And I made sure we were seen in various locales, such as Tehran, Damascus, and Istanbul, and that word got out we would be meeting with the ISIS leader Ghareeb al Taizi. I knew Jaxon would not be able to resist trying to capture me, Nikitin, and al Taizi, so I made it easy to find us."

"You said one of these locales was Istanbul, Turkey," Karp said, as he walked over to the prosecution table, where Katz handed him two manila folders. "What was the purpose of that meeting?"

"One of the main points of the plan was to ensure that U.S., Syrian, and Russian air strikes did not destroy oil facilities that ISIS was operating," Malovo said. "Nikitin had already worked the Russian side with his friends in the Kremlin, as well as Damascus. However, the main player in the conspiracy, in fact the person who came up with the concept and the name, was an American. I did not know his name, only that he was extremely wealthy and had powerful connections in the U.S. government, particularly the administration. We went to Istanbul to work out some of the details with this man's representative."

Walking over to the witness stand, Karp asked, "At one point were you asked by me to view a lineup and identify, if you could, this representative you met in Istanbul?"

"Yes, I picked him out."

Karp handed a folder to her. "Is this a photograph of the man as he appeared that day in the lineup?"

"Yes, that's him, holding the number 6 against his chest," Malovo said, handing the photo and folder back.

"Your Honor, for the record, the witness has identified Shaun Fitzsimmons as the man she met in Istanbul."

"Same objection. All of this is improper," Arnold said.

"Overruled. The exhibit is accepted."

Karp handed the second folder to Malovo. "Did you meet with someone else in Istanbul?"

"Yes. I met personally with the national security adviser, Sylvia Hamm."

"Do you recognize the two women in the photograph you're holding?"

Malovo nodded. "Yes. That's me and Hamm. I had an accomplice take the photograph from the other side of the street."

"Why did you do that?"

"As part of my plan to expose this conspiracy."

"Where was Nikitin during this?"

"In the hotel. He and Hamm did not want to be seen together."

"Why did you need to meet with Hamm?"

"To give her the locations and coordinates of the 'protected' facilities, as well as the transportation routes that would be off-limits to air strikes."

"Did this plan have a name?"

"Yes. MIRAGE, because it is illusory—not just because of the false oil facilities but also the chimera of a united front against ISIS and terrorism, when in fact they were supporting both."

"Were the details of this plan written down and saved to a data storage device?"

"Yes. It was on a flash drive that al Taizi had created. He didn't trust any of the others and created it as a way to blackmail them if they went back on their word. But I'd been introduced to him as Ajmaani, the Chechen jihadi, so he told me about it."

"Why did he tell you?"

Malovo smiled. "I have certain charms that men like him find hard to resist."

"If I understood your testimony, your plan was to lead Jaxon and his counterterrorism team to this meeting in Syria. Did something go wrong with your plan?"

"Yes. Someone tipped off the American, and he'd didn't show."

"What happened to those who did?"

"I killed them all, including Nikitin," Malovo said as nonchalantly as if she was discussing taking out the trash.

"Why?"

"Well, part of it was I had developed a certain . . . affection . . . for Jaxon and his team, and I did not want to see them hurt or killed," Malovo said. "But more important, if the others had been captured, they might have talked, but the identity of the American might have been swept under the rug, and the MIRAGE files would disappear. I had to know who created MIRAGE, and I thought the only way to do that would be to get Jaxon involved."

"Did that plan change at all?" Karp asked.

"Yes," Malovo said. "Jaxon's team was intercepted in Saudi

Arabia and the MIRAGE file was seized, along with many other documents and computer drives. I thought my plan had failed until I was interrogated by Colonel Swindells, who asked me about MIRAGE. Call it female intuition, but I hoped that if I put Jaxon in touch with him, together they would expose the conspiracy, including discovering the identity of the American."

As she said this, Malovo looked pointedly at Constantine. "I regret that Colonel Swindells lost his life as a result."

"Ms. Malovo, did you attend the performance of *Hamilton* at the Richard Rodgers Theatre last night?"

"Yes. It was quite interesting."

"Could you explain to the jury how that happened and why?"

"It was a plan to get Hamm to reveal that she knew about MIRAGE and its connection to Mr. Constantine. I pretended that I was calling from an apartment where I was being held for safekeeping for this trial. I told her that I wanted to discuss my testimony about MIRAGE and that I wanted money and my freedom."

"Did you arrange a meeting?"

"Yes. I told her that I was going to be allowed to attend the performance," Malovo said, "as a way to relax before my testimony today. I also said that following the performance I would get away from my escorts and meet her backstage to tell her my demands and give her a Swiss bank account for depositing funds."

"Did this telephone conversation actually take place in my office?" Karp asked. "And was it recorded?"

"Yes."

"Who was present in my office when this was recorded?"

"You, me, Detective Fulton, and S. P. Jaxon."

"Your Honor," Karp said, again pointing to where Katz stood at the audio machine, "I'd like to play People's Exhibit 71, which is the exact record of the conversation between the witness and Ms. Hamm the witness just testified to. Also, Your Honor, I offer in evidence a court-certified transcript of the conversation, People's Exhibit 72, which I ask to be distributed to the jurors to enable them to follow the taped conversation with greater ease and understanding."

"Same objection," Arnold said impassively.

"Overruled. Go ahead, Mr. Karp."

After the tape was played, Karp turned to Malovo. "Was that a fair and accurate recording of the conversation you had with Ms. Hamm?"

"Yes, every word."

"I'm going to play a recording of a conversation backstage at the Richard Rodgers Theatre last night. Tell me if you can identify these two voices." He nodded at Katz one last time.

"You have not changed since Istanbul."

"I'm not here to talk about Istanbul. . . ."

23

"I THINK THIS CALLS FOR A COUPLE OF FINGERS OF Scotch," Espey Jaxon said that afternoon in Karp's inner office as he pulled a bottle of Macallan out of his briefcase. He looked around at the others in the room: Karp, Katz, Fulton, Marlene Ciampi, and Ariadne Stupenagel.

Court had recessed following the vigorous but futile cross-examination of Nadya Malovo, who'd then been handed over to federal agents waiting to escort her to Fort Dix. They'd all gathered to discuss the case so far and go over Jaxon's testimony the next day. Marlene and Ariadne, who'd been attending every day of the trial, had begged to join them, and Karp had relented.

"I'm not so sure," Karp said with a grin while pointing to the bookshelf across from the desk where a set of tumblers waited. "You have to testify and I have to ask questions without slurring my words."

"Just one won't hurt, boss," Fulton said, eyeing the bottle. "We worked hard for this one, and that was quite an ending!"

"Ha," Katz chortled as he handed out glasses. "I loved it when Arnold kept pounding away at what an evil monster she was—a paid assassin, a terrorist—and she finally had enough and told him that he'd be next if he didn't back off."

Jaxon, who was following him to pour the booze, laughed. "I saw her say something to you, Clay, when those goons were taking her away today. Care to share?"

Fulton frowned. "Yeah, she said, 'I hope this wipes the slate clean with you.' She was talking about when she shot me that time after she and her killers murdered those children and cops."

"What did you tell her?" Stupenagel asked.

"I said I could never forgive her for those kids and cops, and she said a funny thing, she said, 'That's fair. I'll never forgive myself. But I can only pay one sin back at a time. I'm talking about you and me.'" He cocked his head. "I said we're even."

"I suppose we've seen the last of her," Marlene said. "I don't imagine the Russians are going to go easy on her for this."

"I don't know," Karp said, "she's a survivor."

"Well, whatever else she was, she certainly made for a good story," Stupenagel said as she raised her glass. "I hope it's not too politically incorrect to toast a murderous Russian femme fatale, but here's to Nadya Malovo, aka Ajmaani!"

Just then the intercom on Karp's desk buzzed and was followed by the irritated voice of Mrs. Milquetost. "Mr. Karp, there are two federal agents here insisting that they see you."

Karp looked at his wife, Stupenagel, and Jaxon, and motioned with his head to a door leading to an anteroom off his office. As the women and Jaxon scurried out, he pressed the button and replied, "Tell them to wait just a minute while I finish my conversation here with Detective Fulton and ADA Katz, then send them in."

It took less than a minute before the two agents opened the door and stalked into his office to find Karp sitting with his feet propped up on his desk. Fulton leaned against the window behind him on his right and Katz sat in a chair over near the bookshelf. "What can I do for you gentlemen?" Karp asked.

"Where is she, Karp?" asked the taller of the two, a Clark Kent type.

"Where is who?"

"Malovo," said the shorter one, who had the countenance and demeanor of an angry bulldog.

"What do you mean?" Karp asked somewhat quizzically.

"You're the two goons who took her into custody from us," Fulton added. "What happened?"

"You know damn well," said the short agent.

"I have no idea what you're talking about," Karp said. "And you have about ten seconds to explain yourselves or you can go back out the same door you came in. Didn't you take her to Fort Dix to hand her over to Russian law enforcement?"

"We did," the taller said. "We handed her over to some Russians, who put her in handcuffs and then put her on a private jet while we were watching."

"Then what's the problem?"

"They weren't the right Russians, goddamn it!" the shorter agent yelled. "The real Russians, the cops, got a call at their embassy telling them there'd been a delay at the trial and we'd be two hours later."

"You get a good look at the imposters?" Karp asked.

"They looked like Russians," the short agent, who seemed the most put out, said. "Big, dumb Slavic types."

"Like me?" Karp said. "I'm a big Slavic type."

"I didn't mean you, Karp." The short agent backed off.

"I only really remember the leader," the tall agent said. "He's easy to remember. A patch over one eye, scars on the side of his face. Real tall, about your age, looks ex-military."

"He ought to be easy to pick out of a lineup if he ever gets picked up," Fulton deadpanned. "But it looks like you boys screwed up. Now I think you better get your rear ends out of here if you're going to come into the office of the New York County district attorney and accuse him of . . ." Fulton stopped and thought about it before turning to Karp. "Accuse you of what?"

"I don't know," Karp replied. "But whatever it is, I don't appreciate it. Once we turned Malovo over to you, she was your responsibility. Now if you don't mind, we were about to drink a toast to an old friend, and you're not invited."

When the agents left, the others who'd been waiting in the anteroom came in. "So much for writing Malovo off," Stupenagel said. "Wow. What a story! I can't wait to write this one up."

"I wonder who the guy with the eye patch and scarred face was," Marlene, who knew perfectly well, said to Karp with a smile.

"I don't know, but I hope he doesn't commit any crimes in New York County," Karp said with a grin. "Because he'd be easy to pick out of a lineup."

THE NEXT MORNING, as S. P. "Espey" Jaxon walked to the witness stand, Karp smiled inwardly, watching the women on the jury and in the gallery perk up. Close-cropped, pewter-colored hair framing his tan, chiseled face, Jaxon possessed a leading man movie star demeanor with the grace of the trim athletic hero.

However, appearing on a witness stand in open court was not something Jaxon wanted to do, given the secrecy with which he and his people normally operated. He was prepared to do so on this day only because of the national security implications of the case.

"Good morning, Mr. Jaxon," Karp began after his longtime friend was sworn in. "Could you begin by giving the jurors and the court a brief biography of your professional career?"

Jaxon turned to the jurors. "After graduating from law school, I worked for the New York District Attorney's Office as a prosecutor, where I first met Mr. Karp. After a dozen years in that capacity, I began a new career as a special agent with the Federal Bureau of Investigation. Then, following the nine-eleven attacks, I was placed in charge of a small federal antiterrorism agency."

"And is that your role now?"

"Yes."

"Can you name the agency?"

"Not publicly, though I have written it down here," Jaxon said, leaning forward to hand a card to Karp, "for the judge."

Karp approached the bench and gave the card to Dermondy. "Your Honor, for reasons of national security, this counterterrorism agency requires strict confidentiality."

Dermondy looked at the agency designation on the card and said, "This card will be marked Court Exhibit Alpha and ordered sealed. Please proceed."

"Mr. Jaxon, approximately a year ago, did you and your team have occasion to conduct a—for want of a different term—black ops raid near a small village in south-central Syria?"

"Yes, we did."

"What was the purpose of the raid?"

"We had learned that a Russian assassin named Nadya Malovo was traveling with a Russian gangster and former Red Army general named Ivan Nikitin," Jaxon said. "We'd been attempting to apprehend Malovo for some time, but we were also interested in Nikitin. He was known to have close ties with the current regime in Moscow and the government of Syria. In the course of our intelligence gathering, we learned that Nikitin would be meeting with a high-level leader with the Islamic State, also known as ISIS, named Ghareeb al Taizi."

"In addition to Malovo, did you hope to apprehend Nikitin and al Taizi?"

"Yes, especially al Taizi. He was on U.S. intelligence and military most wanted lists and thought to have extensive knowledge about ISIS operations."

"Was the raid successful?"

"Well, yes and no. We were able to capture Malovo, as well as seize a number of computers and documents that have yielded valuable information."

"What about al Taizi and Nikitin?"

"They were both killed, as well as Farid Al Halbi, a Syrian oil company executive with personal ties to the Assad government, and Feroze Kirmani, a senior official with the Iranian intelligence agency VAJA."

"Were they killed by your team?"

"No. They were all assassinated by Malovo before we could get to them, including her employer, Nikitin. She was the only one alive in the room where the bodies were found."

"Did she say why she killed them?"

"Initially, she claimed she didn't want to get caught in the crossfire if their bodyguards resisted my team."

"You said 'initially.' Did she change her story?"

"Yes. She had other reasons."

Rather than delve further into this line of questioning, Karp dropped it and moved on. "You noted that computers and documents were seized that have yielded valuable information. Are you aware of any particular documents that have bearing on this case?"

"Yes. My team located a safe they were able to open," Jaxon said. "Inside, along with other documents, was a data storage device—otherwise known as a flash drive—on which we found a folder containing several files. We were able to open the files. They were written in Arabic; however, the information was encrypted."

"Were you able to ascertain anything from this encrypted material that would be of interest to the jury and the court?"

"Yes. Although the information itself was encrypted, and therefore didn't make sense, one word appeared a number of times, drawing our attention."

"And that word was . . . ?"

"*Sarab.* The Arabic word for 'mirage.'"

Karp was looking at the jurors when Jaxon spoke and saw the word register on their faces. He glanced at the defense as he walked over to the prosecution table and picked up a clear bag containing a small object and a piece of paper. Constantine was doing his best to maintain an air of confidence, but Karp could see that he was shaken.

"And why did that word stand out?"

"The frequency and placement of the word in context with the other information led us to believe that it was being used as a code name."

"What happened to the documents, and in particular that flash drive?"

Jaxon's face grew hard. "We returned from the raid to the U.S. air base in Saudi Arabia, where we were surrounded and detained by a U.S. Army intelligence unit. They demanded that we turn over the material we'd seized during the raid, as well as our prisoner, Nadya Malovo."

"Did you do this willingly?"

"No."

"But did you eventually have to comply?"

"Yes. We received orders from the office of the president's national security adviser telling us to stand down and hand over the items you mentioned, as well as Malovo."

"And did you?"

"Yes. We had no choice."

Karp walked over to the witness stand. "Do you know the identity of the Army unit that detained you and seized the materials, as well as took Malovo into custody?"

"Yes, Troop D of the 148th Battlefield Surveillance Brigade."

"Did you know Colonel Michael Swindells?"

"Personally, no. But I learned his identity later."

"And what did you learn?"

"That he was the commanding officer of the 148th during the events just described."

"Was he present that day in Saudi Arabia?"

"No. Only Troop D, which, although part of the 148th, reports directly to the office of the national security adviser."

"Did you have reason to want to contact Colonel Swindells?"

"Yes. Through back channels we learned that Swindells was concerned about the information seized by Troop D, in particular what we have come to refer to as the MIRAGE files contained on the flash drive."

"Do you know what concerned him?"

"He apparently had learned that the files contained information regarding a conspiracy by an American oil company working with representatives of foreign governments and the terrorist organization known as ISIS to sell black-market oil."

"Do you know where he got that information?"

"It's my understanding that he learned it by questioning Nadya Malovo."

"Did he or you know the details of this arrangement, or the name of this American oil company or the representatives of the foreign governments?"

"No. But we believed that the information might be contained on the encrypted MIRAGE files."

"Did you attempt to contact Colonel Swindells yourself?"

"No. I wasn't sure of his loyalties or of those around him."

"Did you instead try to determine those loyalties and possibly arrange for a meeting through an intermediary?"

"Yes. In the course of our investigation, we learned that a journalist named Ariadne Stupenagel had a personal relationship with the colonel. A member of my team has a personal relationship with Stupenagel as well, and she requested that Stupenagel make contact."

"Was Stupenagel given information by you or a member of your team regarding your purposes?"

"A basic outline and that the information we sought might be connected to the word 'mirage,' that's about it."

"Did Stupenagel contact Colonel Swindells and discuss this information?"

"It's my understanding that she did."

"What happened after that?"

"A few minutes following her conversation, Colonel Swindells was murdered by Dean Mueller."

Karp walked up to the witness stand and handed the clear bag and sheet of paper to Jaxon. "I'm handing you People's Exhibits

47 and 48 marked for identification. One contains a data storage device known as a flash drive. Do you recognize it?"

"It appears to be the same sort of device we seized during the raid."

"Is there a way to ascertain if it is indeed the same device?"

"There is. Prior to handing over the flash drive, we marked it with an invisible solution containing a unique synthetic DNA code that is then entered into a database with a company in the United Kingdom called SelectaDNA. That particular DNA sequence would be found nowhere else in the world and can only be detected by their equipment and specially trained dogs."

"Would you please inform the jury what is contained on the document I handed you."

Jaxon studied the paper and then nodded. "This is from SelectaDNA verifying beyond a reasonable degree of scientific certainty that this flash drive is the one we marked with that particular synthetic DNA."

Retrieving the flash drive and document, Karp held them up to Dermondy. "The People request that Exhibits 47 and 48 be received in evidence."

Arnold rose to his feet. "We object. This so-called evidence has been sprung upon us in the eleventh hour, and we've had no opportunity to have our own experts examine it for authenticity.

We don't even know if the information on the flash drive, if it's indeed the same device Mr. Jaxon and his team seized in Syria, hasn't been altered."

"I believe I can clear up that issue by asking Mr. Jaxon another question," Karp replied.

"Go ahead," Dermondy said.

"Mr. Jaxon, how can the jurors know that the files contained on the flash drive are the same as those that were on the device a year ago?" Karp asked.

Jaxon held up the folder he'd carried with him to the witness stand. "I have here paper copies of the encrypted files, and they are both time- and date-stamped."

"Would you like a further voir dire of the witness regarding authenticity, Mr. Arnold?" Judge Dermondy inquired.

"Not now, Your Honor, but we reserve our right to engage an expert to examine the evidence," Arnold replied.

"Very well, the evidence is received. The defendant's objection is duly noted, and you may proceed, Mr. Karp."

Resuming his position at the jury box rail, Karp charged on. "Would you please explain to the jury to the best of your knowledge what happened to this flash drive after it was taken from you in Saudi Arabia."

"It was stored in a secure location at the air base. However, after Colonel Swindells spoke to Malovo, he removed the flash drive and replaced it with a copy. He then transported the original flash drive to the United States, where he attempted to have it deciphered by Army intelligence. That's when it was discovered that he was in possession of the MIRAGE file."

"What happened then?"

"A member of Troop D was tasked with retrieving the file. He was caught going through the colonel's personal effects and discharged from the Army."

"Do you know the identity of this individual?"

"Yes. Dean Mueller."

"Mr. Jaxon, was the Army, or any other U.S. government agency, able to decipher the MIRAGE files?" Karp asked, looking over at the defense table.

"No."

Karp noticed the visible relief on the faces of Constantine and Arnold. Then he dropped the bomb. "Was anybody able to decipher the MIRAGE files?"

Jaxon smiled. "Yes. It ended up being child's play, so to speak."

Watching the faces of the men at the defense table blanch, Karp burrowed in. "What do you mean by that?"

"They were deciphered by a teenage computer science prodigy at the Massachusetts Institute of Technology. He determined that the sequencing of the coded information was tied to passages in the Qur'an, which he studied and learned by heart with the help of a multilingual member of my team for this purpose."

Karp turned back to Jaxon. "You noted that your folder contains the time- and date-stamped encrypted MIRAGE files in hard copy form. Does it also contain the same deciphered information?"

"It does."

Karp walked to the witness stand, where Jaxon handed his folder to him. "Mr. Jaxon, I won't ask you to go into all of the details included in this folder. The jury will be able to go through it themselves. But would you please give us a synopsis of MIRAGE?"

Jaxon nodded and turned to the jurors. "MIRAGE is a conspiracy between an American oil company with the complicit assistance and knowledge of the office of the national security adviser as well as representatives of foreign governments in Syria, Russia, and Iran to sell black-market oil produced at refineries under the control of ISIS in northern Iraq.

"In addition, it prevents U.S. and Russian air strikes against these facilities, as well as the transportation of the oil. Instead, the American public—indeed, the world—has been shown air strikes purporting to be attacks on ISIS oil facilities but are in fact abandoned refineries and mock convoys of trucks. Thus MIRAGE—something that appears to exist but doesn't."

Karp looked over at Dermondy. "Your Honor, I'd now like to play a video taken from the air over northern Iraq and have Mr. Jaxon narrate what the jurors are seeing."

"Objection. We haven't had an opportunity to view this video or ascertain its veracity," Arnold said tiredly.

"It's rebuttal," Karp said. "This administration, as testified to by Ms. Hamm, has claimed to have destroyed oil facilities owned by the defendant but under ISIS control. This video will dispute that."

"Very well. Overruled, you may proceed."

Karp nodded to Duffy McIntyre, who dimmed the lights. A screen lowered from the ceiling as Katz began the video from his computer at the prosecution desk. Black-and-white aerial images of what appeared to be a large industrial complex with huge storage tanks showed up on the screen.

"Mr. Jaxon, please describe to the jury what we're seeing," Karp said.

"These have been released to the public through the media by the office of the national security adviser, purporting to show the destruction of oil facilities owned by Well-Con Oil. Those flashes were missiles from U.S. aircraft, obviously followed by massive explosions and near total destruction of the facility."

The screen changed to show a convoy of tanker trucks on a highway from the air. "And this, Mr. Jaxon?"

"These were given to the media, purportedly showing the destruction of Well-Con tanker trucks operated by ISIS."

Karp nodded at Katz, who paused the video. "Was that a Well-Con facility that was destroyed by the air strikes?"

"No," Jaxon replied. "As a matter of fact, those belonged to Shell Oil."

"And the trucks?"

"That video was actually shot in Afghanistan eight years ago, not Iraq or Syria."

Karp nodded again at Katz, who restarted the video. The image of another oil facility appeared on the screen. "What are we seeing here?"

"These are images of four Well-Con facilities in northern Iraq," Jaxon replied.

"They appear to be operating as normal," Karp said. "There are trucks driving around, people walking, though they look about the size of ants."

"Yes, it's business as usual at these facilities."

"When were these images taken?" Karp asked.

"Three nights ago."

"And how were they obtained?"

"That same teenage prodigy at MIT specializes in drone technology. He actually flew a drone over there and took these images sitting in my office."

Karp looked over at Duffy McIntyre, who raised the lights and the screen. He then walked over to the jury rail. "Mr. Jaxon, who benefits from this conspiracy?"

"Well, the Russians get cheap oil at far below market value. They also have moved their military into Syria, a strategically important region of the Middle East on the southern border of Turkey with warm-water ports on the Mediterranean. Syria gets some of that cheap oil and gets Russian help going after anti-Assad rebels. In exchange for looking the other way, and allowing the oil to be transported across Iran to the Caspian Sea where Russian oil tankers wait, Iran gets oil and Russian nuclear technology. ISIS gets money and arms."

"What about the U.S.?"

"As with the Russians and Syrians, ISIS is a distraction. They're the 'bogeyman' of the Middle East. As long as they can trot out the occasional atrocity, put everyone in fear of domestic terrorist attacks, who cares about what else is going on. It's also payback for millions of dollars in campaign funding."

"What about the defendant?"

Jaxon looked over at Constantine. "He doesn't lose tens of millions of dollars in equipment," he said. "Plus he gets to sell black-market oil, some of which is shipped from his competitors' facilities that have been shut down, to his. And in the end, it's about power."

As Jaxon spoke, Karp walked one more time over to the defense table and stood staring down at Constantine, whose face was a mask of pure hatred combined with fear. "And did the MIRAGE files name this company?"

"They did."

"And what was that name?"

"Well-Con Oil, a subsidiary of Well-Con Industries."

The words were hardly out of Jaxon's mouth when Constantine leaped to his feet. He struck the table with his fists. "It's a lie!" he screamed at the jurors. "It's all lies!"

"Mr. Constantine, take your seat!" Judge Dermondy demanded as he pounded his gavel on the dais. "Security, remove him if he doesn't."

With the court security officers moving toward him, Constantine slumped back into his chair and covered his face with his hands, panting like a trapped animal.

Dermondy looked at Karp. "Do you have any more witnesses?"

"No, Your Honor."

"Do you intend to recall Mr. Constantine to the stand?"

Karp turned toward the defense table. Constantine removed his hands from his face and looked at him with panicked eyes.

"No, Your Honor," he said. "I don't think there's any reason."

EPILOGUE

THE INTERCOM ON KARP'S DESK BUZZED AND WAS FOL-
lowed immediately by the voice of Darla Milquetost. "Mr. Karp,
the others wanted me to tell you that they're in the conference
room and that the *Nation Tonight* show about the Constantine
trial is about to start."

"Oh, brother," Karp said, rolling his eyes. "Okay, tell them I'll
be right there."

"I will," Milquetost replied. "This is exciting!"

Karp shook his head. It had been a month since the Constantine trial had concluded, and he was still dealing with the fallout,
including the perjury and obstruction of justice trial of now
ex–National Security Adviser Sylvia Hamm. The White House,

which had barely staved off an impeachment attempt by opposition members of Congress after the murder of Sam Allen, was now in full defense mode.

Karp had wanted no part of the media frenzy that had ensued following the verdict. He was uncomfortable enough when Stupenagel's exposé, titled "MIRAGE: The Treachery of an American Mogul," hit the newsstands. He'd cooperated only because of his initial promise to be interviewed once things were settled in court. He'd declined another invitation to be interviewed for *Nation Tonight* but had no say over the courtroom cameras capturing the drama of the trial.

The best part about the trial being over was that Marlene and the boys had returned home. The big excitement there was that while they'd been gone, they'd received their papers on revolutions in the mail from their teacher. Zak had been beside himself when he saw the A+ as well as a note from the teacher congratulating him on his hard work. What made it even better, as far as he was concerned, was that Giancarlo had received "only" an A.

"It might be the one and only time in my life I get a better grade, so I'm going to rub it in for a while," Zak said. But Giancarlo didn't mind. He was proud of his brother and willing to take the teasing.

With a sigh, Karp got up and walked into the conference

room, where gathered in front of a large-screen television were Milquetost, Katz, Fulton, Marlene, Stupenagel, Bryers, and Jaxon.

"You're late," Katz said. "They started with your comment aimed at Arnold: 'The defense in this case is like the old courtroom saw: Weak case on the facts, try the law; weak case on the law, try the facts; weak case on the law and facts, try the DA.' That's classic, and I think the jury picked up on that."

"Shhhh, I'm trying to listen," Milquetost scolded as the camera cut away to two talking-head attorneys discussing the case like a couple of football commentators.

"I think District Attorney Karp took a risk telling the jury that the prosecution has a huge advantage because it gets to move the chess pieces around before the defendant is even indicted. And then the defendant has the option to plead to the indictment, or go to trial when the chessboard has the defendant in checkmate," said one. "I could see a juror—and remember, it only takes one—thinking it's all unfair."

"I disagree, Jack. Jurors like that kind of honesty," said the other. "The way he described each piece of the People's case and how it fit into the overall strategy it took to put Constantine in checkmate was a perfect analogy. But let's listen in to how he wrapped up his summation. It was simply brilliant."

"THAT'S MY MAN!" Marlene yelled as the others in the room cheered.

The screen cut to the interior of the courtroom with Karp pacing in front of the jury. "Their warped mind-set rationalizes their illegality as justified because it serves, and I quote, 'the greater good,' and therefore they commit their criminal acts with impunity. The rules be damned, to serve their own selfish ends. They are the new aristocracy and we are the commoners, the serfs, here to serve them and their avaricious, grotesque lust for power and money."

The screen switched back to the commentators. "That's powerful stuff, Jack. Now listen as he brings it home . . ."

". . . the result of this unbridled ambition, their weak character, is their own enrichment, satisfying their lust for power and riches. A good, honorable man who served his country with distinction was murdered so that this defendant . . ."

Just then, Karp's cell phone rang. He looked at the caller ID and moved to the back of the room. "Ivgeny," he said, "I was wondering where you went."

Ivgeny Karchovski responded with his rich baritone laugh. "I decided it was a good time to take the yacht on a cruise of the Mediterranean," he said. "I just wanted to call and congratulate you belatedly on your victory."

"Hello, Butch!" a female voice joined in.

"Is that . . . ?" Karp asked.

"It is a new member of my crew," Ivgeny said. "Though at times I have considered making her walk the plank."

Karp laughed. "I'd be careful there, Cousin. Or it might be you swimming with the sharks."

"You're right on that," Ivgeny replied. "Anyway, you're probably watching the television show. You're a movie star!"

"Hardly, but I better get back to the gang," Karp said.

"Yes, you do that. Give my love—"

"Our love," the female voice chimed in.

"—to Marlene."

The cell phone went dead. The TV screen now showed Constantine and Arnold standing as the verdict was read.

"We the jury find Wellington Constantine . . ."

"Wait for it, wait for it!" Katz yelled.

". . . guilty of murder . . ."

Constantine's body began to shake, and he wailed, "Nooooooo!" as Arnold placed a hand on his shoulder.

Constantine turned and landed a haymaker on Arnold's chin. The attorney went down in a heap.

"One down, one to go," Katz chortled as Constantine then tried to get to the prosecution table.

"I'll get you, Karp!" he screamed, but was then buried under a couple of heavyweight court security officers.

The television screen flashed back to the two commentators, who sat with amused smiles. "Quite an ending, eh, Jack!"

"You got that right, Frank. Never seen anything quite like it."

As his friends clapped, Karp, never comfortable with accolades, smiled at Marlene. "Fame, if you win it, comes and goes in a minute . . ." he said, nodding at her, and improvised, "Here, *here* are the real things in life to cling to . . ."